MW00573144

BREAKING HER

Book Two in the Love is War Duet.
This is the conclusion of Scarlett and Dante's story.

destruction. betrayal. ruination. True love.

Scarlett

He had done it again. Ravaged me. Burned me. Broke me.

Given me air, only to leave me gasping, writhing.

But then something changed. Something that terrified and excited me both.

Something that utterly destroyed me.

Something that made me whole again.

Dante

Our love was cursed from the start. She didn't know it, but I did.

All she knew was that I'd lied to her, betrayed her. Done unforgivable things. Unavoidable things. Yes, I had broken promises as surely as I had broken her heart. But, just as every war has casualties, and every lie has consequences–every bastard has his reasons.

breaking her

by

R.K. LILLEY

BREAKING HER

ISBN-13: 978-1-62878-046-8
ISBN-10: 1-62878-046-0

Cover photos by Perrywinkle Photography
Cover design by Okay Creations
Edited by The Word Maid
Interior design by Warkitty Formatting

www.rklilley.com

Give feedback on the book at:
authorrklilley@gmail.com

Twitter: @authorrklilley

Instagram: @Authorrklilley

www.facebook.com/RkLilley

First Edition

This book is dedicated to the men out there who aren't afraid to love complicated, difficult women. You aren't afraid of strength. You aren't put off by damage. You aren't intimidated by resilience. You don't see baggage as a deterrent. These are the things that make up a real man.

Also, you like more than an ounce of diabolical sass with your morning coffee.

Dammit. Yeah, okay, I see what I did there, too. This has turned into yet another dedication to Mr. Lilley.

But, well, he is pretty cool.

Dear husband, you wanted more than a spouse, you wanted an equal partner for life, and you got it. Ride or die, boo.

"The heart was made to be broken."
~Oscar Wilde

chapter

one

PRESENT

Scarlett

Anton was over at our place, trying to cheer me up again. He'd brought with him a Costco-sized bottle of Patrón.

It was a good effort.

In return for the tequila, I was making him seven-layer brownies. The two things didn't go well together, but I didn't care. I was only partaking in the one.

Demi's niece, Olivia, was also over for a sleepover. This happened whenever we were home for a good stretch. Demi was a devoted aunt and had a natural ease with children.

I was the opposite. They made me uncomfortable. I hadn't been good with kids when I'd been one myself. Growing up had hardly improved things.

Olivia was a lovely little girl, with Demi's coloring, black hair, and blue eyes. She was very well groomed. Someone, likely every someone in her life, took good care of her.

I wondered briefly what that must be like for a kid.

The girls were planning to take little Olivia to the zoo. They'd invited me, of course, and even Anton, but I was in no mood to be around children, let alone spend a day with one.

Besides, I had some very important, well thought out plans—to stay home and work on my day drinking.

I was doing a stand up job at it so far. Noon had barely come and gone and Anton and I had already progressed to doing shots.

I was in the kitchen, facing Anton across the island.

"Because tequila," we toasted and did another.

I finished that round first, setting my glass down triumphantly in front of him while he was still finishing his.

That was when Olivia skipped up, apparently bored with the cartoons she'd been watching while she waited for everyone to get ready.

She leaned against the counter to stare at me. She was a curious, precocious child. Everyone within her sphere adored her and she seemed to know it well. I guessed no one had ever slapped her for asking the wrong question, so she asked whatever thoughts came to her head.

"Hi, Auntie Scar." She beamed at me. She called all of the roommates auntie. I didn't know where she'd gotten the idea. From Demi, I assumed.

"Hi, Olivia," I returned solemnly.

As I've said, I'm bad with children.

"Hi, Mister Anton," she told Anton.

He blinked at her, scratching restlessly at his bearded jaw and looking as uncomfortable as I felt. Good. This was one of the many reasons I liked having him around. We were so much alike that he had a tendency to make me feel less alone.

And at a time like this, particularly, I needed to feel less alone.

I was not doing well.

This I knew.

Not sleeping. Not getting dressed unless I had to work.

Loafing around my house in my various cat T-shirts (today's gem was a picture of Grumpy cat and read #currentmood) drinking too much, thinking too much. Hating myself *too much*.

What Dante had done, how he'd messed with my head, *yet again . . .*

I won't say it hurt more than the first time, or even that it was more shocking. Once you've been broken, every break after, even when they hurt like *hell*, can never outdo the profound damage of the first time.

I will say that I did not bounce back right away.

It was that feeling again, an old, familiar one. It had always been there, but I'd buried it for a while.

You know that moment when you wake up cold, knowing you've kicked your covers off, and realize someone has tenderly tucked them back around your shoulders?

It was the opposite of that. It was knowing you'd never have that again, that no one would ever care enough to try to keep you warm.

Lately, the feeling was stronger than ever. Consuming. Debilitating.

"Just Anton," Anton finally corrected Demi's niece, bringing me out of my musings and back to the present.

Anton's day drunk was starting to show in the form of delayed reactions.

"My mommy *and* Aunt Demi told me it's rude to address an adult by just their first name."

Anton and I exchanged a glance. How strange it must be to be a child with so many adults around that cared about every little nuance of your life.

"How about Uncle Anton?" she tried. "That counts."

He'd been taking a drink of water when she said that, and he started to choke at her words.

It made me smile, probably the first time I'd done so in days.

Finally he managed to get out a scratchy, "Mister Anton is just fine."

She nodded and bestowed a very charming smile on him.

"What's that?" she asked me, pointing to the giant bottle of Patrón.

"Grownup stuff," I told her, assuming that would settle it.

"Can I try some?"

I made a face at her that made her giggle. "Are you a grownup?"

"Yep," she said quickly.

"Grownups are at least twenty-one years old. Are you twenty-one?" I asked pointedly.

"Yep," she quipped back, the brazen little liar.

"Uh uh," I said.

She nodded at the oven. "Can I have some of those when they're done?"

I shrugged. "I guess."

"Auntie Farrah said you don't like kids. Why don't you like kids?"

"Because they ask too many questions."

"Like what?"

"Exactly."

"Why else don't you like kids?"

"Because they're selfish and mean," just sort of slipped out.

Her eyes widened, watered a bit, and I saw that I'd taken the teasing too far.

"You think I'm selfish and mean?" she asked, voice tremulous, like the very idea might make her cry.

Dammit. "No." I actually meant it. "Not you. I can just remember . . . other kids . . . that were," I finished lamely.

"If you don't like kids, how come you bake me something nummy every time I come over?"

I mulled that one over. I did. I literally baked every time she came over, no exceptions. What the hell was up with that?

"It's a coincidence," I told her. "I bake all the time." That was a lie, but she was eight.

If you couldn't lie to an eight-year-old, who could you lie to?

She beamed at me. "You like me. I knew it."

I curled my lip at her and she giggled. "You're alright," I allowed.

"I like *you*," she offered. "You're really pretty, and you smell nice."

Dammit. Damn Demi and her incorrigible, likable niece. "You're really pretty, too," I begrudgingly returned.

She acted like I'd made her day with that, doing an enthusiastic happy dance that involved a lot of twirling and hand waving.

Was she trying to win me over, or was she really this freaking adorable?

I didn't know, but in spite of myself, I was charmed.

Still, I'd never let her close, never let myself get attached to a kid like that. Even the thought of it spun my mind into dark, fathomless places that I knew well to steer clear of.

Luckily, they all left for a day at the zoo soon after that, and I was spared much more of Olivia's infectious charm.

And dammit, she almost convinced me to come with them. If I had been about two shots more sober or three more drunk, she'd have had me.

Nearly as bad, I packed them a cute little care package full of brownies like I was Betty fucking Crocker.

Of course Anton gave me shit for it. I couldn't blame him.

I shut his teasing up with another shot. It was a sore spot, but in all fairness, lately every damn spot on me was sore.

It was some time later that my phone rang. I was at functioning, non-slurring levels, my day drink game strong. Anton was putting up a good fight, the only signs of how messed up he was, was that he was over-enunciating, and his comeback time was slowing from whip-fast to slightly below average.

I glanced at my lit phone face and grinned wickedly.

It was bloodthirsty, so much so, Anton, even slowed Anton, caught on fast.

"It's him, isn't it?"

I chewed my lip and nodded.

He meant Dante. Of course. Since the funeral and the disaster that followed, he called often, and sometimes

I'd answer. It was a toss-up with me whether I'd chew him out or just hang up.

Sometimes he called to discuss what Gram had left me in her will, but I'd have none of it. "I told you, give it to one of her charities. I don't want anything. I won't *take* anything." I'd never once let him finish his sentence when he brought this up. I'd been called a Durant charity case my whole life, but I'd be *damned* before I'd become one.

Sometimes he just asked me how I was. Like he just wanted to talk, to check up on me. As if he had that right. The bastard.

Those calls ended nearly as quickly as the first kind.

The worst shame of all this was the angry five minutes I spent getting myself off afterwards.

I wasn't sure if it was a comfort or a curse that I was absolutely sure the bastard was doing exactly the same.

Sometimes he didn't even speak. Sometimes he just listened on the other end. This call started as one of those.

"If it isn't my heavy breather again," I said lightly into the phone. "Is there some particular word you're looking for, to get off faster?"

It was a joke, at his expense, but he seemed to take it seriously.

"Say Dante," he told me gruffly.

"Dante," I said gamely. Because tequila. "You're the bane of my existence. Stop calling me."

There was nothing but his disturbed breath on the other end.

"Even that did it for you, huh?" I took the dig at him with relish. "You dirty, old pervert."

"You're in a mood," he finally noted. He sounded

rough. Rough as in terrible. I wasn't the only one drowning my sorrows with a bottle.

But he was right. I was in a mood. And it didn't bode well for him. "Why are you doing this?" I asked him, keeping my tone level. Mellow, even.

There was a long pause on the other end, but he surprised me by finally answering, "You keep answering. If there's a chance you'll answer, I'll never stop calling."

He was right. I'd stopped taking his calls years before our last disastrous reunion. Why couldn't I seem to do that now?

My self-destructive meter was running at full, and I hadn't found a way to bring it down since the funeral.

Maybe a bit of revenge would help.

One thing was for sure. It couldn't hurt.

I didn't really need to, we'd plotted it out several times prior, but just to be safe, I mouthed at Anton, "You ready?"

Anton grinned and gave me a thumbs up.

I held my hand toward him to let him know that he should wait.

"Okay, fine," I finally responded to Dante, my voice hardening, going from light to dark. "I'll stop answering, so you stop calling. This is pointless. Stop wasting my time. I've moved the hell on."

My nostrils flared as I pointed at Anton.

"Come back to bed, baby," his perfect actor's voice rumbled loudly at the phone, right on cue. God, he was good. He sounded sleepy, horny, just fucked, and ready to fuck again. The man deserved an Oscar for that one little sentence.

On the other end Dante made a noise, something indecipherable but unmistakably, unpleasantly, *unbearably* filled with pain.

Agony. Torture.

I think I had the phone to my ear, staring into nothing for at least five minutes after he hung up. I wasn't sure what I was feeling. Which was the problem. That little stunt had been designed to torment him, but, above all, to improve my mood.

Why had it done the opposite? Why did hurting him *always* hurt me?

"You know, we could just do it," Anton said sometime later.

I stared at him. "What? Sleep together?"

He shrugged. "Why not? What would be the harm? We're so much alike, it might actually turn into something, and if it did, it might be something good. And if not, no harm, no foul. We'd stay friends and forget about it, end of story."

I mulled that over, but I knew myself too well to fall into that trap. I decided to let him have the full, brutal truth of it, the fatal flaw in his harmless plan. "Here's how that would play out: the sex might be good for me, would be great for you, but the only way it's great for me is if I'm picturing you as someone else . . . Someone I hate. And then, in the morning, you'd be hopelessly in love with me, and it'd get weird, because I fucking hate it when guys fall in love with me, and then I wouldn't enjoy hanging out with you anymore. How sad would that be for both of us?"

"Is he really that good?"

"He's the best I ever had. And the worst thing that ever happened to me."

True love is a bitch.

"And it's really that . . . hopeless? You can't even get off without him getting in the way?"

I was well aware of how pathetic, how epically fucked up it was, and hearing it aloud hardly helped.

"It's hard to explain," I warned him. "But, basically, yes. I can't even eat a fucking apple because of him."

"What?" he asked, sounding baffled, which was understandable.

"He even ruined apples for me," I explained.

"What?" he repeated.

"I have a memory, a very clear one, of biting into an apple—we grew up surrounded by orchards—and so we got the best apples. And I just have a memory of eating one fresh off the tree, sharing it with him actually, and thinking it was the best thing I'd ever tasted."

"Okaaay . . . And?" he prompted.

"It was a . . . special day, and every time I ate an apple after that it all came fresh to my mind.

So when it ended between us, horribly, I could never . . ." There was nothing quite so demoralizing as recalling your sweetest memories and feeling utterly bitter.

"That blows." His voice was succinct. He poured us another shot.

"They were my favorite fruit," I lamented. "Love sucks."

"And now your favorite fruit is the lime that chases our next tequila shot."

As far as pep talks went, it wasn't the worst one I'd ever had, so I toasted it. "Bottoms up."

"She burned too bright for this world."
~Emily Brontë

chapter two

PAST

Dante

I'd always had a soft spot for her. Since I could remember her flashing eyes and stubborn face were dear to me.

Even before she'd decided we were friends, before our first fateful bonding moment outside of the vice principal's office when she first realized I was in her corner, I'd admired her.

Admired that she never backed down. Admired that, with the way she was treated by nearly everyone around her, she never bent, not one iota, let alone came near to breaking.

Her strength galvanized me, made me see the world in a different way.

I had it so easy. My mother was awful, my father dismal, but my life was pampered and I could escape any time I wanted, which was often, and visit my gram, who lived a short walk away and made up for both of my pieces of shit parents and then some.

I had an anger problem and a bad attitude. This I knew. But it was Scarlett who inspired me to give those things purpose.

The first time I tried to help, she didn't even notice me.

We were in the cafeteria at school. I was in line to get lunch, stealing glances at her.

She was by herself. She always was. She was less interested in talking to other kids than any kid I'd ever seen besides myself. Once, I'd even taken a seat across from her to eat, and she'd still barely said two words to me.

Her thick brown hair was endearingly messy. She had the perfect face of a doll, but it was always set into hard lines, an incongruous, arresting look but one that I couldn't stop looking at. And I looked a lot. I enjoyed watching her. She wasn't like anybody else, didn't react to things in the same way. I got a kick out of expecting the unexpected from her.

Every inch of her tiny frame read: This girl is tough and she does not plan to deal with your shit. Do not mess with her.

So why was everyone *always* messing with her?

They loved to tease her about the trashcan stuff, and I thought that was about the most messed up thing ever. It set my teeth on edge. What an awful thing to tease someone about.

No part of me understood, but then, I'd never felt like someone who fit in, either.

They were serving cheese zombies and tomato soup

for lunch, one of my favorites, and I waited in line just watching her and not particularly paying attention to anything else.

I couldn't help but overhear the boys in front of me, though. There were two of them and they were snickering. It was the type of laugh where you knew there was something bad behind it. Something mean, and so I focused on them, listening as they revealed themselves to be just the kind of little shits I had no patience for.

"I swear to God, Jason," one said to the other. "I have five dollars in my backpack, and if you do it, it's all yours."

Jason laughed harder. "I'll get into trouble."

"It's five bucks! Just say you tripped and spilled it. Hell, some tomato soup on her head might make her smell better."

They both went into loud peals of laughter. I thought they sounded like nasty, little hyenas.

I felt sick. I didn't even have to hear any more, I knew what they were planning and to whom, but I did hear more, I listened and collected my food, then quietly followed them.

I set down my tray on the first table I passed.

Jason's giggling friend sat down at the next one and waved him on.

With an evil grin, Jason approached Scarlett from behind, still holding his tray.

With quick furious steps I caught up to him, grabbed his tray, stepped on his foot, and sent my elbow hard into his chin all at once.

He went down with a gratifying cry.

Very calmly, I took his tomato soup and poured it right into his bratty, dismayed face.

"Is it funny now, you little shit?" I spat at him right before a teacher started dragging me away.

I glanced at Scarlett as I went.

She'd turned at the commotion, looking bored with only a touch of interest in her big, dark eyes as she looked at me, but no comprehension on her face that I'd just saved her from a headful of soup.

Still, that didn't deter me. Her plight ate at me. I'd lie in bed, hands clenched into fists, and stew about it.

I was a lonely, solemn boy, more sensitive than I'd ever admit, and I couldn't stand what was happening to her.

Anytime something was really bothering me, I took it to Gram.

"It's not right," I told my glamorous grandmother. "It's *wrong*, the way she's being treated. The kids are monsters, and the teachers don't care until it's gotten so bad that Scarlett gets herself into trouble. It's every *day*, Gram. Every *day* she has to put up with these little *shits* picking on her."

She was studying my face in a way that I liked, the way she always did when I was reminding her of Grandpa. She didn't even reprimand me for cursing, that's how intently she was listening to me.

"You've gotta help her, Gram. It's bad enough the way they talk, but she's got no one at home taking care of her. She needs *clothes*. Soap. Someone to wash her hair and brush her teeth, or yanno, teach her how to do it."

She touched a hand to my hair, purest love pouring out of her eyes. "Yes, yes, of course she does, Dante, my sweet, sweet boy. We will work on all of that."

"They're *awful* at school. They won't let up on her.

Maybe if you talk to her about . . . taking a bath or somethin', it'd make it easier on her."

"I will. I absolutely will, you darling boy. I'm ashamed that you even had to point it out, but you leave it to me, okay?"

I nodded. I had absolute faith that Gram would do anything she promised, so I was done worrying about that part of it.

"Thank you," I told her. "But . . . what should I do? How do you think I can help her?"

"How about just being her friend? Friends can make life a lot better."

I flushed and looked down, embarrassed to tell her that the girl I was so worried about would barely say two words to me. "I'll try," I muttered.

"And Dante?"

"Yes?"

"You're strong. And brave. I have faith in you. I know you will find a way to help her. If you see she needs defending, *defend* her. Do what you think is right and you won't have any regrets."

A few weeks later, I pounded a guy that I heard making a joke about her, and I got my first smile out of her.

I loved that smile that seemed to belong only to me. I felt like I'd been invited into a special club that consisted of just the two of us, and I wanted to stay there. It was the *only* place I wanted to be.

From that day forward, it was my job to protect her. Her feelings. Her body.

Her freedom.

I look back on it all often, I think about it too much, and my life has fallen into categories—in spite of everything—gradations of *her*.

Life before Scarlett. Life with Scarlett. Life after Scarlett.

Wanting her.

Needing her.

Having her.

Losing her.

But always, *always*, there's a cloud looming over our heads, a storm on the brink, and in my mind, at least, there is only one person to blame for it.

From my earliest memories, I had a complicated relationship with my mother.

She taught me to knot a tie, play chess, and to never, ever turn my back on her.

I kept Scarlett from my mother as much as I could for as long as I could. Hid the one I held most dear from the one I most feared.

I sheltered Scarlett from her. Protected her as much as I could. She had enough to contend with in her life without my terrifying mother adding to it.

I kept her hidden as best I could, but of course, that couldn't last forever. Scarlett and I were inseparable. There was bound to be some overlap.

It was the strangest thing, if you ever caught my mother off guard it was like walking in on a corpse. There was not one ounce of animation to her. She was inanimate, staring off into nothing, and if you startled her, her face went on like an alarm going off.

Like stepping on a snake, she struck before you fully understood what you'd done.

I'd caught her like that once and learned to avoid it.

Still, I thought about it. It creeped me the hell out. What did she do when she was so deep in her own mind that she seemed to leave her body?

I was young when I pondered that, very young, and the older I got the more apparent the answer was.

She was plotting. Always plotting.

An enemy's downfall, a friend's humiliation, a rival's shame.

A husband's misery.

A son's ruin.

She never lived in the moment. She only lived for her latest trap to spring.

And she always had some web to spin. Everyone in her sphere played some part in the spinning, whether they knew it or not.

There was one thing of value about being her only son; I did learn to deal with her.

Or so I thought.

When I was young and stupid, I thought I'd gotten the best of her, thought I had the keys to keeping her in check for the foreseeable future.

She let me think so, I later realized. She was playing a longer game than I could have anticipated.

The key when it came to my mother was control. If you broke it all down that was all she wanted from anyone, to have power over them.

But that didn't work until you had a weakness to exploit.

The answer to controlling me was always there, from the time Scarlett became my first and best friend, but I was too naive to see it.

I thought I had it all figured out. I thought *I* was in

control. I thought I was the one that had something on *her*.

I found the thing my mother found the most important without even trying.

For her, the woman who had no animation when she was by herself, it was all about appearances. Her entire life was a sham, a play, and that's all she wanted it to be. She cared more about what the world thought than she did the actual reality of it.

Once I knew that it was a simple thing to figure out what she wanted from me. And once I had that, I figured I had the power to keep her from taking what was important to me.

She loved to bring me out at parties, loved to show off her strapping boy, with his perfect teeth, his good looks, his blond hair, blue eyes, and straight posture— the very image of his handsome father. Thanks to her expectations, I was better at making conversation with adults than other kids, and her 'friends' found this endlessly charming.

She was very happy with that.

I let her have it for a while. She'd taught me well. I even went out of my way to ham it up, her charming little boy, but I made a note of how it pleased her, how she expected, *needed* my impeccable behavior to help illustrate how perfect, how *complete* of a person she was pretending to be.

I kept that little card to myself until I needed it, because I always knew I would.

And I did. It was the first time she got an inkling of how close I'd grown to what she referred to as, "*That Theroux girl,*" in her most derisive tone.

She didn't beat around the bush. The day she found

out we walked home together from school, she forbid me from ever speaking to Scarlett again.

With a somber face I told her calmly and simply, "No."

She smiled smugly, like she'd been expecting that. "I'll talk to that little piece of trash myself. I'll keep her from ever wanting to so much as look at you, that I promise."

That set me off into the biggest rage of my young life. I could see I even shocked my always a step ahead mother as I began to throw things, going from calm and somber to livid and violent between one breath and the next.

I did have a temper, and it was an ugly thing, but on this particular day there was more than a trace of calculation in it. I'd been expecting this for some time.

I'd been preparing for it.

Plotting it.

There would be no do-over. I'd only get one chance. I couldn't risk not taking it far enough, so I let her have it.

We were in her favorite sitting room. Every single thing in the room was meticulously placed, chosen by her. On a normal day, I knew better than to so much as misplace a pillow in this particular room.

This was not a normal day.

I began by reaching down and picking up a prized object on the glossy mahogany coffee table.

It was a Fabergé egg, worth a lot of money, I knew. It was possibly the most valuable thing in this room full of valuables, and that's why I went for it first.

Our eyes met, hers narrowed and disbelieving, mine full of pure, desperate spite. I held her gaze for one meaningful moment just before I turned and threw the thing, with all my might, straight into the wall.

She gasped and started screaming.

I started screaming louder.

That was only the start. I kept going, breaking things until I felt I'd adequately gotten her attention.

That was when I really let her have it. "FUCK. FUCK. FUCK. FUCK!" I screamed into her face.

"What the hell is wrong with you?" she screamed back.

My voice got deadly quiet to show her that I was in control of myself. "If you embarrass me to Scarlett I'll make you sorry. Every time you want to show me off at some stupid party, I will put on the stupid suit, I will let you do my stupid hair, and then the second you try to introduce me to someone." I pitched my voice louder suddenly, back to near hysteria. "I'm just going to shout FUCK at the top of my lungs."

Her hand was at her throat. She looked horrified. "What has gotten into you?"

"FUCK! FUCK! FUCK! FUCK!" I repeated, again and again.

"What is *wrong* with you?"

"FUCK! FUCK! FUCK! FUCK!"

"I don't even—"

"*CUNT!*" I brought out the very worst curse word, which I'd only ever heard from my dad when I was eavesdropping on my parents fighting. "CUNT! CUNT! FUCK!"

I won that round. She couldn't stand the thought of anyone thinking her perfect son might be disturbed, mentally challenged, or worse, ill bred.

I thought I'd won the war with that silly display. I thought it was enough to keep her in check, to make her leave me alone to live my life, to pick my own friends, to make my own choices and take my own path.

I was so foolish.

"Every girl should use what Mother Nature gave her before Father Time takes it away."
~Laurence J. Peter

chapter three

PRESENT

Scarlett

We were having a beach day. All of my roommates had conspired to drag my cheerless ass out into the cheerful light of day.

Fun in the sun. Yay.

I actually did try to be a good sport about it. I put on a tiny bikini with a sexy gold sequined cover up, piled my hair on top of my head in a thick, messy bun, and put on my best knock-off designer shades.

And, of course, my game face.

We all brought a guy along, though it wasn't planned.

I took Anton. He had a break in filming from his show, and he loved the beach. And the company.

Leona brought her still-boyfriend pilot, Ed. I still didn't like him, but I kept my mouth shut about it. There's a point when your girlfriend has fallen too far for a guy to be turned back with any sage advice, and that was the point when I stopped giving it. I wouldn't alienate her. We were put on this earth to support one another, not tear each other down, and so I was resigned to watch, worry, and wait. There was nothing I could do but be there to pick her up off the ground if she fell too hard.

Demi brought her friend, Harry. He was an adorable college kid with messy brown hair and thick, black hipster glasses. I kind of loved him. He was sweet and shy, and innocent enough to be just perfect for a bright and shiny young soul like Demi.

Farrah brought along Mitch, a guy she'd been dating on and off for at least a year.

He wasn't her boyfriend, per se, but he was certainly a regular, and all of the roommates liked him.

Even me. He was a cop—LAPD—so I'd just avoided him at first, aggressively so.

As I've said, I have a very healthy fear of the police.

But over time, Mitch had just sort of grown on me. He was nice, and he seemed fair. Honest. Sincere and straightforward, particularly so when he talked about his work. He was one of the good guys. It was as refreshing as it was baffling to run into one.

Still, I'd never get over being paranoid around law enforcement, and I knew that he would always make me nervous.

Of course I could never let that show.

We took two cars, and Anton and I ended up in the car with Mitch and Farrah. Which is how I found out that Anton did not share my opinion about Harry.

"What a smarmy little punk," he muttered as we parted ways with the other group, climbing into cars to head to the beach. His eyes were on Harry, who was opening the door for Demi, so I didn't have to ask whom he meant.

Mitch was driving, Farrah in the passenger seat, and I was sharing the backseat with Anton, so I had an unimpeded view as I shot him a look. "What is your problem? Harry is a doll." I hadn't been aware there was any animosity between them, and I couldn't for the life of me figure out where it came from.

"I guess. If you like pretentious little mamas' boys."

I blinked at him slowly, letting him see how crazy I thought he was. "What the hell, beardo? Leave the poor kid alone. What'd he ever do to you?"

His arms were crossed over his chest, biceps bulging in a way that would have been very distracting if I wasn't starting to see him as a brother, and his face was set in what I would have called a pout if he weren't a huge dude with a man-bun and amazing facial hair.

Nope, I decided. It was still a pout.

"He didn't do anything," Anton finally answered, "but there's no way he's good enough for Demi. She's out of his league."

I don't know why, but I still didn't connect the dots. I was preoccupied, had too much going on in my head, and yes, I was being self-absorbed, were the only excuses I could come up with later.

At the time, though, I only said, "She's out of everyone's league. She's a perfect fucking angel, but a girl's still gotta date."

Anton just curled his lip. "I bet he doesn't even need to wear those glasses. And the douchebag called me his fucking bruh." He snorted. "Bruh. I bet he uses the word hella."

That made me laugh, because I'm a little bit evil (on a good day), but I quickly stifled it. "Just be nice. Jesus. If I can pull myself together and be pleasant for a day, so can you."

"I don't even think they're dating," Farrah added helpfully from the front seat. "They're just friends. She likes to hang out with him. Kind of like you two."

That seemed to improve Anton's mood dramatically, but again, I still didn't catch the significance.

"And us," Mitch added.

Farrah gave him one of those looks you can only give to a lover who has just said something that offended you. "Not like us. We have sex. Sometimes."

I saw Mitch's baffled expression in the rearview and it almost made me laugh.

"You guys aren't sleeping together?" he asked either Anton or me or I guess both of us.

At that I did laugh. Maybe I should have been offended at such a personal question, but I knew he wasn't trying to be rude. He was genuinely shocked.

Anton was smiling and shaking his head as he answered, "Not at all."

"Like ever?" Mitch seemed unconvinced.

"Never," I added. "We're literally just friends. So un-L.A. it hurts."

"Dude," Mitch said, and it was definitely directed at Anton.

"Dude, I know," Anton shot back, still grinning.

Farrah and I looked at each other and rolled our eyes. "Relax, bruhs," I said, mocking them. "You don't need to feel sorry for Anton. He gets around plenty. Just not with me."

"Dude," Mitch commiserated again.

Whatever. I gave up. Men were from Mars, and Mars was stupid.

The reason for our beach day wasn't just to get my depressed ass out of the house on our time off. It was also an ongoing PR project for Anton, whose publicist insisted that he be seen more at all of the 'spots.' His show was building a steady and loyal following, and every time he showed the world how hot he was off the set, it invariably got them a boost of viewers. And on a beach day, where he could show off the killer body he worked his ass off to perfect, the rewards would undoubtedly be tenfold.

We were only too happy to help him. It was, after all, exposure for each one of us. We'd all gotten roles, albeit small ones, from opportune TMZ moments.

These little outings used to be fun for me. The attention. The potential exposure. The hope of being discovered.

Not anymore. I played the game, acted the part, but the crushing weight of reality was too oppressive for me now. Growing up, when fame had been my dream and I'd envisioned a future in Hollywood, it'd been all about doors opening and directors fawning over my incomparable talent and beauty.

The reality was nothing like that, and it felt as though the magic was gone. I was broke, nowhere near famous, and I sure as hell wasn't having a good time.

Still, for whatever reason, I hadn't yet given up. Likely because I was too cursed stubborn.

I spotted a few paparazzi camped out at the entrance to the beach as we were still parking. "Did your publicist call them, or is this a coincidence?" I asked Anton.

He looked annoyed even with his sponsored shades

covering his eyes. "I told her what I was doing, so I'm sure she called."

He seemed salty about it. "It's all part of the job," I reminded him. Small price to pay for the world to know your name, as far as I was concerned.

"I know, I know," he said, already shrugging out of his shirt. "You mind playing it up with me? The photographers always love it when we're affectionate."

I grinned wickedly, all too ready to play that role for anyone that cared to watch, in particular my oldest stalker. "It will be my pleasure." I was glad I'd worn makeup, dressed scantily, and had brought a spare pair of killer heels for the short walk from the car to the sand. I was decked out in metallic hues, head to toe, and it brought out the new gold ombré color in my hair.

I was ready for my close-up.

I waited for Anton to come around and open my door because it made for better pictures. I let him pull me from the car and up into a brief press of our bodies.

I giggled gamely when he kissed me on the neck, my hands stroking intimately over his hair, playing with his little man-bun like it was foreplay, then let him lead me with a familiar arm wrapped cozily around my waist, his big hand on my stomach.

I gave the paparazzi my warmest smile when they called out for Anton. Hell, they even called my name. That's how long and how much we hung out together.

"When will you finally make an honest woman of her?" one of them called, all good humor. We'd been encouraging on again off again rumors for years.

We laughed on cue. "Who says she'll have me?" Anton called back, flashing his perfect white teeth.

"Who says he's up to the challenge?" I said.

They got a kick out of the banter, laughing with us as one of them got it all on video, another snapping pictures of us and our entire entourage.

We walked past them leisurely (for better pictures), but we didn't linger. The idea was that we were in a bit of a hurry, like the photographers weren't half the reason we were there. It would never do to seem too desperate, even if desperation *was* half of our profession.

At least half.

We'd chosen a particularly nice day to visit Carbon Beach. Only a dozen or so other people were lounging about, giving us plenty of room to play.

"Did they follow?" Farrah murmured as we laid out our towels.

I glanced around surreptitiously. "Yes. At ten o'clock."

"Looks like the show must go on," Demi added, her tone flat.

I glanced at her, studying her face. She didn't seem like herself. Not at all.

I moved under the shade of the umbrella that Anton was propping up for me and closer to Demi. "Is everything okay?" I asked her.

She sent me a sheepish smile. "Yes. Of course!" she rallied, shrugging off her purple cover-up. Underneath was a lavender string bikini that was tinier than anything I'd ever seen her wear.

I checked her out. "You look fucking hot, Demi," I pointed out. It was not her usual style, but she was knocking it out of the park.

She blushed, and it was as adorable as it sounds. "Thank you."

"I second that," Harry said with a grin.

I shot a glance at Anton, who had the balls to be eyeing

her bountiful chest, the lech. Some devil got ahold of my tongue. "Do you third it, Anton?" I asked him archly.

"She's basically naked, but yeah, the view is *fantastic*," he said succinctly, sounding downright bitter about it.

I glanced down at myself, then at Farrah and Leona, who were already laying out. It was skimpy for Demi, but she wasn't showing more skin than anyone else was.

My eyes narrowed on Anton as my preoccupied brain finally caught up to what was going on.

He was jealous. Over Demi. Uh uh. Nope. He was a shameless man-whore, and he was not allowed to go there. Not with my too innocent, too sweet friend.

"Hey, beardo," I called to him, already moving away and toward the water. "A word."

He joined me in the surf. We were up to mid-calf in the water, and, mindful of the photographer that still had us in his sights, I threw my arms around Anton's neck, leaning into him.

He gripped my waist lightly with his big hands, very familiar with the routine.

I wondered if he could tell that I was glaring at him through my dark shades. "You know Demi is off-limits, right?"

His mouth twisted like he'd just tasted something sour. "What are you talking about?"

"My friend. *Demi*," I emphasized.

"She's my friend, too. What about her?"

"She's too innocent for you. She's not a casual girl. You'd break her heart. You know that, right?"

He lowered his shades enough to shoot me a belligerent glance. "I'm well fucking aware."

"I'm not sure you are. You're acting possessive about

her. And I saw the way you were looking at her in that bikini."

"I was looking at all of you like that. You just didn't see it. I like bikinis. And skin."

I wasn't buying it. "So we're clear? No messing with Demi?"

"Message received. I get it; you're a mama bear with your friends. How about you give this speech to Mr. Hella Bruh that's pawing her over there?"

I glanced over at Demi and Harry. Anton was exaggerating. Mostly. Harry was just helping her apply sunblock.

"You're only proving my point right now," I pointed out.

"Fine. I'll drop it. I'll try my best to stay away from our sweet Demi from here on out."

I studied him. The way he said it made me wonder if something had already happened between them.

I glanced at Demi, who was indeed getting more and more cozy with Mr. Hella Bruh and decided against it. There was no way she'd be so nonchalant around Anton if that were the case.

That settled, we put on a great show for the cameras, frolicking in the surf, canoodling in the sand.

I'm not sure when it happened, but at some point the day went from faking fun for the cameras to actively enjoying myself.

It was possibly around the time that we broke out the bottles of pre-maid cocktails we'd packed in lieu of a picnic lunch. Who needs food when you can have liquor?

We chatted about nothing and everything as we pretended to lay out to tan, when in actuality we were all sun-blocked into oblivion and reapplying every quarter hour. Because wrinkles.

"I was sure that Lacy was going to get killed off in the season finale," Farrah was saying, referring to her recurring role as a biker groupie in Anton's show. She was such a hit that they kept bringing her back. "But I just got the script back, and they're keeping her! They're giving her a bigger role than ever in a story arc that goes into the next season!"

"That's amazing!"

"Congrats!"

"They know their audience!"

"Awesome!"

We all congratulated her and meant it. I personally thought she was brilliant in the role. She was a valley girl and an ex-cheerleader, so it was a testament to her talent that she could pull off the role of a hardened biker chick so perfectly.

"Eventually we'll all be on your show, Anton," Leona joked, though who knew if it *was* a joke. I myself had made a few appearances, though nothing with a speaking role, mostly I'd been an extra with a lot of close-up body shots. Leona had been cast in a similar way, if less times.

That left only Demi, but even as I had the thought, she said, "I'm actually going to be in it too. My agent called me earlier. That role I was up for, the rival club's daughter. I got it."

I blinked at her. How had I missed this?

We all rushed to congratulate her, and I felt like a dick for having no clue about such huge news.

"That sounds like a big role," Harry said, hugging her. "Wow. That could really turn into something, right?"

"She's already scheduled to have sex with me," Anton said, his tone flat and more than a touch riled.

We all looked at him. Okay, I *glared*, and Demi blushed and looked everywhere but at him.

"What?" Harry asked him, wide-eyed.

"Our characters have a star-crossed affair. She's going to be on the show quite a bit, from the sound of it. They have lots of story planned for her character."

"You don't sound thrilled about that," Demi almost mumbled the words, not looking at him.

"I just don't think the show is a good fit for you," he said brutally.

For that, we were *all* glaring at him. "What the hell?" I asked him.

"You can get typecast, doing a show like this," he tried to explain. "I just don't think it fits your image. You should be trying for more family friendly stuff. Like one of those princess live-action flicks. Something like that."

"That's why it's called acting," Demi said to her feet, her face red. "I should be able to do both."

Anton was not letting up. He was in a hell of a mood. "This is a *cable* show. Did you know they're already talking about having you do a topless scene? With *me*. A topless sex scene in front of the world. That what you were going for?"

Demi, looking more miserable by the second, responded with a forlorn, "Topless? Oh no. My parents are going to kill me."

"I told you not to audition," he continued relentlessly. "This is *not* a good fit for you. Mark my words."

"Knock it the hell off," I told him. "She's an actress and the path she takes is her business." We had a pretty aggressive stare down, but eventually he broke the gaze. "Now quit being an ass and congratulate her."

"Congratulations," Anton looked very pointedly at

Demi, who still wouldn't look at him. "In a few weeks, I'm going to be playing with your naked tits in front of an audience. Hope you're okay with that." He got up and stormed away.

"What the ever-loving *fuck*?" I asked anyone that might know what Anton's problem was.

"Asshole," Leona breathed, shrugging off her quiet but clingy pilot boyfriend to go put her arm around Demi. "You okay, sweetie?"

Demi nodded, but she was chewing on her lip. "I think he thinks I'm intruding on his territory. It's his show, he's the lead in it, and I don't think he wants me being a part of it."

That was it. I got up and went after him.

His long stride had covered a lot of distance fast, but he'd stopped as soon as he hit the nearest bar, which was about a foot away once you hit the street, so it wasn't hard to catch or find him.

I took the barstool next to him, glancing around. We were getting some stares. It was a quick walk from the beach, but no one else in the place was wearing swimsuits. Also, they may have recognized Anton.

Whatever.

"That was so out of line," I told him quietly after the bartender left our earshot. "Were you trying to make her feel like shit?"

He sighed heavily. "No, but I think she'll feel like worse shit if her perfect family sees her topless in her first big role. And topless is just the edge of it. They've got a scene written of her . . . servicing me in a bathroom. It's not what I want for her. Is that what *you* want for her? Her biggest role to date and the world gets to see her topless and on her knees?"

Jesus. It did make me feel overprotective, but ... "That's beside the point. Regardless of how you feel about that particular subject, do you think you're handling this in a good way? She's out there looking like she might cry because she thinks you don't want to work with her. You need to go apologize, and you need to make it stick."

He cursed, long and fluid. He finished his beer with one long swig, standing up. "Fine. Fine. You're right. I'm an asshole. I'll go apologize."

He settled his tab and we left.

When we got back to the group, he quietly asked Demi to take a walk with him.

Farrah and Mitch went swimming, and Leona's pilot and Harry went to grab a beer together.

It was just me and Leona sitting side by side, watching the water when she said, "It's so peaceful, isn't it? The ocean, I mean."

Peaceful? I did not find the ocean peaceful. I found it troubling. I didn't see the calm waves or the beautiful water, I only saw the chaos underneath, the dangers lurking in the depths. Riptides, strong currents, high tides. Sharks. Other things that bite and/or sting you.

Today on Scarlett looking at the world with fear and pessimism: Oceans.

It also didn't help that it reminded me of a certain bastard's eyes.

But all I said was, "It certainly gives the world perspective."

Which was true, and yet another thing about the ocean that I hated. If you stared at it for too long, it made you think. Reflect on your life. Your choices. Your state of well-being.

My current state was clearly not well.

My foul mood, uneven temper, and damn near steady drunk. Is that who I was becoming? Fucking Glenda? Was I really letting myself turn into someone I despised? Pitied? And for him?

Not fucking likely.

"Did you know about Demi getting that part?" I asked Leona.

"Yeah. It's so awesome, isn't it?"

"It is, but I had no clue she even auditioned. I'm such a shit friend."

"Stop that right now," she said sternly. "You are a good friend. The best kind of friend. You found out a few hours later, so what? Who was the first one to get on Anton about being an ass to her? Who was the one that got him to come back and apologize?"

"That's just because I'm good at being the bitch."

"No. *No.*" She was shaking her head. "I don't agree with that. You're a lioness, not a lamb, and you don't need to *apologize* for it. You're overprotective and fiercely loyal. None of those are bad qualities. They're your strengths and I've always admired you for embracing them.

The best kind of friend is one that makes you feel like a better version of yourself, and Leona was an absolute pro at that. "Thank you," I said quietly. I hadn't been fishing for a pep talk, but I realized just then that I'd sure as hell needed one.

"Familiarity breeds contempt."
~Aesop

chapter four

PAST

Dante

I was packing for a dreaded overnight stay with my dad in Seattle when I heard my mother yelling.

With a long-suffering sigh, I dropped what I was doing and went to investigate.

Sure enough, there she was, laying into Glenda, Scarlett's grandma, with particular viciousness. My mother was never nice to the staff, but sometimes she got truly out of control. This was a case in point. From what I'd gleaned as I made my way to the yelling pair, Glenda hadn't polished the silver properly, and now Adelaide was rapping her on the forehead, over and over, with a small spoon, each contact punctuated with an insult.

"Useless woman. *Why* do I keep you around? No one else will hire you, but is that my problem? Some people *deserve* to be out on the streets."

The older woman was cowering away, looking pathetic.

I used to like the way my mother treated her. It was petty, I know, but it seemed fair with the way she treated Scarlett that she'd get a bit of it back.

But as I grew older, and began to understand a bit more of how humans worked, I became more and more troubled by it. Not because I had much pity for the woman.

It was that every slight she received seemed to only go one place. She never gave it back to my mother.

Instead, she passed it on. To my girl.

"Mother," I said loudly, my tone curt. "Enough. Get away from her."

"Stay out of this," she snarled at me, looking deranged.

"No," I said firmly. "Let the woman do her job and leave her be."

"This woman is too *stupid* and *simple* to do her job," my mother told me tremulously, and I wondered which personality I was dealing with today. "That is my *problem*. This is what I get for hiring *trash* to clean my house."

"Just stop. Go to your room," I softened my tone, because sometimes that worked with her, though nothing inside of me remained soft toward my mother. She'd stomped out every tender feeling I had for her a very long time ago. "I think you need to lie down. Maybe take something? This isn't like you." That was a lie, but sometimes lies worked with her too.

My mother studied me like I studied her—like she wasn't quite sure how to handle me today.

"Perhaps I will." She dropped the spoon and moved to me, taking my arm. "Walk me. I feel a bit weak."

I walked her dutifully to her room, because I knew well to keep up appearances, even in front of the staff.

I thought that was the end of it, but as I began to move down the hallway, she called me back into her room.

"Yes, Mother?" I asked her. She was lying on her bed now, looking like a delicate doll against the pillows.

She smiled serenely at me. "If you correct me in front of the help again you *will* be sorry. Scarlett will be even sorrier. I'll make sure of it. You're little cum-dumpster will pay the price for your insolence."

Fucking triggered. I went for the jugular. "Stay the *hell* away from Scarlett. If I catch you saying or doing one fowl thing to, or about her, here's what's going to happen: Your friends at the country club are all going to hear every awful thing you've ever said about them. I've been paying attention, *Mother*. I've been taking notes. I'll tell them everything. Who will even talk to you again after they've heard what you think of them? It's bad enough you're stuck holding court in this rinky-dink nowhere town—you think if you get ostracized here, that you will *ever* live it down?"

I had her, I saw it. Still, I took it a step further. "And leave Glenda alone. Quit abusing the staff. I catch you doing it again, I will tell at least one of your *friends* something *interesting* that you've said about them. Is that clear?"

She nodded, her face a careful mask.

Round for me.

I went back to packing. My dad was supposed to pick me up at two, and I had to rush to be ready on time.

Still, I was ready at two. Two came and went, then three. Then four.

At five o'clock a car and driver showed up.

"Do I really have to go?" I asked my mother, who had only just emerged from her wing of the house.

"Of course you do. It's part of the deal."

"He didn't bother to show up himself, and even his driver is three hours late."

She shrugged, completely unaffected. "So? A deal's a deal. He has you for the weekend. Go."

"I don't want to go. I want to stay with Gram instead."

"It's interesting that you think any of us care what you *want*. Now go."

It was hopeless. My mother had never been any help in dealing with my father, and she clearly wasn't interested in changing that.

I went with the driver.

I hated visiting my father. Living with my mother was obviously no picnic, but I'd learned how to deal with her and stay largely out of her way.

Leo was a different and less familiar challenge. Who knew what awful things he had planned for me this time?

A selfish part of me wished I could at least have brought Scarlett with me, but even if I could have gotten her away, the fact was that I didn't like to bring her around my father.

I didn't like the way he looked at her. It was unsettling and infuriating, some strange mixture of distaste, recognition, and animal lust. It made me want to hurt him.

I'd taken to sheltering her from my father even more diligently than I did my mother.

I only had to stay with Leo a few weekends a year, but they were always particularly dreadful.

This one was no exception.

I wasn't greeted at the door of his penthouse apartment. I had to ring the doorbell several times before a redheaded woman in her underwear answered the door.

She smiled when she saw me. "You must be the

birthday boy," she said and took off her bra. "I've got a present for you, D—" She paused, then called over her shoulder, "Leo! What's your son's name again?"

"Dante," he called back from somewhere in the large apartment. "Happy Birthday, boy!" he shouted.

At least he's here, I thought wryly. Drunk off his ass, but here.

It wasn't even my birthday. That'd been over a month ago, and I'd seen him at least once since then.

The topless woman started moving closer, and I warded her off with my hands. "No, thank you. I have a girlfriend."

She giggled and went down to her knees. She put a finger over her mouth and said in what I think she thought was a quiet voice. "I won't tell her if you won't. Now come here. Let me see if big cocks run in the family. Don't be shy. I don't have a gag reflex."

I wanted to leave right then, but I was too proud. My father would say I'd run away like a pussy or something along those lines. He always turned everything into a test for me, like *he* was some standard to be held to, which was a joke.

"No, thank you," I told her, coldly and politely. "Which room is my dad in?"

Another woman walked into the entryway, this one blonde, wearing a corset around her middle and nothing else. The blonde was not natural.

"I'll show you to him, baby," she purred at me. "You guys are into some fucked up shit—the father/son kink, but I'm down. Ever double penetrated a woman? If you're into that, I'm your girl."

I was genuinely horrified. I didn't consider myself a prude, but she'd more than shocked me.

"I want to talk to him," I clarified. Translation: I wanted to chew him the hell out.

She nodded her head toward the billiard room. "The party's in there, birthday boy. You're in for a treat, let me tell you."

It was not a treat.

Well, not for me, at least. Leo seemed to be enjoying himself.

I hadn't thought I could have less respect for my father, but I'd been *wrong*.

The first thing I noticed was the two girls on the pool table. They were naked, on hands and knees, facing away from each other, and they were *moving*. When I realized what they were doing, I felt myself blush.

The next thing my eye caught was my depraved father. He was sitting on one of the low leather couches with a glass in one hand, while the other was tucking himself back into his pants, his eyes glued to the pool table. The woman beside him, his mistress, I realized in shock as she straightened up from his lap, was wiping her mouth.

"Can I have a word?" I asked him sharply.

He sent me a glare that made him look like a spoiled child told to put down his ice cream. "Oh what *now*? You're not happy with your birthday party?"

"I'll be in the kitchen," I told him and left the room, having to shrug off two half-naked prostitutes as I went.

He didn't make me wait as long as I thought he would, only ten minutes or so, but in that time I had to kick five working girls out of the room.

"It's not my birthday," I said when he finally made his way leisurely into the kitchen.

He leaned against a countertop, his dirty blond hair

mussed, part of it standing on end. I don't think he noticed.

He folded his arms over his chest, glass of liquor still in hand, staring me down. It wasn't very intimidating considering he was swaying on his feet. "It's not?"

"It's not." But that wasn't even the point. "You do know I'm only fifteen?" I asked him, curling my lip with the question. I wanted him to know how disgusted I was with him.

I always wanted that. It was the focal point of our relationship for me. I wanted, always, to establish how different I was from him.

How I was *nothing* like him.

He blinked a few times slowly, his mouth opening in what could only be described as a vaguely shocked, drunken pout.

I'm not even sure why his reaction surprised me. It wasn't at all out of the question that he'd forgotten how old I was.

"Fifteen?" he finally got out, taking a long swig of his drink and pursing his lips. "I thought it was fourteen. How the years go by. Damn, I hope you're not still a virgin?" He laughed. "Have I neglected my fatherly duties?"

I wanted to punch him right in his smug, drunken face. I was shaking with the urge.

"You're sick, old man," I sneered instead.

"Don't tell me you're queer." Something bright entered his eyes, and he smiled. "Actually, that would be just fine with me, as long as you can still manage to produce an heir. My God, that would be justice. Adelaide would lose her cunt mind."

I'd been rolling my eyes pretty hard, but he didn't seem

to notice, so I finally just interrupted his strange tirade. "I'm not gay, and I don't want a whore for my birthday."

"I wasn't offering you a whore, son." In spite of everything, my heart jumped a bit when he called me son. It was pathetic. "I was offering you a room full of them. An *apartment* full. I was offering you as many different whores as you could stick your squeaky clean dick in between now and your next school day."

"No, thank you. I have a girlfriend."

"So? Is she here now? Grow some balls, boy, or at least get yours back. Gotta be a man sometime."

"Even if I didn't have a girlfriend, I'm not interested in prostitutes," I sneered.

That had him lifting a brow and calling, "Heather! Get in here."

"Why does *she* need to be here?" I asked him. I had no reason to like his longtime mistress. Just the opposite.

He grinned and it was unpleasant. "You're not interested in whores." Heather walked into the room, looking unfazed.

Well, dead behind the eyes if I was accurate.

The things she must see on a daily basis, I thought. I should have more pity for the woman.

"Heather, Dante says he's not interested in whores, but I still owe him a birthday present."

I still didn't catch on until she started to strip, her dead eyes on me. I was more naive than I'd realized.

"What are you doing?" I asked both of them, backing up a step, then another.

"Her tubes were tied after she had Lorenzo, so you don't have to wear a condom. You're welcome."

"You're disgusting," I told him.

"Is he gay?" Heather spoke for the first time.

Leo shrugged. "You prefer anal? Go for it. Heather's up for anything."

"Fuck no. Fuck you."

"He always was a brat," Heather noted.

This from the woman that had tried to smother affection on me in front of Leo when I was a child, then had shown me nothing but cruelty when his back was turned.

I gave my despised father the coldest stare I could muster over my rage. "I said I'm not interested in prostitutes. Get her out of here."

She left in a huff, like I'd deeply offended her.

"I'm going to tell Mother about this," I told him when she was gone.

I hated that I sounded like a child as I said it.

"Ha!" He got a real kick out of that. "Go for it. You think she doesn't know what I'm up to? I can't divorce the cunt, but she sure as hell doesn't get to tell me where I put my dick."

I stared at him, glared, and hated that aside from the eyes, I was the very *image* of him. *Only on the outside,* I told myself.

It cannot be stated strongly enough—I *hate* my parents.

"I'm going to Gram's for the rest of the weekend. Any objections?"

He shrugged, waving me off. "Whatever. More for me. Have my driver take you."

One good thing came out of the weekend: He never insisted that I stay with him again.

"If love is the answer, could you please rephrase the question?"
~Lily Tomlin

chapter five

PRESENT

Scarlett

It wasn't an easy drive to get to my friend Gina's house. It would've taken a solid hour without traffic, which was a laughable assessment. There was *always* traffic. It was an hour and a half if traffic was good, two and counting if it was the alternative, which it almost always was.

I loved driving, loved going fast, even in my shitty old sedan I wreaked havoc on the streets like I was racing every stranger I passed. God help me if I ever actually owned a car that could perform to match my mood.

I loved driving, yes, but no one loved driving in *this* town. It was a chore to get to my dear friend's house, but when she called, I answered. When she asked, I came if I could.

It was a one-sided kind of friendship. I never called

her, never asked or invited myself. But some friendships are just designed that way. It's unavoidable. A give and take that we *need* even if it's not what we *want*.

Some people are put into our lives at just the right moment. Of this I am certain.

And the why of it was this woman. Gina.

Gina was the kind of nice that made everyone around her uncomfortable. If I so much as mentioned a hardship I had suffered, even a casual one that was years old, her eyes would water as though it was a fresh wound. There was nothing I despised more than receiving someone else's pity. It literally made my skin crawl, but I knew that she couldn't help herself.

Eugene, her husband, was not much better. He was more in touch with his emotions than a Care Bear. And not in an annoying way. Well, not completely. He had a method of disarming that was rare. He brought out the soft side in everyone, asked just the question that let you know he was in tune with your mood. That he cared, that he felt.

He was one of those sensitive men that had more of a hard-on for Adele than Angelina.

I secretly loved that about him, and I tried my best to behave when I came over to visit. I kept the more acidic side of my tongue to myself.

Mostly.

They lived in a mansion in the hills. A dream house beyond even my overinflated dreams. They were both successful entertainment attorneys that came from money, and everything about their life was a bit of a fairytale, but that didn't make me jealous or covetous. Unworthy, perhaps, but never jealous.

No one deserved a perfect life more than they did.

They greeted me as a pair at the door when I arrived, opening it before I could knock. Gina pulled me into a tight, long hug. She was a short, heavy blonde woman with a pretty face and at least fifteen years on me, though I'd never been so ill mannered as to actually ask her age. "How are you, gorgeous?" she said, beaming as she let me loose.

"Hanging in there," I said with a rueful smile, my best version of looking at things on the bright side.

Eugene gave me a warm hug. He was a big man with a soft voice. "You've lost weight. Luckily I made pasta."

I tried not to groan in dismay. The last thing I needed was carbs. I fucking hated carbs. They made me feel bloated and sleepy. And fat. "Yum, my favorite," I said, trying, as always with them, to be a good sport.

"Had any interesting roles or auditions lately?" Gina asked politely as we stepped into the house. She was always very interested in my career, or lack thereof. She'd been the one to connect me with my agent, years ago.

My mood brightened slightly. "Actually, yes. I had an audition last week that felt like it went really well. I've got my fingers crossed."

She clutched her hands together, face brightening like I'd just made her day. "That's wonderful! What sort of a part is it?"

I shrugged. "It wasn't really clear. Some kind of a character role. I wasn't even sure if it was major or minor, but the director is Stuart Whently, so I'm pretty excited."

"Love his movies!" Gina exclaimed.

"We *love* his movies!" Eugene chimed at the same time.

I smiled nervously and found myself ringing my hands. "Well, cross your fingers. He was at my audition—it was a call back—and we actually hit it off pretty well. He said some nice things to me and it felt like, I don't know, like he at least *wanted* to hire me."

"That's awesome!"

"Brilliant!"

I smiled ruefully. I imagined that this was what it felt like to have your mother compliment you. I appreciated it, even if it didn't mean anything. But even so, I felt better, enough so to elaborate. "He said I had defining characteristics. That I would give the movie panache. Like I said, it felt like we hit it off."

They overreacted.

Eugene made me give him a high five as he congratulated me as if I already had the part. Like I even knew what the part was.

Gina put both hands to her cheeks and teared up.

It made me feel silly, like I'd overstated things, even though I had actually understated them.

These people were way too nice to me. It made me so uncomfortable that I felt awkward in my own skin.

I tried not to let it show and allowed them to fawn over me.

We went straight to the dining room. I was just in time, and I knew that they'd have dinner ready. They were always very prompt, never taking too much of my time when we had these dinners. It was ironic that they valued *my* time when they were both worth much more per hour than I was.

But they did value it, I knew. I was equal parts flattered and baffled by that.

Their daughter, Mercy, was already in the dining room. They had a house that was elegant and extravagant enough to have come straight out of a magazine, but they let their precious little girl have the run of it. Currently she was finger painting on a child-sized easel, her colored fingers dripping generously onto their expensive marble floor.

Neither parent so much as scolded her. They were doting to a fault, which wasn't at all surprising, since they even doted on *me*.

Mercy was the most beautiful child I'd ever seen. She just was. It wasn't any one thing about her face that made her so, but the way each feature fell together like poetry. To describe her was to do it no justice. Masses of streaky, dark blonde hair with just the right thickness and wave to it that it fell in a perfectly arranged waterfall down her back.

Big blue eyes, again something that sounded so plain, but made stunning on her. Thick lashed, almond shaped, and heavy lidded. They were bright and fathomless at once.

Her cheekbones were high and colored as though someone had taken blush to them, though I knew her mother, of all people, would never do such a thing to a child. Her lips were a perfect little rosebud, her nose small, straight, and shaped appealingly.

"Scarlett!" she said excitedly, rushing at me.

Her mother caught her halfway, guiding her toward the powder room. "Oh no you don't. First, let's wash up for dinner. Remember what we talked about? That not everyone likes paint all over their clothing?"

"But it's purple!" the little girl returned. "Purple is pwetty!"

Her parents both cracked up at that, and I tried my best to smile with them.

Mercy rushed to hug me when she was paint free, throwing her little arms around my waist.

I patted her on the head tentatively, letting her touch me but not knowing what the proper response was on my part.

As I've said, I'm bad with children. Luckily, I didn't know many people with kids, so it wasn't often a problem.

Eugene smiled at me fondly and threw a friendly arm around my shoulders, an embrace that never seemed to get less awkward, at least for me.

"So how are you guys?" I asked him. Gina had gone into the kitchen to ready dinner.

"Wonderful," he replied with no hesitation. "Just wonderful. We're blessed. *So* blessed." He sent me a warm, fond smile.

This was his usual response, and I actually believed it. They had a wonderful life and they felt it was all a blessing. Even pessimistic me couldn't fault them for it.

"No one deserves it more," I returned sincerely, though the words came out stiffly. "You're the best parents I know." It wasn't saying much, most of my friends were single and childless, but it was still the truth.

He stammered out a thank you at that, eyes misting over.

Oh Jesus. I had to look away. He was such an emotional, open book that I didn't have a clue how to deal with him. Mostly I just tried to pretend nothing was happening when we had 'a moment.'

Dinner was delicious, as always, and the conversation was pleasant. It was so positive, in fact, that I didn't know how to contribute to it. Sarcasm felt wrong in their presence. Snark felt inappropriate, so I tried my best to be politely neutral without being fake.

It was a difficult line to balance. Particularly so for me.

I wondered, not for the first time, why these perfect people wanted so earnestly to be friends with me, to have mean, negative, *flawed* me in their lives on a regular basis.

Of course, I didn't voice the thought aloud. I knew more than anyone did that, when it came to these two that would be the equivalent of fishing for compliments.

I escaped them right after dinner, as soon as it was politely possible.

I had to pry Mercy, and then Gina, off me after hugging them. They were an extremely affectionate family.

"She has your smile," I told Gina as we said goodbye, and it was true.

Gina beamed at me, and it was a grownup version of the one Mercy had just bestowed on me. "You think so?"

"I do."

"Oh, thank you. What a sweet thing for you to say. Her smile is so beautiful."

"Just like yours."

She flushed in pleasure.

Normally I took their perfection with something approaching good grace, but lately I had been thin-skinned and emotional, and being around the three of them made me dwell on every bittersweet thing I'd ever lost.

I'd just fastened my seatbelt when my phone started ringing.

I checked the screen. It was Dante. Typical.

I ignored it, foul mood gone fouler.

It stopped and started again almost immediately, and for some reason, I answered that time.

"Does he know he doesn't have a chance?" his silky voice bled over the phone. "That he never did?"

Hello, temper.

That opening salvo had hit its target perfectly and even I could admit that he'd won the round.

But the bastard wasn't finished.

"You've never been soft for anyone else. You've never been vulnerable. Those things belong to *me*." He launched each jab at me without pity, hesitation, or remorse. The *bastard*. "They *always* have. They always will. You've never given the you that's *mine* to anyone else, and you *never* will. Even your lying lips can't convince me otherwise."

It was so callous, so profoundly *cruel*, even for him, that my breath caught at his words. It held in my chest for a few chaotic beats before I could pull it together enough to breathe again.

In, out. In, out. In, out.

Of course every word he'd said was true. That's why they hurt so much.

Finally, I found my voice to ask, "Why do you do this? What do you want from me?"

"That's a pretty silly question. I think you know."

"No. *No.* No, I sure as hell don't know. Whatever goes on in that manipulative brain of yours is so beyond me that I don't even *try* to guess anymore."

"I do this to remind you—there's no one else for you." His voice had thickened as he spoke, so rich now that it felt like a physical touch. "There's only *me*."

"You're such a bastard," I managed to choke out around the thick ball of hatred that had formed in my throat.

"I'm a complete and utter bastard," he agreed ruthlessly, "but you *never* get to stop loving me. I *need* you to stay *incapable* of moving on."

The sheer gall of him, the utter nerve . . . I was so

furious I was trembling with it. "I hate you," I said, my voice ragged, the words feeling like they'd been wrenched out of me.

I hung up before he could respond.

I was so thoroughly pissed off after that that there was nothing to do but go shopping.

Because retail therapy.

I had another bad moment as I was driving through the winding mall parking lot when I spotted the huge Durant's department store sign and had a near overpowering urge to drive my car through its shiny glass doors.

It was pure hell to be a broke shopaholic with an ex whose family owned one of the biggest department store chains in the world. It was salt in the wound that I couldn't afford to shop there. Not even close.

Still, feeling contrary, I parked near the entrance, went inside, and started trying on overpriced designer dresses. I wasn't sure if it made me feel better or worse that they all looked fabulous on me.

Eventually I moved on to shoes, and that definitely made me feel better.

Someday I'll be successful, I told myself. *Someday I'll be able to buy myself whatever the hell I please.*

Someday I won't hate myself. Someday I won't be hung up on a guy that messes with my head for fun.

Someday I'll be rid of this weakness in my bloodstream that is my love for Dante.

By the time I'd exhausted all of my contrary shopping urges I felt decidedly better.

The magic of shoes.

I was heading back out to my car when my agent called me. With news. Amazing news. Life changing.

I was still stunned by it as I made the long, traffic-filled drive home.

Could this be it? Finally? My big break?

I was almost afraid to hope.

"There is always some madness in love. But there is also always some reason in madness."
~Friedrich Nietzsche

chapter

six

PAST

Dante

There were three of them to my one, but adrenaline had ignited in my bloodstream right along with my temper, so it felt like good odds to me.

Also, I was bigger, meaner, and angrier than all of them put together.

Jock #1 went down like a chump. I'd have bet a good percentage of my trust fund that he'd never even been in a real fight before. He came left, and I blocked him, jabbing under my own upheld arm for a vicious gut punch. Shock overtook his face as he doubled over, the breath whooshing out of him. He was out after that, more focused on his own pain than coming at me again.

Good. Onto the next. Jock #2 wasn't so easy to take

down. He was bigger than the last and better at throwing a punch, but it just wasn't enough. He lasted about thirty seconds longer before I brought him low with a brutal fist to the chin.

Jock #3, fucking Reese McCoy, was the best fighter of the bunch, but he also happened to be the one I most wanted to beat the shit out of, so it didn't do him a whole lot of good.

His big mouth had started this.

He got in a few good clocks before I took him down, but I wasn't going to give him too much credit for it. I never was much good at ducking.

Luckily, he wasn't either. I cornered him and started whaling, the sound of each punch barely louder than the blood rushing through my ears.

I used to get into fights for her because they called her trash and tried to hurt her.

It got better for a time as kids started to understand that I wouldn't stand for that, but over one summer her body changed.

She went from being my best buddy—my partner in crime, then boom, she changed shape, she was a girl, and then, right on the tail of that, a woman.

She didn't just get boobs before any other girl in our school. She got *fantastic* boobs. They were out of this world. Big, perky, pointing right at you, mouth-watering breasts.

And her hips and ass drove me possibly more insane. She became shapely all over, but her waist stayed as tiny as ever.

And her face—it was much the same as the dear face I'd known for so long, but something happened to it, to her pouty lips, her dark, dark, drown-in-me eyes, even her voice changed, got lower, raspier.

She walked into school that year and it was comical to watch the way the boys couldn't take their eyes off her. Even the ones that had been the cruelest to her, the ones that hated her still, couldn't manage to hide their reactions.

Well, it would have been comical if it didn't make me want to kill someone.

A lot of someones.

I'd watched the entire shift, witnessed every minuscule change in her as it happened.

But for the rest of the boys it seemed to happen overnight. One day they all looked at my girl and saw what I saw.

It was not a good year for me. I got into fight after fight, same kids, just calling her different names now. And looking at her. And talking about her. And mentioning her name with the wrong fucking tone in their voice.

The only upside to fighting these days was that kids rarely told. Teenage boys had too much pride to tattle.

And meanwhile, Scarlett didn't even have a clue that she was the sexiest creature on the planet. She'd been a bona fide sexpot at fifteen and completely oblivious to it.

Well, not *completely*. She seemed to have at least some idea about what she did to *me*, and she'd had no problem practicing her wiles on me rather ruthlessly for the last few years.

I was a willing lamb to the slaughter. Anything she wanted to do to me I wanted done. I'd lie on my back and let her sharpen her claws on my underbelly as long as she let me look at her while she did it.

I was that far gone.

But she was mine, fucking *mine*, and only I had the

right to think of her that way, let alone speak about her that way.

Which brought us to this fight, and the things I'd caught these punks saying about her in the locker room. They hadn't even been trying to hide it from me, the thickheaded idiots.

We'd just finished football practice. Scarlett had come to watch from the stands, but everyone knew she was there for me. Every single one of these guys knew what was up.

I'd been on my way out, practically to the door, hell, maybe that was it, maybe they'd thought I was already gone, when I heard them talking.

They didn't even have to say her name. And a few words in I nearly lost it just by the tone in scumbag Reese's voice.

"Did you see what she was wearing today?" he was asking his buffoon, jock friends.

That's all it took. I knew who he was talking about.

I stopped in my tracks, my entire body going stiff. Reese I had a *particular* problem with. This was not his first offense, or even his third. He had a thing for my girl, a thing that involved him degrading and coveting her both, and I had a major fucking issue with it.

"Fucking A I did," one of his greasy buddies answered.

"She's such a fucking tease," another one said.

"No," Reese replied. "She's no tease. She's been giving it up to Durant since sixth grade, I heard."

From my shoulders to my fists, I felt myself begin to shake.

"No shit?" one asked.

"Doesn't surprise me one bit," the other added.

"Yeah, it's the truth," Reese said, like he knew it for a

fact. "She's a little nympho, too, man. Can't get enough cock. I heard she'll spread her legs for anybody. There's just one thing you have to do."

Fucking triggered.

I knew I was about to get myself into trouble, but I'd heard too much. I couldn't walk away.

"What?" his friends chimed on cue.

"Just take her out back to the dumpster. Makes her feel right at home."

Fucking.

Triggered.

They started laughing and I lost my shit.

"She'll let *anyone* plow her if you don't mind a little garbage with your puss . . ." Reese trailed off as he saw me coming at them.

The rest was a domino effect of violence. I took the punks out, one by one.

"Don't talk about her. If I hear another fucking word come out of your mouth that has anything to do with my girl you will make me have to hurt you." I was spitting each word into his face I was so unrepentantly angry.

The two cohorts were down, and I was straddling a struggling Reese, one hand holding him in place, the other cocked back for another blow when my friend Nate's voice got through to me.

"Coach is coming. Dante, he's coming! Walk away!"

I let my fist fly one last time with relish before I got off him.

The first thing I saw when I walked outside was Scarlett. She was waiting for me, looking edible, living up to every fantasy that every one of those fuckers no doubt had about her on a daily basis.

I was a hypocrite. Even if she hadn't been mine, even

if she'd been with someone else, I'd have fixated on her, obsessed about her.

It was the wildness in her. She could never hide it. Not in her eyes, not in her smile, not in her masses of wavy hair, or her out of this world curves. Every part of her led the mind to the same conclusion—this beautiful creature cannot be tamed.

It drove guys out of their minds, I knew firsthand. I'd been mad for her since we were ten years old and she gave me her first conspiratorial grin, the one that told me we'd be giving the world hell.

Adrenaline was still pumping through my system, endorphins going wild, as I approached.

Her brows drew together in concern as she saw my face. "Fighting again?" She touched my cheek when we were in reaching distance. "Are you okay?"

"Fine," I said shortly. Reese's words were still echoing through my head, still drawing me back to fight him.

"Who was it?" she asked.

"No one important," I replied truthfully.

"Let's get out of here," she said, taking my hand.

"The cabin's ready," I told as her we broke into the woods, moving swiftly along the familiar trail that took us home.

She shot me a look. "Are you . . . up for that? Is this really the best time? I can tell you were hit in the face— your cheek is red. Where else are you hurt?"

"I'm fine. You can check out my other bruises . . . at the cabin." I grinned at her. She blushed and looked away.

I felt myself getting hard.

"Isn't it a long hike?" she asked her feet.

It was. The cabin was on Gram's land, that's how I'd

found it, but it was deep in the woods. No roads led to it, just one grueling hiking trail. That's why it was so perfect. It was a place that could be ours alone. "About an hour and a half hiking, less if we set a good pace. I'm up for it if you are?"

She chewed on her lip, still blushing. "I'm up for it. It certainly feels like we've waited long enough."

We had, and then I'd made us wait longer, finding just the right spot, cleaning it out, stocking it up.

The hotels in town were shit, and nowhere else felt private enough for our first real time together.

"I just need to grab one thing from Gram's," I explained.

"We'll be back before it's dark, won't we? We can't hike back in the dark. Do we have enough time?"

"It's a Friday. You *always* stay out late enough for Glenda to pass out and then you leave before she wakes up. Do you really think she's going to notice if you're away for one night?"

She looked uncertain. Her grandma terrified her to an unreasonable degree. It made me sick to my stomach to think about. She was so helpless when it came to that hateful woman.

"I don't want to rush," I added. And when that wasn't enough, I used the magic word. "Please."

"Okay," she agreed instantly. "But if I catch hell for it, I'm blaming you, and letting you deal with my grandma."

"Deal." I didn't hesitate. Her grandma pissed me the hell of, but she didn't scare me.

I grabbed the key to the thick padlock I'd put on the cabin door. It was on a key chain, but as we started to leave, an idea struck me.

"One sec," I told Scarlett, leaving her by the front door.

I found Gram. It didn't even occur to me that she wouldn't have what I needed. "Do you have a gold chain I could borrow? Something sturdy, to hold a key."

She studied me, her controlled face frankly curious. "Is it for you or for Scarlett?"

"Either or both," I said cryptically.

She smiled. "I'll dig up one. You can have it. You don't need to *borrow*."

When I approached Scarlett again, still waiting by the door, I draped the key on its chain casually around her neck.

She fingered it. "What's this?"

I smiled, kissing her briefly. "It's the key to our first place together. Hope you like what I've done with the place."

She laughed, and I took her hand, pulling her into the kitchen. We put together a backpack full of food, enough for days, though we'd only have one night. There was no telling how hungry I'd be, though, so better safe than sorry.

The walk was long but idyllic. Since we'd be staying overnight, we took our time, stopping at Gram's huge orchard and picking as many apples as we could carry, keeping one out to eat as we walked. I took a big bite, the sound of it echoing through the trees.

We grinned at each other as I passed it to her. She took a bite and handed it back.

Watching her eat did things to me. Base, primal things. By the time we ate to the core, I was throbbing hard and ready to burst.

I took off my backpack, dragged her to the ground, and started kissing her.

"You taste like apples," I told her, smiling into her mouth.

She smiled back. "Well, gee, I wonder why."

"I'll never be able to taste one again without thinking of you. It's impossible. You do this on purpose, don't you? You leave your mark on everything. You love that I'm this obsessed with you."

She laughed and laughed. "Well, yes. Of course I do. If I was this obsessed on my own it would be pretty damned depressing."

I smiled and kissed her again, then forced myself to climb off her. "Not far to go," I told her. "If you can control yourself for a few more miles we just may make it."

She mock glared at me. "Look who's talking." Her eyes shot down to my crotch. "It can't be Mr. Walking Erection calling me out today, can it?"

I couldn't stop laughing for a solid five minutes, and she couldn't stop smiling.

On we walked.

I meant to make it good for her. To be tender, that first time more than any other. I meant to go soft and slow. I had my mind made up on the matter. Making it good for her was the priority, because I knew that regardless of the pace or the tone, it was sure as hell going to be great for me.

I had so many notions on how it was going to be, how it had to be. I'd done so much planning, even down to hard physical labor, thought out every detail to make it memorable for her, to make it perfect.

The first thing was the location. I'd found the perfect place, private and remote. I'd cleaned it out, brought fresh linens, every necessity I could think of.

I'd added a new lock and a thick bolt across the door, both of which fit the key around her neck.

I let her do the honors, my adoring eyes on her smiling face all the while.

The cabin was just right, I saw by her reaction when we walked in the door. She was delighted, moved, touched almost to tears.

It really wasn't anything fancy. It was instead something thoughtful, which I knew meant much more to her.

"It's ours," I told her softly. "Our first home together. Of course it won't be our last."

"It's perfect," she said, throwing herself at me.

Fuck. Triggered. The moment our bodies touched in that intimate place, it was like a bottle-rocket shooting off. I couldn't have stopped if I'd wanted to. And I didn't. Oh Lord, I didn't.

We started kissing, passionate, open-mouthed, tongues delving as we peeled each other's clothes off, piece by piece.

Everything was going right according to plan up until the moment my dick decided it'd had enough.

I knew I should've jerked off first.

I was on top of her, naked, condom on, a prayer away from being inside of her, still determined to do things right. I was just starting to breach her, my tip barely in, when it happened. It wasn't that I didn't want to take it nice and easy, but I could not stop myself after that. I just snapped, lost complete control of my body, thrusting, rutting, sucking on her tongue, and jackhammering in and out of her like I'd never have another chance at it.

And worse even than that, I didn't last thirty seconds.

Still, it was the best thirty seconds of my life. Spectacular. Magnificent. Perfection.

"Jesus," I panted into her face when I could finally

speak. "I didn't mean to do that. I wanted to go slower the first time."

She pulled my face even closer to hers. Tears were running down her cheeks, but they weren't from pain. "We'll just have to practice more."

"I wish I were a girl again, half-savage and hardy, and free."
~Emily Brontë

chapter seven

PAST

Scarlett

"A pom-pom girl?" The words sounded as ridiculous coming out of my mouth as they had coming out of his.

Dante shrugged, opening the locker that his 'pom-pom girl' had decorated for him. "I don't know what to tell you. It's a tradition and that's what they're called. I sure as hell didn't come up with it."

Somehow that didn't make me feel better, especially when he pulled a plate of cookies out of his locker as he said it. He snagged the plastic wrap off, grabbed one, and took a big bite, closing his eyes as he chewed. He'd always had a sweet tooth.

He offered me one and I turned it down with a glare.

"Another surprise from your pom-pom girl?" I asked him with a curl of my lip.

"I assume. Sure you don't want one? They're really good."

"I'll pass," I said dryly.

I didn't understand the tradition. Personally I found it degrading. Cheerleaders assigned to football players for the sole purpose of serving them.

"Why do they do it?" I asked Dante, who had finished the first cookie and was on to the second.

"I have no clue," he said absently.

I studied him. I didn't believe him. Dante studied everyone and everything. He was always looking for motives. "I don't believe you."

That made him pause and look at me. "Okay, fine. I think they do it for attention. I think they do it for popularity, social standing, a new boyfriend, a random hookup. You name it. They become pom-pom girls for the same reason they become cheerleaders. They want to get close to the football players."

"And you're okay with this random pom-pom girl getting close to you?" My tone was icy with disdain, enough so that it hid my anger, and my hurt.

"There's no chance of that, so I'm indifferent. I won't be rude to the girl, but c'mon, who cares what she does?"

"You ate her cookies."

He smirked. I'd amused him. "I like cookies, and I don't turn down food. I'm pretty sure you know that."

I was opening my mouth to speak, to say something scathing, in fact, when a petite little blonde came bouncing up in a cheerleader uniform.

She didn't even look at me. She hadn't come for me,

obviously. She was after Dante. Her vacant, smiling eyes aimed up, up, up adoringly at him.

"Hi, Dante. I'm Brandee." She drew out the e. "And I'm your pom-pom girl. I'm here for anything you need, from food to laundry, to after practice massages. I'm great with my hands." She giggled. "Anything you need, I'm your girl." She giggled again. "I'm here for you, day or night, so don't hesitate to ask."

She'd had the luck to be assigned as a pom-pom girl to the hottest guy in school, and she was sure as hell going to give it her best shot. You had to almost respect it.

Except that I didn't. I hated it. And her. And football. And cookies.

I was just about to get myself into a whole lot of trouble when Dante stepped in.

He threw a muscular arm around my shoulder, pulling me close, squeezing me hard enough to trap my arms.

I glared at him. I knew what was up. He was worried I was going to hit her.

Because he knew me.

"Hi, Brandee," he said. He didn't smile but his voice was light, casual. "I won't be needing anything, but thanks anyway."

She pouted, looking genuinely crushed. Her sulky lower lip seemed completely unfeigned. "Really? Not anything? Did you hear my list? I give a killer massage."

"No, thank you. I have a girlfriend, if you didn't notice."

She barely spared me a glance. "It's not like that. It doesn't have to be girlfriend stuff. This is just pom-pom girl stuff. You know, the stuff you *need* on game days."

Whore, I thought at her.

As though sensing my thoughts, Dante squeezed my

shoulder firmly. "No, thank you," he said again, voice slightly less polite than the time before.

She flushed, biting her lip. It was degrading enough that she wanted to wait on him, but the fact that she had to ask him for it had to be a tough pill even for an empty-headed pom-pom girl to swallow. "You don't even need me to clean your uniform for you?"

"Nope. I don't. You're off the hook."

She didn't look happy about that. "What about food? What's your favorite? I'm a great cook."

"I'm all set on food too. I'll make it real easy on you—I don't need anything at all."

She was persistent, I'd give her that. "Not even sweets? You didn't like the cookies?"

That made him hesitate and look down at the plate of cookies he'd clearly been enjoying. "They were great, but you don't need to make me anymore."

"You really thought they were great?" she beamed, flirting right in fucking front of me.

Dante's arm squeezed me tighter. "Yeah, they were great, so thanks, but like I said, I don't need anything else."

She was smiling like she'd gotten what she wanted. "Wait until you try my cupcakes. And my muffins are to die for. Just you wait. I won't disappoint you."

She flounced off.

Dante held me back from going after her.

"What a little whore," I grumbled at her back.

"Stop. C'mon. She's not worth it. Calm down."

I shrugged his arm off and he let me. I glared at him, then at the plate of cookies he still held in his free hand. I knew that he was going to keep eating them. He'd basically been a human garbage disposal for food since we were twelve. He ate everything.

But he seemed particularly keen on these cookies.

I grabbed one, taking a bite. I wanted to see what all the fuss was about.

And it was good. Peanut butter, with just the right amount of crunch and chew. I wasn't even a big fan of cookies, but little miss pom-pom's were pretty awesome.

Dante grinned at the look on my face. "She can bake. You have to give her that."

I didn't want to, and I hated the way he said it, like he admired the skill.

I decided right then and there that I would learn how to bake, for the simple reason that I could not stand the thought that Dante might have a need I couldn't fulfill myself.

For a solid month I spent more time with Gram's housekeeper, Mrs. Stewart, than I did with Dante. It drove him crazy, which I saw as icing on the cake. Kind of literally.

Mrs. Stewart was nice and happy to teach. She'd been a trained pastry chef once, but rarely got to practice the skill as Gram liked sweets even less than I did. In fact, she called them evil. I figured it was damage from her Hollywood days, when keeping her figure on point was part of her job.

Mrs. Stewart patiently taught me how to make just about every kind of cookie I could think of, cake, pie, muffins, cream puffs, crème brûlée, chocolate mousse.

The list was large, and though it took me some time to get the hang of it, to understand how exact each instruction and ingredient needed to be perfect, over time I became very good.

A neglected Dante cornered me one afternoon in

Gram's pantry when Mrs. Stewart was grocery shopping, and Gram was at a friend's house playing cards.

"I'm busy making macaroons," I told him, warding him off with my hands when he tried to move close.

"You made your point," he said, catching me when I tried to go past him and back into the kitchen. "I won't eat anyone else's cookies." There was a smile in his voice. He was teasing me.

"I'm busy," I said again. My voice came out almost singsong lyrical, like a taunt. I hadn't quite meant it that way, but I wasn't all that sorry.

Teasing him back when he was in this kind of mood rarely disappointed.

"You're not, but you're going to be."

I eyed him insolently. "What's that supposed to mean?"

He crowded me deeper into the walk-in pantry, one step and another, past the long shelves until my shoulders hit the wall at the very back of the room.

"Oh, I think you know. Macaroons are off the menu for today."

"You don't like macaroons?"

"Right now, I *hate* macaroons."

I bit back a laugh. "Now you *hate* macaroons?"

"I hate everything you bake if you ignore me to do it."

"Fine, then. You can't have any." I tried to move past him, to leave, but he got in my way, bumping his chest into mine. "Excuse me," I said.

"I don't excuse you," he said, and there was heat in it. Past teasing into outright foreplay.

"Let me out," I ordered.

"No," he taunted back.

"You can't keep me in the pantry forever. What's your

plan here?" I renewed my efforts to squeeze past him, rubbing against him in the attempt.

With a groan, he backed me up to the wall again, this time advancing until our bodies were flush, and I could feel beyond a doubt what he wanted to do.

He gripped my ass with both hands, hoisted me up against the wall, and said, sounding nearly out of breath, "I think you can guess."

He slanted his mouth over mine and I was lost.

It was some time later and we were straightening our clothes when I said smugly, "So you know that you basically promised me you wouldn't eat anyone else's cookies."

His smile was warm as he crowded me back against the wall, rubbing his big, hard chest against mine. "Angel, I promised you that a long time ago."

"If you prick us, do we not bleed? If you tickle us, do we not laugh? If you poison us, do we not die? And if you wrong us, shall we not revenge?"
~William Shakespeare

chapter eight

PRESENT

Scarlett

I was drunk. Good and stinking drunk.

We were at the crew hotel in Seattle (not my favorite town) on a layover and we were trolling the lobby bar.

Okay, *I* was trolling the lobby hotel. My girls were just there for moral support.

I was planning to make up for the fact that I'd just spent a solid month being a pathetic, lovesick fool moping in my room, crying in my bed.

Staying at home. Hating myself. Wanting to disappear.

But I'd decided tonight that I was done with that.

I was on the hunt for a stand-in punching bag. I had decided about three drinks ago that I'd feel much better about myself if I put at least one man between me and my last memory of Dante.

I was looking around, a pout on my face. "No cute boys," I told the girls.

Demi agreed.

"I'm not sad," Leona said, studying me. "I don't think I want you to find a cute boy when you're in this shape."

They were sitting in a booth and I was standing next to it. I was not in a sitting mood. I was in a get some male attention mood. I just wished there were some males around worth being noticed by.

I'd already shot down two that just weren't cute enough. More specifically: reject number one wasn't tall enough and reject number two looked too wholesome.

I didn't like wholesome, never had. I craved sinister categorically.

"Don't speak too soon," Farrah said, eyes aimed at the door. "I'll let you have him if you want him, but damn, I sure don't want to."

I turned to see. And smiled.

It was my lucky day.

Either he was actually looking for me or it was a hell of a coincidence but, Dante's half-brother, Bastian, had just walked in the door.

He was standing there, scanning the room, and it didn't take him long to zero in on me.

He grinned.

I tilted my head and grinned back, then pointed my chin at the bar, heading there with a bouncing little strut.

He beat me to it, and watched me approach, his eyes all over me.

I was glad I'd turned myself out well.

My minuscule nude dress was basically man catnip. It

hit all the right buttons: deep cleavage that left very little of my abundant breasts to the imagination, short skirt that showed off my sky-high legs. The whole thing was fitted to show off my flat tummy and hourglass figure.

Pink platform stilettos and sexy bedroom hair didn't hurt my situation, and my makeup had been on point before I'd gotten sloppy drunk. Who could say now? Who could care?

Not me. I felt sexy as hell either way.

"Hello, stranger," I said when I got within earshot of Bastian. "You look good enough to eat."

And he did. Three-piece suit, dark, messy hair, five o'clock shadow, a handsome as hell Durant face, and a devilish smile.

Yeah, he'd do.

"Look who's talking," he retorted, eyes on my catnip dress. "My God, woman, you are trouble, aren't you?"

I went to hug him, because drunk, and breathed into his ear. "You have no idea."

"Unfortunately, I don't." He sounded truly regretful about that as he put his hands on my hips and set me back just the slightest bit. "I'm sure you've guessed, but I came here to talk to you."

"How did you know I'd be here?" I asked him, cocking my head to the side.

His mouth twisted ruefully, and when he did that he reminded me so much of Dante that I wanted to smash something over his head. And cry. And run away. And kiss him.

"Facebook. You and your friends love to share your locations, and, you know, I live here."

I scrunched my nose up. "Facebook stalking me, are you?"

He was unapologetic. "Yes. It's a helpful tool. Actually, I was going to fly down to see you soon, but this worked out much better. Well, it did if you're up for a serious talk that I'd like you to remember in the morning."

"I'm not up for a serious anything," I told him and, because drunk, I pressed my mouth to his.

He made a little noise in this throat, a hungry one, and I licked his lips, brushing my breasts against him.

He set me away, but he was breathing hard.

"You taste good," I told him.

He smiled but not like he was happy. "Do I taste like revenge?"

"Exactly like that. Yum."

"Trust me, you beautiful, edible, dangerous creature, I would love to take you up on that, but it's a line we can't cross."

"There's no line I won't cross," I said, meaning it. I was feeling self-destructive to a dangerous, limitless degree. "God, do you know what he did to me the last time I saw him?"

"I heard a bit about it," Bastian said solemnly.

That surprised me. "What did you hear? And from whom?"

He sighed. "From Dante. I'm sure you won't be surprised to hear that he's in rough shape."

That bit of unfair bullshit only made me more determined. I moved closer and he let me. I rubbed up against him, my lips in kissing distance of his again, teasing him. "Let's make it rougher for him, huh?"

"*Jesus,*" he said, and it reminded me so much of Dante that I wrenched away.

I leaned against the bar, flagging down the busy bartender.

He didn't make me wait, in fact stopped what he was doing and came to do my bidding with a smile.

I'd been flirting with him all night, but he wasn't my type. He was tall but his shoulders weren't broad enough. Still, the right smile got me some amazing service.

"Hey, Scarlett," he said, his tone when he said my name making it sound like we were old friends or new lovers. "Another Black Label for you?"

"You're the *best*, Benny," I told him, leaning forward, shamelessly teasing him. "Can you make it two?"

He nodded, eyes on my cleavage. "Anything you want, gorgeous."

"Wow," Bastian whistled when Benny moved away to get our drinks. "If I was Dante, I would *lock you up.*"

"Well, that's *not* what he did," I said, and it was an effort to keep my voice steady. "He threw me away. Again."

"Oh, Scarlett," Bastian sighed. "I have a few things to ask you, and so much to tell you. I'm not sure just how drunk you are, but I'm pretty positive that what I have to say will sober you up."

That was an understatement. What he had to tell me didn't just sober me up.

It changed *everything*.

"No one can make you feel inferior without your consent."
~Eleanor Roosevelt

chapter

nine

PAST

Scarlett

I was so mad I was shaking.

It'd been a hell of a morning.

It was my own fault, I knew. It was a Saturday. My grandma was off work on Saturday and Sunday, and on every single one of her days off, no exceptions, she went into a calculated and steady drunk.

She was unpleasant and surly when she was sober. Drunk, she became outright hateful, and if I was stupid enough to stick around, I was automatically the go-to target for all of her animosity.

When I was being smart, which was most of the time, I didn't come home until she was passed out cold, and I left quietly in the morning before she roused.

This morning was one of the exceptions. I'd overslept, somehow even more so than her, and boy was I in for it.

Of course I'd been out late with Dante. Out doing all of the things that would drive her the most crazy, and she always seemed to know it.

But this morning was worse, because instead of her usual tirade where she accused me of things she couldn't prove, this time she'd actually found something to vindicate her venomous rant.

In our defense, Dante and I *had* hidden the evidence. The crazy woman must have gone outside and dug into the trashcan to find the handful of used condoms that she threw in my sleeping face.

"At least you're the kind of *whore* that uses protection," she spat.

I was still blinking awake, automatically batting off the sticky objects that she'd flung at me.

When I realized what I was touching, I recoiled, my face drawing tight in distaste.

"What the——?" I grumbled.

"I suppose you think I should be happy? You're one step up from your slut of a mother," she continued, screeching the words.

I wasn't sure what smelled worse, the day old-plus used condoms, or her breath, which was a combination of her usual halitosis, mixed with vomit and liquor—a particularly putrid, if familiar, stench.

"What time is it?" I asked her, voice flat, even, not letting her know that no matter how old I got, she still terrified me. "What are you doing up already?"

My casual tone just set her off more. "What the hell does it matter what time it is?"

"Because usually I'm gone long before you wake up from one of your blackouts. Did you never notice?"

I got a sharp slap across the face for that bit of sass.

"That's all you have to say for yourself? Not even defending your behavior now? Shameless!"

I supposed she was right. I was a bit shameless about what went on between Dante and me. I just couldn't see at as wrong.

Maybe a part of me even wanted to rub it in her face. She'd been telling me I was going to be a whore since I was too young to know what the word even meant.

Now here I was, a sex-obsessed teenager that spent as much of her free time as possible underneath or on top of her equally sex-obsessed boyfriend.

I wasn't sure if you could really call me a whore for having sex with one guy, no matter how *many* times we'd done it, but I knew my grandma would have no problem doing so.

"You know there's something wrong with you, don't you?" she asked me, voice gone deadly calm, which I knew from experience was even worse than her shouting.

"You're the one digging around in trashcans, looking for used condoms," I muttered back. Sometimes I just couldn't help myself.

I was rewarded with another ringing slap, and then another.

"You think you're so smart," she said, punctuating the words with another slap. "But you're as stupid as your mother. You think you're special, spreading your legs for a Durant? Every girl in the county gave it up to his daddy, and I'm guessing the son's not much different. That boy is going to use you and throw you away, just you watch."

"I'll take my chances," I told her stubbornly, not so much as flinching from her slaps.

"Your mom threw you in a dumpster because even *she* thought you were trash, but that's not what made you trash. You've done that to yourself."

And there it was. Her slaps weren't the terrifying thing about her. Her words were without a doubt her best weapon.

She didn't just exploit weaknesses, she opened them wide, put her unfeeling hands inside, and sifted through you until she unburied new ones, uncoiled them, and let them plop down at your feet.

"Y-y-y—" I tried, but my temper, and my fear, and her damned slaps, had gotten the better of me. I was so frustrated by it that I just got up and left, wearing nothing but a now soiled T-shirt and the first pair of jeans I grabbed off the floor on my way out. I couldn't even get to a bra, she was blocking that part of the room with her body, and I needed out *now*.

"Good. Get out!" she shouted at my retreating back. "But remember, if you're running to that boy, he doesn't care about you! He thinks you're trash, too. You're just the little trailer girl he sticks it in. Mark my words! He'll leave you for one of his own kind, I promise you that! He's never going to stay with some piece of filth that came from the dumpster! Especially not a slut like you that gives it up for free!"

I ran and didn't look back. I was trembling in rage as I made my way up to Gram's house, but in the short time it took, I'd nearly calmed myself, because I knew that as soon as I saw Dante, I'd feel better.

That was the point of him.

He made the world make sense again with just a look.

I was so caught up in thinking about him that I forgot I was a complete mess.

I remembered again as I caught sight of a pristine looking Dante. He was already at Gram's house, hanging out in her front yard, wearing a suit and tie; his hair combed, parted, and slicked back.

Oh, that's right. He'd had some country club thing he'd told me he had to attend this morning. He hadn't invited me along. He never did. He claimed I'd hate the country club, and I believed him.

I didn't care about any of it—how clean he was or how filthy I was. I nearly ran as I made my way to him.

But as I watched, the front door of Gram's house opened, and out came Tiffany, looking even more pristine in a lacy white dress.

I stopped in my tracks, lingering at the tree line, feeling my temper begin to re-boil.

She beamed at Dante, and he smiled back, his hands in his pockets like he didn't have a care in the world.

She said something I couldn't make out and he laughed.

My vision went red, and I must have made some noise because Dante, *finally*, noticed me.

His smile didn't falter, in fact it widened, and he said something I couldn't hear to Tiffany and started moving toward me.

I began to back away, painfully aware of the picture I made—bed-mussed hair, slapped red face, in a tight, soiled shirt with no bra.

I couldn't have looked more different from the two of them in their country club uniforms if I'd been trying to.

Still, Dante didn't even notice at first. He was already talking as he approached, too intent on what he was saying to notice how I looked. "Listen. I have an idea. I think you and Tiffany should spend more time together. I had a long talk with her—"

"When? Why?" I interrupted without even meaning to, moving deeper into the woods. *What the hell was going on? Hadn't we been over this?*

Never. I would *never* give that girl a chance.

"She caught me on my way out at the country club brunch this morning, and I gave her a ride. She asked me to hear her out, so I did. She's never done anything to either of us. She has nothing to do with my mother's schemes. She's as baffled as we are about the things my mom claims. We had a good laugh about the fact that my mom says I'm going to marry her after college. Trust me, she's no more interested in that than I am."

I was glaring at him, hands clenched at my sides, and it was only after he'd finished talking that he seemed to notice something was wrong.

Well, something other than the idiocy he'd just spouted that he had to know I wouldn't be swallowing as easily as *he* had.

Tiffany *wanted* him. I knew it in my bones. Like recognizes like.

He blinked a few times, eyes running over my face and down my body. He took a step closer, his hand darting forward almost unconsciously to palm one of my breasts. It was a casual touch that spoke of absolute intimacy. He was so accustomed to having me under his hands that it was second nature at this point.

His brows drew together. "Why aren't you wearing a bra? Do you realize how revealing that top is like this?"

His mouth twisted up in distaste as his roaming hand

made contact with one of the still sticky stains on my shirt. "What's all over you?"

I wanted to punch him in the face. "Long story," I gritted out. I didn't feel like telling him anything. I was just too frustrated by then. The morning couldn't have been going worse.

He wiped his hand on his immaculate suit then brought it back, this time slipping it under my shirt to fondle me. He backed me farther into the woods, until we were well hidden. "I woke up dreaming about last night," he said, voice thickening, eyes on his hand inside my top. "I wish you could have been with me." He stepped closer. "I wish we didn't have to sleep apart. It seems wrong, doesn't it?"

He had no idea. I'd have given anything for that.

Also, he was a master at manipulating me. He'd nearly made me forget why I was so upset with just a few drugging sentences.

Still, I tried to rally, to get back on point. "It's semen," I answered his earlier question.

"What?" he asked sharply, his hand still kneading at my breast, his thumb rubbing circles around my puckered nipple

"On my shirt. It's cum. My grandma went digging through the garbage can outside this morning, found a bunch of our used condoms, and woke me up by throwing them on me."

His free hand came up to finger my cheek, and he seemed to notice my face for the first time. "She was slapping you again, wasn't she?"

I shrugged, dislodging his hand. "Does it matter?"

"Of course it matters! If she's putting her hands on you again, I'm going down there—"

"What are you going to do that you haven't done before? Even if you talk sense into her, she'll forget it all the next time she's drunk."

"Are you okay?"

I shrugged again, not looking at him. "I'm fine." Code, of course, for not fine.

"We're going to go down there, and I will call the police."

"You think that will help? Last time we did that, she turned it on me, said *I* was hitting *her* and nearly had *me* arrested."

"*Fuck*," he cursed, because he knew I was right. The cops were never on my side. I'd been in too much trouble to ever ask the authorities for help. "Well, I'll walk you down and keep her away from you while you grab some clean clothes. In the meantime, though, take off your shirt."

"Excuse me?"

He grinned, shrugging off his jacket, loosening his tie. "I'll give you mine. You shouldn't have to wear that dirty one for another second." He was already unbuttoning his before he'd finished speaking.

I took off my shirt, and in spite of everything, or maybe because of that, the way his eyes moved on my bared body, I was suddenly ravenous for him—insanely, madly, *starved*.

I licked my lips, hands going to the button of my jeans. "Dante," I rasped.

He dropped his shirt and jacket on the ground, crowding close to me. He still had his undershirt on, unfortunately, but I took care of it in short order.

"Do you have anything on you?" I asked, rubbing my chest against his.

He was flushed and panting into my face. "Yeah. I was just about to come find you." He pulled a wad of condoms out of his pocket. "Please, *please*, get on the pill."

I'd had some weird paranoia about my grandma figuring out I was having sex if I went through all the steps of getting on the pill, but that cat was evidently out of the bag. "Okay," I panted, stroking him through his slacks. "I will. Soon as I can."

We didn't even kiss, which may have been a first, but I was too far gone. I braced my hands against a tree as he worked my jeans off, got us both ready, and took me from behind.

He kneaded my breasts, mouth rasping in my ear as he pushed into me.

It was quick but still more tender than rough. I came with a fast and quiet intensity, shutting my eyes tight, barely making a sound.

He came louder, much louder, calling out my name as he rooted deep and finished.

He was still rutting inside of me, milking out every last twitch when he stiffened suddenly.

"Fuck. Tiffany," he said, voice pitched loud.

That, of course, made me stiffen. I was craning my neck around, heart already wounded with just two words, absolute murder in my eyes.

Had he really just said *Tiffany?* I couldn't quite believe it.

But as my eyes caught on movement in the woods, it all made sense. There she was, backing away, eyes wide. Our gazes met an instant before she turned and fled.

"What the fuck was that?" I asked no one in particular.

"She accidentally walked up on us, I think," Dante

said, coming way too fucking quickly to her defense. "She couldn't have known we'd go twenty feet into the woods and start having sex."

"She clearly doesn't understand us at all, then."

"We need to stop doing this. That's twice now someone's been creeping on us in the woods. I don't like it." As he spoke, his weight lifted off my back and he slipped out of me.

I turned, leaning my back against the tree as I looked up, up, up at him. "I can control myself if you can." It was probably a lie, but one I doubted I'd ever be tested on.

As though proving my point, his eyes were on my body, one hand going to cup my breast, the other to my sex. "Did you get off? You were so quiet I couldn't tell."

I bit my lip and lied, "I didn't."

"I'm sorry. Want me to take care of you?" he asked, voice gone quiet and dark. He moved closer, thumb circling my clit as he pushed a finger inside of me.

I gasped and nodded. "Please, Dante," I pleaded, because he loved that, and as a sort of penance for the selfish, pointless lie. I hadn't had to make him feel guilty to get him to go down on me, but for some reason I'd wanted to. *Needed* that element of repentance in his touch.

He wasn't the only manipulative one here.

He lowered to his knees, perched one of my legs onto his shoulder, and buried his face between my thighs. He pushed two fingers into me and went to work on my clit with his tongue, his free hand sliding up to fondle my breasts.

I gripped his hair with one hand, the other covering his on my chest, feeling at my body with him. There was something unutterably sensual about experiencing his touch on me through my own fingers.

I was calling out his name less than quietly, eyes pointed beseechingly up at the sky, when a movement caught the corner of my eye.

My head snapped to the side. It was Tiffany. Again. Peeking at us from behind a thick pine.

I glared at her.

She smiled back, turned, and fled. Again.

Dante was standing, wiping his mouth before I told him. "Tiffany came back to watch round two."

He looked infuriatingly confounded. "*What*? Are you sure?"

I was so pissed by that, by the fact that his mind worked that way, that somehow me imagining seeing her was even vaguely possible, that I just stopped talking.

I shrugged on his shirt, put on my jeans, and started walking determinedly back to my grandma's trailer.

He was on my heels. "Why would she come back? I don't get it."

To see you naked, I almost replied, but bit my tongue. It was becoming apparent that he needed to figure out for himself who and what Tiffany was. I was sick and tired of trying to show him myself. I'd lost all patience.

He dropped the subject, which was for the best, because I was *brewing* for a fight.

"Women are meant to be loved, not to be understood."
~Oscar Wilde

chapter ten

Thankfully, my grandma was passed out cold when we got back to the trailer.

Dante waited for me on the sofa while I showered and changed into clean clothes.

I was rubbing my wet hair with a towel as I walked out of the bathroom.

"Let's go see a movie with her this afternoon," he greeted me with.

I knew what and who he meant immediately, though I wished I hadn't. More like, I *hoped* I'd misunderstood. "What? Who?"

"Tiffany. I think we should all go out. Grab a movie and pizza, or whatever."

I gave him my best drop-dead glare. "No. *Hell* no."

"Just try this once. For me."

It only took a few words to take all of the steam right out of me. "For you? She's that important to you?" I tried hard not to let him see how much that bothered me.

"Oh, stop. It's not like that. I honestly believe that you two will be friends. You could *use* some more friends, Scarlett." He said it kindly, and so it hurt all the more.

Ouch. He hadn't been trying to be mean, but the pity in his voice was worse to me than just about anything else.

And I was furious again, that he didn't see her for who she was. For God's sake, she'd just spied on us having sex. Twice. And still he thought she was some innocent girl who wanted to be *my* friend.

I knew very damn well that Tiffany wanted nothing so much as for me to disappear forever. I *knew* it. In my gut. In that bitter little spot where instinct and hunches go to *flourish*.

Still, in this instance, my instincts did not seem to be enough for the both of us. I'd let him see for himself. "Fine," I gritted out. "What time?"

"The movie's at one thirty."

I tried not to grit my teeth when I realized he'd already planned the whole thing. With her.

I was about to lose my temper, but I held on to the very last thread of it as I spoke. "Fine," I said again, cursing him in a thousand different ways in my head. "I'll meet you there."

His brows drew together. "No. I'll take you, of course. What are you even thinking?"

"I'd like to be alone for a while," I said, trying to be reasonable when I wanted to scream at him. "I'll meet you there," I repeated.

"No," he repeated, making every thought about being reasonable fly right out of my head. "I'm not leaving you here," he said firmly. "Are you *kidding* me?"

"Glenda's passed out cold. It'd take a miracle to wake

her up before four p.m. And besides that, I'm planning to lock myself in my room and read. If she gets up before I leave, I'll climb out the window. You don't need to worry about me."

He stood, the look on his face telling me that he was finally beginning to comprehend how badly he'd messed up. My last sentence had clued him in. "Don't. Scarlett, *stop*. I'll cancel, okay? Let's go to Gram's. I'm not leaving you here."

I raised my chin. "You are. Go. I'll meet you and *Tiffany* at the movies."

He started cursing, and I left him to it, locking myself in my room.

"How will you even get there?" he eventually asked me, voice muffled through the thin wall that separated us. He'd been standing there for a while. I pictured him clearly on the other side of it, eyes closed, leaning forehead first into the door.

I hated that question, hated that I didn't even have a way to get around, that I was *so* dependent on him, and had never even given it a thought until now, because we did *everything* together.

"Like I said, you don't need to worry about me," I told him with stilted bitterness. "I can figure out how to get to the movie theater without your help, Dante."

I just hadn't done it quite yet. I'd gotten my license, but I sure as hell didn't have a car. Could I borrow my grandma's and have it back before she woke up? I wondered.

She'd kill me, I decided instantly. She was absolutely possessive about her junker of a car. She'd only ever let me be a passenger in it maybe five times, let alone drive it myself. The thought was laughable.

Still, I wasn't backing down. I was too far gone. My temper was officially running the show.

Dante made a noise of utter frustration. "You know what? Fine. I'll be back to pick you up at one."

I wanted to punch the door. My fists were clenched in preparation for it. "Don't. I won't even be here by then. Like I said, I'll meet you there." My mouth was working independently of my brain, it seemed. I felt separate from the words, like they had more meaning for him than me.

This made sense, I supposed, because half of what I was saying was for effect alone. I really had no way to make it the thirty-minute drive to the movie theatre.

Eventually he left, and though I'd told him too, that did not help my temper at all.

It got worse the more I tried to calm it. Simmered hotter the more I tried to turn it off.

It was unfortunate that Reese McCoy just happened to call my house right when I'd nearly talked myself out of going at all.

Reese had been persistently pestering me for at least a year. I'd never encouraged him in any way whatsoever, but I knew he had a crush on me. He was a nuisance, but at least he was nice to me, which was more than I could say for most people.

"I told you not to call me again," I told him right away. It came out naturally. "I'll tell Dante that you're bothering me if you don't stop." I'd told him this at least a dozen times, but I'd yet to actually follow through. Dante would *pulverize* him, and I didn't truly believe that he was anything but harmless.

But then Reese, in his timid voice, said, "I just wanted to see if you wanted to go out, or whatever. We could, like, go to the mall, or whatever."

It was ridiculous of him to ask, but no one could fault his timing. On any other day, I'd have skewered him for asking.

But today, well, I really needed a ride. "Do you have a car?" I asked him.

I swear I felt him smile through the phone.

"Do you know Tiffany Vanderkamp?" I asked Reese when he picked me up in his old Toyota truck.

"That rich, new girl? Yeah, I've seen her. Doesn't she live close to here?"

Too close, I thought. "She does. Do you like her?"

He was driving by then, but he looked away from the road to shoot me a guarded look. "She's alright. Why?"

"She's going to be at the movies. Maybe you could take her out afterwards."

He chewed on his lip for a long while, finally getting up the courage to say, "I'd rather take *you* out afterwards."

I rolled my eyes. "You know I'm with Dante."

"Not right now you aren't. Right now you're in my truck, if you didn't notice."

That shut me up. I'd just gotten into a car with a guy I barely knew just to piss off Dante. I was helpless, and I'd done it to myself. The thought was sobering.

Luckily Reese didn't pull anything, taking me straight to the movies, like I'd asked, unaware that I was bringing him on a double date whether he liked it or not.

Or a trap, depending on how you looked at it.

But I wouldn't be letting him drive me home. Something in his tone had me worried. He was definitely less of a pushover than I'd always assumed.

Dante's reaction was predictably gratifying when I walked in the door with Reese.

He wouldn't even look at me. His cold eyes were on Reese. "Let's take this outside."

Tiffany, who'd been standing next to him, watched the guys leave, looking troubled.

"I tried to bring you a date," I told her. "I guess it didn't work out."

She studied me. "I don't mind being a third wheel."

I smiled at her and it was smug. One thing I could guarantee; Dante would stop setting her up to be my 'friend' now. "I mind. One thing I also mind is you watching us having sex. Do you even know how sad and pathetic that is? How desperate?"

Her nostrils flared. I'd finally found a crack in her fake pleasant facade. Good. I'd been looking for a while now.

"What can I say?" As she spoke, her voice changed, her entire demeanor did. It was fascinating and reminded me, like a lightbulb going on, of his mother. "He is awfully nice to look at, even if you did keep getting in the way of my view."

"Like I said, pathetic," I said in disgust, though deep down what I felt the most deeply was satisfaction. *Finally* she was showing her true colors. "Look your fill, but that's all you'll ever get."

"You really think that," she said slowly, tasting the words. "You're confident, I'll give you that. You're wild in bed, sure. But you're also a manipulative bitch. How long do you think that will keep him entertained? How long do you think it'll take him to realize he could do better?"

I really hated that her words made me ask myself that same question.

It was spooky how much it felt like I was speaking to his mother. Every nuance of her words was crafted in the same way. She had that precise, killer, imminent threat to every syllable of her speech. And *exactly* like Adelaide, she had a talent for pointing out an insecurity you didn't even know you had.

She *created* insecurities.

Just like with his mother, I held that against her. By this point, I had a whole list.

"And when he does, I'll be right here," she continued. "I'm not going anywhere, and I'm very patient."

"He doesn't even think you're interested in him," I told her with incredulous hostility, though I wasn't sure who that was aimed at. Dante, most likely. The blind fool.

Yeah, okay, it was definitely aimed at him.

"Good," she said, the word filled with warm satisfaction. "I don't want him to. He'll come to me when he's ready. Just you watch."

I almost punched her, but I managed to maintain my composure enough to just walk away.

Dante came back inside sooner than I'd have thought possible, and looking mad enough to breathe fire, he strode right to me. "Okay," he gritted out. "Message received. We'll stay away from Tiffany, so long as you *promise me* you'll stay away from Reese McCoy."

"I promise," I told him solemnly, feeling like I'd finally, *at last*, been heard.

Sometimes drastic measures pay off.

"Let's get the hell out of here," he said, snagging my hand.

I smiled at Tiffany while he made our excuses, turning my head to hold her glaring gaze with delight as he wrapped a solicitous arm around my waist and pulled me outside.

I felt I'd won, because back then I didn't know it was more than a battle; it was a war.

It was sometime later, deep into the night, before I brought it up again.

Dante was in a much, much better mood by then. We were in the backseat of his Audi, parked deep in the woods, several miles from his house. He was on top of me, catching his breath, kissing my temple every so often, his big, firm, edible chest right in my face.

I wriggled underneath him, and it made him groan. He was still inside of me. "I need to get home," I told him.

"No," he said as he pulled out. "Not happening. I'm keeping you."

I was in a serious mood, but that made me smile. "Promises, promises."

He kissed me lightly. "Seriously, though. It's not right that we can't sleep together. There has to be a way. I'm moving in with Gram. I think you should, too."

"You think I wouldn't love that? But my grandma would *never* agree, and I'm not eighteen yet."

He kissed me again. "We'll find a way."

I didn't share his optimism, but I kept my peace.

He was driving me home when I asked, "She's crazy, you know that, right?"

"Who?"

"Tiffany." Duh.

He didn't roll his eyes, but it was close. "Yes, I'm aware you don't like her."

"She's a clone of your mother," I told him. Maybe that would get through to him.

It didn't. He just looked more annoyed. "Please. You're exaggerating. Tiffany is harmless."

Famous last words, I thought dramatically at the time. But I was more right than I knew.

"Don't allow your wounds to transform you into someone you are not."
~Paulo Coelho

chapter eleven

PRESENT

Scarlett

I woke up feeling strange. I was at home, in my own bed, but I didn't know what to do with myself. I checked my phone, saw several missed calls and texts from Bastian, and recalled that I'd promised to call him the day before.

Had an entire day passed? It didn't seem possible but it must have been. I'd woken up the day before in Seattle with a raging hangover and an aching heart.

What was I supposed to do now?

As though answering the question, my phone began to ring.

It was Bastian.

"Hey," I greeted him.

"Are you okay?" he asked, sounding more worried than he should have.

Was I okay? No. Was I going to be? Who knew? Not me.

"I'm fine," I told him. Girl code for *don't ask a silly question, of course I'm not okay.*

"I still need to do some digging around, and I have more questions for you, but I just needed to make sure you were all right."

"Where's Dante?" I asked.

"Here. Somewhere in Seattle, I believe. I'm going to try to find him today."

"Find him? You didn't tell me he was missing." It seemed like something that should have come up considering how much we'd talked that night.

"I told you he's been having a rough time."

I didn't bother to point out that one had nothing to do with the other.

"Listen," he told me somberly. "Don't do anything rash. Don't confront anyone. In fact, it would be best if you act as though everything is normal. I still have a lot of digging to do. The less they think we're onto them, the better."

I felt a little nauseated. This man was kicking a beehive, and he didn't understand, not fully, what was about to come out to swarm him.

But what he was doing—I needed it done.

"I won't confront anyone," I assured him. "Everything will stay normal on my end. Good luck. And . . . thank you."

"You don't have to thank me," he said, something hard entering his voice. "I'm doing this for myself as much as anyone. I'll be in contact soon."

I felt strangely better after we hung up, a little lighter. My stomach grumbled and I realized I was hungry.

I couldn't remember the last time I'd had an appetite.

I was digging through the fridge, scrounging up breakfast, when Demi arrived home with some woman I'd never seen before. Both had armfuls of groceries.

Demi beamed when she saw me. "This is my friend, Moonbliss. We met at Om Nom Organics last week and hit it off."

To be fair, Demi hits it off with everyone. And if I guessed correctly, she'd just adopted another lonely person. They came from all walks of life.

I greeted her friend politely, even though I could tell with one glance that she was one of *those*.

Sallow complexion. Thin to an unhealthy degree. Wide, glassy eyes. Un-dyed, untreated, product-free, brown hair.

She was a vegan. No, worse. Much, much worse.

A juicer. A raw, vegan juicer.

Also, *Moonbliss?*

"Oh, you're having breakfast?" Demi noted. "Perfect timing! We're just about to cook something."

I eyed their reusable grocery bags dubiously. "What were you about to cook?"

Moonbliss looked horrified at our exchange. "Cook? Oh no. We don't *cook*. Cooked food is valueless food. We *prepare*."

I was too tickled with amusement to even think of rolling my eyes. "What were you about to *prepare?*"

"Green shakes."

"Sounds delicious," I said dryly.

Moonbliss didn't catch the sarcasm. "Oh, it's simply nirvana. I make it with goodness greens and activated almonds."

I was still mouthing *'activated almonds?'* at a confused looking Demi when Moonbliss spoke again, "Would you like one, Scarlett? You look as though you could use some brain dust."

"Brain dust." I wasn't asking about it so much as trying the words out in my mouth. "Did you just say brain dust?"

"Wait, what? Are you serious? You don't partake of brain dust?"

Was *I* serious? It was getting harder and harder to give her straight answers, but the longer I let her go, the better the payoff. Clearly.

"Was it made by a virgin?" I asked, deadpan. "On the third day of a new cycle?"

Demi bit her lips to keep from laughing, looking away from me.

Moonbliss gave me a look that told me I'd just made her moon decidedly less blissful. "Do you want one or not?"

"Are you making anything else?" I asked hopefully. "Maybe something with solid food, or even meat?"

"I consider myself a purist," Moonbliss explained haughtily, "and there's nothing pure about meat."

"A good steak tastes purely awesome," I offered.

"I don't eat anything with a face. As humans, I think we've evolved past that. Don't you?"

I sure as hell hadn't. "Oh, me? I don't eat anything that points west. That's asking for trouble."

She studied me with narrowed eyes for a moment, then went back to her preparation.

I took a seat at one of the barstools lined up against the counter that faced into the kitchen. Amos crowded my legs, and I patted him absently. He licked my knee, and I let him, because he did it with love.

I felt a little bad for making fun of Moonbliss, so I said, "I'll take a green shake, thank you."

"Moonbliss has been teaching me to coo—prepare some amazing recipes," Demi told me brightly. "She's about to publish her first cookbook."

I was not the least bit surprised. "That's great. Congratulations. What's the name of it? I'll be sure to pick it up."

"My Soul Mission is Raw: Healing the Wounds in the Universe One Human Digestive Track at a Time."

I blinked. "That's a mouthful. Oh look, I made a pun."

Even Moonbliss laughed at that. I guess even she liked puns.

"This shake is best complemented with an hour of Kundalini yoga," she explained to us.

I'm ashamed to admit it, but I actually did know what that was.

"But there's simply no time today. Tomorrow morning, Demi?"

"Sure," Demi said. Damn, she was a good sport.

"Want to join us for yoga tomorrow?" Demi invited me.

Yoga had never worked for me. I was a boot camp fitness kind of girl. Running, pushups, sit-ups, squats. Things that hurt but did the job. I kept it simple.

"Oh, no thanks," I said blandly. "I like to do mind yoga."

"*Mind* yoga?" Moonbliss asked, rightfully suspicious.

"I just think about it really hard until the results manifest themselves."

At least it cracked Demi up. Can't please everybody.

It took Moonbliss for-freaking-ever to make the

shakes. She talked us through every step, but it was so complicated that I doubted I'd retain one bit of it.

There was no sugarcoating it—the shake was horrible—everything from the color, to the taste, to the texture—but I drank it anyway. It was worth the price of admission for this crazy train.

Also, I'd been treating my body like hell lately and it couldn't hurt to start remedying that. Baby steps back to being a normal human again.

As we drank, Moonbliss (she opened up and admitted her parents had actually named her that—poor girl had never had a chance) walked us through her day to day eating. It sounded very time-consuming and confusing to me, and I *liked* cooking.

Oh, but wait, she didn't cook. I guess I just wasn't that into *preparing*.

"When do you find time to manifest your heart's purpose?" I broke in cheekily at one point just to let her catch her breath.

She didn't skip a beat. I was kind of impressed. "Oh, that's easy. I never miss my hour of Kundalini meditation first thing in the morning. It's crucial to the progressive cultivation of my soul. *Crucial.*"

She was a bit of an acquired taste, much like her green shake. One thing I could say about her, though: she loved Amos. A lot. She couldn't keep her hands off him after she finished her shake, rolling around on the ground with him, rubbing his tummy how he loved. Amos, as always, couldn't get enough affection, and I had a soft spot in my heart for anyone that could love our homely, adopted mongrel.

"I think your dog is my spirit animal," she said at one point.

I just about choked on my shake, but recovered quickly. "Mine is that half-empty, Costco-sized bottle of Patrón on the counter."

Moonbliss gave me an odd look, but let me have it. "What about you, Demi?"

"Yeah, what about you, Demi?" I repeated.

"I never thought about it. Maybe a purple unicorn? A baby one."

I smiled at her. Damn, I liked her. We had grown particularly close lately. I chalked it up to her tender heart, especially when it came to wounded creatures.

She had a way with us all.

Moonbliss couldn't stay long. She had a lot of world wound healing still to do for her soul mission before the sun set, but she was thoughtful enough to write down some recipes that would energize my chakras before she left. She handed the piece of paper to me with a flourish, as though it were a prescription. "Always, for you, add spirit dust; you need all the help you can get for the path to inner peace."

Fair enough. No one had ever accused me of being peaceful.

I studied the list.

"And if you're having a craving for sweets, dose yourself with a bit of bee pollen. It's divine."

"Is bee pollen vegan?" I asked, just for the hell of it.

"My soul feels untroubled by it," she said by way of an answer.

Doesn't that make your chakra sticky? I almost asked, but held back, if only barely.

"Buckwheat soba noodle salad. Roasted kabocha soup. Denuded feldspar. All of these should be staple meals for you."

"Should they be . . . activated or . . . regular?"

She cocked her head to the side and studied me like *I* was the weird one.

Or maybe she actually realized that I was messing with her.

"I pray your afternoon is as carefree as a juniper breeze," were her parting words.

"Buh-bye," I said back

"See you tomorrow," Demi replied.

"You don't like her, do you?" she asked me when we were alone.

I was surprised she'd gotten that impression. "I do, actually. And I like having her around. She puts my improv training to good use."

I'd had a good laugh, but it did get me thinking. I had not been taking care of myself lately. Usually I tried to practice a good balance of exercise and eating healthy, with a dash of alcohol on party nights.

I needed to start taking care of myself again.

Because I needed to start caring about myself again.

"Is she for real?" I asked Demi. "Did you set that up just to mess with me?"

"I found her looking hopeless in the produce section. Her boyfriend dumped her for a younger woman, and she's feeling lost. All of her energy is going into finding something, real or fake, that makes her feel better. She can be . . . opinionated and eccentric but she is a nice person, and I want to help her. You know me. . . I just like to help. It gives me purpose."

Well, hell. Schooled by a twenty-two-year-old with a pure heart. You'd think it'd be demoralizing, but it was actually kind of enlightening. It never felt bad to just be nice to people.

In my case, I knew I needed to start with myself.

"Are you going to try one of those recipes for us tonight?" I asked her.

She flashed a dimple at me with her smile.

"If you do, just please, for me, be sure that the buckwheat has been de-hulled by an Amazon Chieftain during flood season on a blood moon. It's very important."

I couldn't help it. Being a smartass was part of my DNA.

We both lost it, laughing until tears were running down our faces.

"Got it," she gasped. "And you don't have to worry about the feldspar, either. I'll make sure myself that it's denuded by a virgin during flood season and pointing west, of course."

I wasn't the only one who'd had improv training.

"That sounds like something that will boost my blood irony levels," I said in parting, feeling something akin to carefree for the first time in I didn't even know how long.

I'd been planning to spend the day marathoning Vanderpump Rules so I could feel better about me and worse about humanity, but I felt a renewed sense of purpose (that I refused to blame on the green shake), so I went for a long, satisfying run instead.

"If you would be loved, be lovable."
~Ovid

chapter twelve

PAST

Scarlett

He'd done it again. Made me so mad I couldn't even look at him. He'd promised. Promised that he wouldn't have anything else to do with Tiffany, that neither of us would. But then right before last period, he'd mentioned oh so casually that she was coming over to Gram's house for dinner that night. Her parents were out of town, and he didn't think she should have to eat alone.

It felt like a double betrayal, since Gram was in on it. Did Gram like Tiffany now, too?

How long before they both preferred her to me?

I couldn't stand it. How insecure I felt, how completely Dante disregarded my feelings out of consideration for someone else's.

I didn't even confront him. I just walked away. He followed me to my class, then to my desk.

I sat down, looking straight ahead.

"You're upset," he said, and had the nerve to sound annoyed.

"Go away," I said stiffly just as the bell rang.

Dante's class was across campus, nowhere close, so he had no choice but to drop it. "I'll be back before practice. *Don't* take off," he said in a tone I found insufferable. He'd have had more luck ordering me *to* take off. "We're going to talk before you blow this out of proportion."

I glared at his retreating back with absolute murder in my eyes, waited a beat, just long enough for him to leave, and stood.

My history teacher, Ms. Banks, called my name once, then again.

"Not feeling well," I told her. "Going home." She didn't try to stop me, though I'd probably regret it later. My attendance was always a problem on account of me hating school and loving to leave it before it was over.

I made my way home almost blindly, looking down at my feet, following the trail, my mind somewhere else. Several places in fact, but mostly on Dante's reaction when he realized I hadn't stayed put. He'd be pissed. He'd likely even skip practice to confront me right away.

Pathetic as it was, I hoped he would. I needed, over and over, like a broken record, for him to show me that he'd never get sick of me, no matter how flawed I was. How insecure. How unlovable.

I had never made peace with being abandoned. I was certain that I never would. I still looked the reality of it in the face every day, wondered why I was so worthless, wondered when I'd be abandoned again.

My response to that was to unleash my helpless rage on the one person who would take it. Who wouldn't leave me. Who cared enough to chase me when I ran.

I was deep in thought as I approached the creek. There was a longer trail home, with a bridge over the small body of water, but when it was this nice out, it was never worth taking when you could just hop the rocks on the shorter route. It was tricky, but I'd gotten the balancing act down years ago.

It was an unseasonably warm day just a few weeks into the school year, and so I'd worn shorts. The sun was shining, a teasing breeze drifting through the forest. My mood was starting to improve the more I had some time and space away.

I poised myself to take the first big lunge. Once you started, it was best just to skip straight across, no stopping.

It happened fast, so fast that more of it was processed in retrospect than real time.

The creek was small, but it was loud. Loud enough to drown the sounds of even a large man moving directly behind me.

It happened fast, *so fast*, all of it. Something hard struck me in the back of the head. I saw stars, and my world took a turn for the darker.

It was hours later and I was still pissed. I'd been shuffled from the police station to the hospital. I was in a patient bed now, and they wouldn't let me *leave*. All I wanted to do was go home, shower, and curl up into a ball, but I had a bad concussion so that would not happen until tomorrow at the earliest.

And in the meantime, two cops, one male who'd introduced himself as Detective Harris, and one female who'd introduced herself as Detective Flynn, were asking me the same questions, over and over again. They didn't seem to want my answers, because every time I answered the same question the same way, the female cop looked increasingly more disgusted.

I took a strong disliking to both of them almost right away.

Her first and it started the moment she spoke to me. There was just something in her voice I didn't like, some undercurrent of hostility. No, it was more than hostility. It was judgement. Cold and final. This woman had an opinion about me and it was set in stone.

I wasn't sure why I didn't like Harris at first, but I didn't. Perhaps my instincts were trying to tell me from the start that something was wrong with him.

Looking back, it's easy to think so, but if it was so in the moment, I can't honestly say.

And worse than all of that, they wouldn't let Dante in to see me. I'd heard him, several times, making a fuss about it, getting himself into trouble somewhere in the hospital, trying his best, I knew, to make it to me, but so far he was losing.

I needed him to win. I needed to see his face, feel his hands holding mine, absorb his presence comforting me.

One upside: the detectives seemed as over it as I was. Finally, Flynn pulled the male officer to the other side of the room, the side with a second, currently vacant bed, shutting the curtain behind them.

The detectives started talking to each other about me, voices pitched low, but not low enough.

Flynn had made clear early on that she thought the whole thing was a colossal waste of their time.

"She's the daughter of Renee Theroux and Jethro Davis," Flynn was saying. "Can we really believe any story she's spinning? What do you expect? Who knows what kind of trouble she got herself into, and with whom. Should we just take her word for it that some homeless guy that's been living in the woods just walked up and attacked her?"

I felt my face getting red, I was so angry.

"It's obvious she was attacked, and that there was a sexual assault," Harris replied. "Nothing else is relevant. We need to figure out who attacked her. And you know as well as I do that this isn't the first time we've gotten a report like this."

"So we're supposed to just start digging around in the woods and grab every homeless guy with a spot by the river?" Flynn said impatiently. "On her word? That girl gets into fights with everyone, all the damn time, now we have to investigate one of her altercations like she's a *victim*?"

"Yes, we have to investigate it. That's our job. This was an assault, not a fight. Don't forget, we do have evidence, and there are several sex offenders that have gone off the grid around here. Not to mention all of the unsolved cases we're sitting on. It wouldn't be bad for us, in general, to start checking out some of the transients that have set up shop along the water."

Was this what good cop, bad cop sounded like? I'd never experienced it before. All cops were bad to me.

And it didn't make sense. I couldn't figure out why

they'd be using this tactic on a victim. *Oh wait, that's what it was.* Flynn had decided I wasn't one.

God, I hated cops. I hated that I'd even had to call the police, but I was *furious* and I wanted the creep caught.

"Fine," Flynn said curtly. "Let's get back to the station and start the paperwork."

"Okay. You go ahead. I'm going to have a quick word with her."

I watched Harris warily as he approached me again, looking apologetic. "I'll be back to follow-up soon." He set a card on the high nightstand beside the bed. "Call me if you need anything at all."

I nodded, chewing my lip and looking down at my hands. "Thanks, Detective Harris."

"Call me John."

I didn't particularly want to, but . . . "Thanks, John. Do you think this guy has done this before?"

"I think it's very likely we are dealing with a serial attacker, yes."

"Do you think you'll catch him?"

"As long as you cooperate, I'll make sure we do, Scarlett." That struck me as odd, but I was too distracted to think about it for long. "You take care. I'll be in touch."

He left, and Dante, *finally*, came in. He moved to me silently, looming over me, then softly took each one of my hands in his.

I couldn't even look at his face after the initial glance. It was like staring into an open wound. I was pissed, hurt, and embarrassed, and again, *pissed*, but he'd gone into another realm. I knew this was his worst nightmare.

"Are you okay?" he asked, voice shaking.

"Yes," I said, because it was true. I'd been attacked, yes, but I knew that it could have ended much, much worse.

"Who was it?" he asked, and I'd known he would.

I closed my eyes. I didn't want to tell him. He was too far to losing it, and if he had a clue just how much the police did not give a damn about finding the guy, he would to do it himself, I knew it. "Don't," I said quietly. "The police will handle it." I didn't believe it myself, but that wasn't the point. "I'm just a little bruised and pissed off, okay? Let's not make this a big thing."

One of his warm hands had moved up to cup my cheek. "Do you want to talk about it?" he asked. "I don't know what to do. I feel so helpless."

I did not want to talk about it. It felt like I'd talked about it *too* much, but I figured it would be better to let him know what had really happened than to let him speculate and think the worst.

He gripped my hand a little too painfully amid the retelling, but stayed very quiet and still, and I knew without having to ask that he was going through his own personal hell.

Gram came in soon after. Between the two of them, they made a big enough fuss over me that I felt truly cared for, and, though I was embarrassed by it, I was comforted.

Dante stayed the night with me in the hospital room, even after an initial standoff with my nurse. I think she decided it just wasn't worth the trouble.

I was discharged the next day, and things were almost starting to feel normal again, or at least like normal was on its way.

We were talking as though nothing had happened, joking, teasing each other as I prepared to leave for home.

As Dante was helping me to dress, we had another bad moment when he saw my bruised torso.

I glanced down at my breasts. They were black and blue. No wonder they hurt so damn much.

Dante had been holding my bra but it dropped out of his hands, his breath gone ragged. "Jesus. Look what he did to you. I'll fucking kill him."

The nurse walked in as he said that, and she sent him a startled look.

"I can't wear a bra right now," I said practically. "Just grab me a shirt."

"I'll do that," the nurse told Dante, her tone sharp, as he renewed his efforts to dress me.

He was gently sliding my arms into an oversized T-shirt as he tersely replied, "I've got her." The two didn't get along. It'd been awkward since their standoff about him staying the night before.

But the nurse only cared to a point. She clearly decided that we weren't worth the hassle and left us to it with one last glare.

We didn't even discuss it but he took me straight to Gram's house instead of mine, and she was waiting for us, a large corner suite upstairs prepared for me. I pulled Dante into bed with me and went instantly back to sleep.

"I fucking hate that guy, the male detective," Dante said abruptly at dinner.

I was surprised. "He's the only one that seems like he's trying to help me."

"I don't like him. I don't trust him. There's something wrong with him."

I was so used to him being jealous that that was the first conclusion my mind jumped to. Detective Harris was a very good-looking man, even distracted and shaken I had noticed, and then he'd had the nerve to keep Dante from me for hours after the attack. Of course Dante didn't like him. I didn't much like him either.

"We are terrorized and flattened by trivialities, we are eaten up by nothing."
~Charles Bukowski

chapter thirteen

The worst thing about the attack was how it made me question everything around me. Made me see it all differently. The forest surrounding our houses had been the home to many of the good memories in my life, a source of nothing so much as joy and enchantment, but all of a sudden, it was the opposite.

It was a dark, mysterious place now, the shadows more oppressive and menacing.

Within a few days, I was still more shaken than I'd admit to anyone, but more or less back into my daily routine, and I thought I was happy to put it all behind me. The police would do their job, and I would go on with my life just as before.

Well, not quite. I didn't leave Gram's, and we didn't walk to or from school anymore. Dante started driving us, and I was more than fine with it.

I knew I'd be in trouble as a few days passed, and I still didn't leave Gram's house.

It just felt so good to stay in a place where I was wanted, so I put off going back home.

Finally, I made Dante take me back to the trailer after school. If he'd had his way, we'd have just avoided the place, entirely and forever.

"Go back to practice," I told him. "You can come get me when you're done."

He wasn't pleased about that. "Fuck practice. I'm not leaving you."

He was immovable on the subject, and I was secretly relieved.

"Oh look who decided to come home after three fucking days," was my greeting from Glenda as I walked into the trailer for the first time since the attack. "No word from you, not even a phone call, and you come waltzing in like you still live here."

"Didn't Gram tell yo—?"

"She's not your gram, and *you* should have told me. Something like that happens, and you don't even call?"

I hadn't even considered it. When I needed someone or some comfort or support, I never thought of her.

"You want to stay up on that fancy hill, you go right ahead, you little brat! I never wanted you here anyway! Collect your shit and get out!" she said and left with a slam.

Oh that's right, I thought. *It was Friday.* I was interrupting her weekly binge-drunk, and I assumed she was heading to a bar to remedy that.

Dante pressed his chest against my back, leaning down to kiss my temple. "Are you okay?"

I mulled it over. "She told me to leave. I get to *leave*."

He threaded our fingers together and nuzzled his face into my hair. "Jesus. It's about fucking time. Just think, we get to wake up together every morning. Let's pack your stuff and get the hell out of here."

I was kind of amazed at how much stuff I actually had. We filled up his entire car and we still weren't even done, but I was tired, so we quit. I could get the rest later.

I couldn't quite believe I got to leave the hated trailer dump to stay permanently with Gram. I was reeling, almost giddy about it. It felt like Dante and I had been waiting our whole lives to live together, and finally it was happening. We could be together, day and night. Just the idea of it overshadowed everything else that had happened, for a time, and I was almost lighthearted.

But it wasn't meant to last.

I borrowed Dante's car the next day while he was at football practice, telling him I was tired and going to Gram's to lie down.

"I can skip out. I'll take you home." He looked like he wanted to. Football had fallen very low on his priorities since the attack.

Everything had a silver lining of some kind.

I waved him off. "No, don't bother. Unless you mind me borrowing your car?"

"Of course not. Be careful. And I can just walk home."

I was worried about him doing that, not because I thought he'd get attacked like I had, obviously. I was worried because I thought he wanted to. He'd been relentless and had finally gotten it out of me who the attacker was.

It was a homeless guy that we saw most days on our

walk home. No mistaking him. Dante didn't just know who he was, he knew where to find him.

I knew he'd go after the guy given half a chance.

"I'll come back to pick you up," I assured him.

I didn't head straight to Gram's. I had a few things yet to get from Glenda's trailer, and I figured the sooner I did it the better. She was liable to burn the stuff if I left it there for long.

I was nearly finished packing one last little box of pictures and keepsakes when I heard the loud sound of a car pulling onto Grandma's loose gravel driveway.

I glanced out a window. It was an old, brown sedan, and as I watched, Detective Harris stepped out of it.

I was not happy to see him.

I wanted the creep who'd attacked me caught, but I'd had more than my fill of dealing directly with the police.

Still, I went to the door and greeted him.

He smiled and asked how I was doing, citing that he hadn't wanted to intimidate me by pulling me into the station again for more questions, which I thought was supposed to be nice.

Nice, but nerve-racking. I didn't want to be alone with a strange man after what had only *just* happened to me.

Still, I did hate the police station. It always made me feel paranoid. I was so used to being in trouble that it just felt instinctual to stay away from a place like that.

"Where's Detective Flynn?" I asked him warily. I really didn't like her.

"She's back at the station, doing some paperwork. I got the impression that you'd be more comfortable without her." As he spoke he was looking down at his notepad, jotting down something that I couldn't make out. "Can I come in?"

I didn't want to let him in. Felt a powerful urge to refuse him, in fact. "Can I call my friend?"

He cocked his head to the side. "Why?"

"To, you know, have a friend here with me for this."

"I don't understand."

"It would make me feel better."

He smiled kindly at me. "I'm your friend, Scarlett. And I don't think it's ... appropriate to have some teenager involve themselves in an official police case. Listen, this will be quick, and I promise you it is necessary. Can I come in, or would you rather go to the station?" he asked again.

"I suppose not," I said stiffly, truly rattled. "You can come in." I knew it was just the fear from all that'd happened, but I did not want to be alone with this man, cop or not, or any man at all just then, for that matter.

"Can I call Mrs. Durant—Vivian—and have her join us?" I tried again. She wasn't a teenager, and I knew with certainty that she'd come if I needed her.

He'd been jotting something on his pad again, but he looked up at that. "Also not the best idea. All of this is sensitive information about an active case. I really can't allow you to divulge any of these details to anyone not actively involved."

Should I tell him that I'd already told Gram and Dante virtually everything, or would that get me into some sort of trouble? I wondered.

"Now have a seat, Scarlett," he said, perching himself on the sofa. He patted the spot next to him.

Trying not to visibly shudder, I sat down, getting as far away from him on the couch as I possibly could.

"Dear girl," he said, still giving me that benevolent smile of his. "I know you've been over all of this, but

I want you to do it again, for my direct ears this time. Maybe I'll catch something that Detective Flynn didn't."

My original statement at the station had been given to Flynn alone out of sensitivity to the fact that I was a teenage girl who had just been sexually assaulted.

Where the hell was that sensitivity now?

Harris shifted closer to me, and I had to fight not to cringe away. "I know this is hard. Just take your time and explain it to me as best you can. Every detail you can recall. Details are very important. Crucial in a case like this, if you actually want us to catch the culprit. You want that, right?"

I just froze, staring down at my hands. I did not want to go over it all again, and certainly not here.

"Here, let me try this again," he said gently. "I'll start with some questions, so it's less daunting, okay?"

I glanced at him and he smiled again. He had a great smile framed by an even greater face. His teeth were straight and white, his features even and handsome, his skin olive-toned, his eyes deep set and so dark that his pupils blended seamlessly into his irises.

I studied him closely for the first time.

He didn't look like a small town cop. He looked like a hard as nails sexy cop from a TV show.

Even so, I didn't want to be alone in a small space with him. And I particularly didn't want to tell him what had happened to me in detail.

Mostly what I wanted was to be left alone for a very long time.

But I wanted the creep that'd attacked me to be caught most of all. I didn't want to be scared every time I took a walk by myself, if I could ever bring myself to walk alone again.

"Okay," I finally said, looking back down at my lap.

"Did the man penetrate you?"

I jerked at the word, bewildered eyes flying back to his face. "N-n-no," I finally and with great effort got out.

"What *did* he do?"

I touched the back of my skull, eyes aimed at my lap. "I didn't see him coming. Something hard hit the back of my head—a rock, I guess?—and then he pinned me on my stomach. His arms reached around me, and he was trying to take off my jeans. He was clumsy and out of breath, *strong*, but he couldn't get the button undone. His mouth was at my ear. His whole . . . body was on my back. I always thought he was skinny, but he was so *heavy* on my back."

"Don't stop," Detective Harris said when I'd paused for too long. "Continue."

"He kept trying, for a while to get the button open, and while he did that he was . . . grinding against me."

"Where was he grinding on you? And *what* exactly was he grinding against you?"

I was red with shame. This retelling was even more embarrassing than the first one, which had been horrible. "My . . . butt."

"Stand up, turn around, and show me where exactly."

My bewildered eyes shot to his.

His eyes were apologetic. "I know it's embarrassing, but it's for the case. I need to work through every detail. Exhaustively. The more you cooperate, the more likely it is that the D.A. will have a good case against this guy once we catch him."

I was shaking as I stood and turned. I wished I'd worn something other than short cutoffs, but I hadn't been expecting a detective at my door.

I pointed to the spot on my butt then quickly sat down.

He was watching me, studying me so relentlessly that I couldn't look at his eyes.

"And what did he grind there, right against your asshole?"

My eyes shot back up to him at that. My shame and bewilderment working together to nip at my volatile temper.

What the hell was wrong with this cop? Was he *trying* to embarrass me?

"Answer the question, Scarlett."

I looked down at my hands. "His p-p-p-penis."

He cleared his throat. "Was it hard?"

"I think so. Yes."

"You think so? Why the uncertainty? Do you not know what a hard dick feels like?"

My snapping eyes were meeting his sympathetic ones now. Hello, temper.

"I do. It was hard. Are we done?"

"Not at all. Semi-hard or hard?

"Hard."

"Hard. Completely hard, not semi-hard, and he was grinding it against your butt, trying to shove it in your asshole through your jeans. Is that accurate?"

I nodded, shaking with fury. With shame. Fear.

"Had he pulled his hard dick out of his pants, or was it grinding against you through his pants?

Nausea moved through me, because I'd felt it enough to know the answer to that. "He'd pulled it out."

"So it was bare and hard and grinding against you?"

"Yes."

"I'm just trying to get every bit of information I can,

sweetie. Details are more important than you think."

"Are we almost done?"

"Almost. And you were just lying there? Or were you fighting him?"

"I was stunned at first. I think the blow to my head maybe knocked me out for a second or two. And I was just trying to breathe. He'd slammed the breath out of me. But after a while, when I realized what was happening, I started to struggle.

"Did he get the button undone? On your shorts?"

"He didn't."

"How tight were those shorts? Were they as tight as the ones you're wearing now?"

I shrugged, hating that he'd pointed something like that out, wishing that my shorts were *less* tight.

"Stand up again, sweet girl," he told me, voice careful, gentle.

I did it, wondering if I could refuse to do this. Whether they caught the guy or not, this interview was starting to make me feel sick to my stomach. Something was very off about all of it.

Something was very wrong with this cop.

He stood up, looming over me.

"Lift up your arms," he ordered softly.

I did it, trembling.

The motion brought my shirt up high enough to expose my stomach.

His eyes were on his hands as he fingered the waistband of my jean shorts. "So tight. Not an inch to spare here. Were your shorts that day as tight as this?" he asked again.

"Yes," I said through my teeth.

I wanted to sock him, but I refrained. I had a healthy fear of police. Even *I* had never hit one before.

"Keep going. What did he do then?"

"He started pulling at my pants, trying to get them down over my hips with the button still fastened."

"Did he succeed?"

"No."

"Those tight jean shorts of yours might have saved you, you know. Were you a virgin?"

I flushed and sat down without asking.

He moved to stand directly over me, and I regretted the decision. "Are you a virgin?" he repeated when I'd been quiet too long.

"I have a boyfriend," I finally gritted out in answer.

"It's a yes or no question, dear girl. Have you had sex?"

"Yes."

"Yes, you've had sex? Or yes, you're a virgin?"

"I've had sex. With my boyfriend."

"How many times? Just once? A few times?"

I blushed and shook my head. "More than a few times."

"How many?"

I shrugged. "I have no idea. I haven't been counting."

"Guess for me. More than a hundred times?"

I glared at him. "Probably. Does it matter?"

"Yes. All of this matters. Guess a number for me, sweet girl. Approximately how many times have you had sex with your boyfriend? Vaginal sex."

"Two hundred."

He looked strange, like I'd riled him.

I started shaking harder, wondering if I could get past him and out the door, or if he'd stop me.

"Two hundred?" he breathed. "Are you messing with me?"

"Like I said, I haven't been counting, but I'd guess

closer to two hundred than one hundred." My tone was defiant to hide the fact that he was terrifying me.

"With his dick in you? Two hundred times?"

I barely nodded.

"So your boyfriend puts his dick in your pussy pretty much every spare moment of the day? What else do you do? Does he fuck you in the ass?"

"What the hell is *wrong* with you?" I whispered at my lap.

"Did this other guy, the one that attacked you, put it in your ass?"

"He didn't," I said through my teeth.

"Did he penetrate you anywhere?"

I was blinking hard, trying not to cry. I was so angry, and ashamed, and confused. I felt so helpless that I didn't know how to react. This wasn't right. None of this was right.

"I t-t-told you, he c-c-couldn't get my jeans off."

"So the jeans stayed on. What happened then?"

"He -k-k-kept . . . g-g-grinding against me.

"His bare dick against your asshole, but over your jeans."

I nodded, glaring at him. "There." I paused. "And against my thigh."

"Where on your thigh? Get up and show me?"

I shook my head, tears pouring down my face. "N-n-n-no. P-p-p-please. I don't want to, sir, please."

"Dear girl, if you want to catch this guy, you're going to have to do your part." His voice hardened. "Stand up now, or I'll assume you aren't serious about catching him. Did you know we've been studying a string of serial rapes over the past decade? A violent man attacking women in the woods across three cities. And a few women have even disappeared. Did you know that?"

I'd heard about one attack locally but it'd been years ago, and several more attacks, but not here, in other towns, if close ones. I'd never heard a word about the disappearances, though.

On trembling legs, I stood.

"Show me where on your thigh. Was it more toward the back? Turn around and show me."

I turned, and bent, and touched the very vulnerable spot where my groin met my thigh, deep up into my shorts.

He was a very large man with a badge and a gun. I was out of my depth. Helpless. Completely. And the way he was acting was *not right.*

"So he got it up that high? Damn, he was close. A few more moves and he'd have had it in."

I might've been in shock, but I went a little numb after that, my mind got a little hazy. Distant.

"But you're saying, even though he got it right there, one quick shove away from your pussy, he still couldn't figure it out, still didn't penetrate you?"

I shook my head, chin to my chest, eyes pointed down, tears falling silently. Not tears of sadness. Tears of terror.

Because I felt terrorized.

"What next?"

"He was grabbing my chest, hard, hurting me."

"Your breasts, you mean?"

"Yes."

"He bruised you up good, I heard. He really did a number on you. How are they healing up? I bet they're sensitive. Big breasts like yours usually are."

I felt exposed, mortified.

I couldn't stop trembling. The tears wouldn't stop leaking out of my eyes, and my hands went up instinctively, covering my breasts.

"They still hurt?"

"I guess," I said. They hurt like hell. I still couldn't put on a bra.

"You know, sweet girl, it's impossible for a busty girl like you to go around without a bra without it showing. They must hurt. How tender are they?"

"T-t-tender."

"Okay, so he was grabbing your big, soft tits and grinding his hard, bare dick against your asshole, over your jeans, and down lower, against your thigh, right into your shorts, just a quick prayer from that tight little pussy. It's still tight, right? Even after letting your boyfriend put it in there two hundred times?"

"D-d-d-d-do you have to say it all like that? C-c-c-could you please try to be a little more p-p-p-p-professional?"

He didn't answer, and though his eyes were still kind on mine, I was quickly learning not to trust them.

"I was screaming by then, and struggling, trying to fight him, but it was hard, being on my stomach like that."

"Was he saying anything to you? Was his mouth still at your ear?"

"Yes. He was saying all sorts of horrible things into my ear. H-h-he called me names, a c-c-c-cunt, a wh-wh-whore, a b-b-bitch, a s-s-slut, and told me to take my jeans off or he'd k-k-kill me."

"Did he have a weapon?"

"I never saw one."

"Did he say *how* he'd kill you?"

"No."

"Did you take off your jeans for him?"

"No. I kept struggling until, um, he was done. And then he got up and ran away."

"Do you know what made him leave?"

"He was *done*, I think."

"He finished on you?"

I nodded jerkily.

"Where did he finish on you? Where did his cum go?"

I shuddered.

"Turn around and show me, as best as you can, where his semen went."

I did it fast, pointing from my rear all the way up my back, where I'd felt it and seen it when I'd taken my clothes off.

"All on your clothing? Or some on your skin?"

"S-s-s-skin t-t-t-t-too."

"And you got a good look at him? I remember you said that. But nothing you just told me indicates that you were looking at anything but the ground."

"When he g-got up and started running, I stood. I was dizzy, but I saw him. I recognized him. He's the homeless guy that always hangs out by the river, at the bridge right by the middle school. I thought he was harmless before, he usually just ignores everyone that passes him, but I guess I'd never encountered him alone. I usually walk to school with a friend of mine."

"Okay. So you got a good look at him running away. Did you see his face?"

"Yes. He looked back at me as he was running. It was definitely the same guy that's usually hanging out there. I've probably seen him on the way home from school, camped out by the river, a hundred times."

"Okay. I think we're done for now. You did a good job today, sweet girl. We're going to find this guy. I promise."

I was so relieved I started crying harder.

He seemed to take that as an invitation to pull me into his chest, embracing me.

It was almost comforting. The size and shape of him, so big and hard, reminded me of Dante.

But this was not Dante. This was a middle-aged cop who I knew I couldn't trust.

Was he going to leave soon? *Please, please leave soon.*

I tried to pull away, but he held me fast. I started to struggle, and he let me know how strong he was by bear-hugging so hard that I couldn't move.

If only I could stop crying, maybe he'd leave.

"Hey now," he murmured into my hair. "You're safe here, sweet girl. I'm just trying to help you. Just cooperate, okay? And know this: You can tell me anything. I know you're a good girl, right? I can see that, and I want you to know that if you have any questions about what happened to you, you can always come to me, with anything, okay?"

"I just want to be alone," I gasped into his chest.

"Okay. Okay, I get it. But you call me if you need anything, okay?"

I agreed to, just to get him to leave.

When he was finally gone I stood shaking at the door, twisting the bolt, again and again, to be sure it was locked.

I may have been in shock. I didn't feel right. I wasn't sure what to do.

I felt dirtier, more raw than I had even after the attack. Somehow, this had felt like even more of a violation.

I took a shower and rubbed my skin until it burned.

What had just happened hadn't been normal

procedure. I knew that, of course, but what could I do about it?

Who could I tell? The police? He was, sadly, the nicest one I'd met so far.

I knew absolutely that I could not tell Dante. He was a maniac when it came to that sort of thing. He'd fight anybody. He didn't give a *damn*. Cop or not. Adult or not, he'd go after this creep and end up in jail. I was certain of it.

It took a few days, but I worked up the nerve to call his partner, Detective Flynn, to try to tell her how he'd acted toward me, but she quickly put me in my place.

She was not inclined to believe anything I had to say, in fact she wanted to give me an earful.

She told me in no uncertain terms that I was nothing but a troublemaker, just like my mother, who she enjoyed informing me, spite in every word, had stolen her boyfriend from her in high school and was still feeling the sting of it.

Just my luck.

And who else did that leave? The sheriff? One of the other cops? It was just a list of people that hated me, that thought I was trash, people who had become absolutely convinced a long time ago that *I* was the problem.

I thought that interview was the worst of it, and the worst had been bad enough.

But the blows just kept coming.

"She's mad, but she's magic. There's no lie in her fire."
~Charles Bukowski

chapter fourteen

PRESENT

Dante

What was I doing here?

I didn't have a good answer to that question. Not even for myself.

Certainly I had no hope. No more than I ever did.

But mostly, I couldn't help myself.

I could not stay away.

She was the siren that called men to their destruction, and I was the first and most eager to answer that deadly call.

Every fucking time.

Always there was a debate in my mind when I did this, when I gave in and went to her again.

Was this heaven or hell?

I'd never been able to answer that question, and that was the whole fucking problem.

It was both.

I'd pulled strings to gain access to her trailer while she was on set. I'd done so promising I was just leaving her a gift and then I was supposed to go.

I didn't do that. I set her gift on the small table then promptly sprawled out on her sofa, loosening my tie, kicking off my shoes.

She had to have a break at some point. I had time. I'd wait.

I was dozing when the door opened some time later. I sat up with a start.

It was her, and for some reason she didn't call security on me.

Instead, she stepped in and closed the door behind her.

I took her in, let her presence wash over me, my eyes devouring her in nonconsecutive bites; her face, her legs, her hands, her lips, her feet, her eyes, her shoulders, her ankles, her chest, her neck, my eyes darting all over her like she might disappear.

Nothing I'd ever seen could touch her. She was as ravishing as she was unattainable.

So heartbreakingly lovely that I ached with it.

A familiar, gnawing pang started throbbing in my gut, and I let the pain wash over me for a moment, indulged in it.

There'd been changes since the last photos I'd seen of her. She'd colored her hair, for the part no doubt, lightened it up just a touch, but enough so that gold streaks overtook and dominated the color, making her some deep, tawny version of blonde.

She was dressed simply, outfitted for whatever scene she'd been doing in a soft white button up blouse tucked into a high-waisted, well-fitted light gray skirt. It was an almost conservative ensemble, until you took in the shoes. They were glittering ivory platform stilettos with a peep toe, and she wore them like a weapon.

I'd have bet money she'd made friends with the wardrobe person, that she'd had at least some say in those man-eater heels.

My eyes shot up to her face as her luscious mouth turned up mockingly at the corners, her fingers going to the front of her blouse, fingering the top button.

Without a word, she started to undress.

"Scarlett." Two syllables. Utter devastation.

She undid one button, and then the next, revealing silky cleavage, a lacy white bra.

"I didn't come here for this," I told her, trying my best to sound convincing.

We always said our lines, played our parts, but that didn't mean I wasn't sincere.

The problem was, no matter my intentions, when it came to her, I did not have one measly ounce of self-control.

She smiled and it was so vicious that it made me flinch. "Once again, you're a fool. What did you come here for then?" She asked the familiar question with an unfamiliar something in her voice.

Something soft, *or did I just want to hear that?*

Something forgiving? No, certainly I must have been imagining that.

"I wanted to ask you a question."

She'd finished unbuttoning her shirt and shrugged it off nonchalantly. Without pausing her fingers went to the front clasp of her bra, snapping it open.

My jaw went slack, my mind blank. I may have drooled.

"What was the question?" she asked, sounding so annoyed that I knew she must have asked it several times before I heard it.

But seriously, what did she expect? She was topless now, playing with her incomparable breasts while she spoke. Of course she knew what she was doing. The amused glint in her eye told me that she was messing with me and she loved the results.

And even knowing she was toying with me, even knowing she thought it was all a battle, a game of war, none of that calmed my reaction to her. None of it quelled my undying desperation for her. It never had.

Just the opposite.

Panting, I answered, "I can't concentrate on anything when you do that."

She bit her lip, her brows drawing together in a fake coy expression that I fucking ate up with a spoon. Slowly, teasingly, she inched out of her skirt. "Is this better for your concentration? What did you come here for, *lover*? What was your question?"

She continued to strip, so slow and languid that I could hardly stand it.

But of course that was the point. She knew what she was doing to me. She always had, at least in this.

I tugged at my collar, outright sweating now. "Jesus, you're merciless."

Her expression did something at that, something vulnerable and twisted, her smile deepening and hardening, turning both more brittle and more real. "You have no fucking idea. Now ask your question."

She was naked now, wearing nothing but her fuck me

heels. *Jesus*, this woman and her shoe-porn would be the end of me.

I tried to ask it. I really did, but before I could get a word out, she was straddling me, every inch of her perfect, bare skin suddenly within reach of my eager hands.

Lust charged through me like a ram. I felt the sharp, sweet ache of it deep in my loins, desire so thick and acute it'd turned painful.

I'm sure she thought I would touch her breasts, her hips, her ass, her cunt, some part of her outrageously beautiful body that she'd so generously draped over mine.

I did not. Both of my trembling hands went up to cup her perfect, oh so beloved face. My voice was somehow steadier than my hands as I asked her my question. "Do you love me at least as much as you hate me?"

That was all I needed, just that small aching bit for me.

Had I kept even some tiny piece of her love?

It made me wretched to ask and worry at her answer. Even so, I *had* to know.

But there was no mercy in her, not today.

She smiled, a gentle smile that made me tense up more than any of her venomous ones had.

I knew her. Knew the hatred she carried around inside of her. I was familiar with it. I'd studied every angle of it. Every harsh plane, every bitter hollow, every rough edge. Like everything about her, that hatred was only at home with extremes.

I knew where it began, what made it thrive, and why it had decided to focus so squarely on me.

I owned my part of it, my share of the blame, but that didn't make it easy, or even okay. It was simply a fact of life that I'd had to accept along with many others.

While I bided my time.

But the smile she gave me then, that one *particularly*, one almost as gentle as it was condemning, *Jesus*, I knew in an *instant* that it meant something had changed.

And I was terrified.

"I'll answer that," she said in a voice so throaty and resonant it could choke your soul. "I will. But not yet. First, I have a question of my own."

I was shaking my head before she'd even finished.

No. No. *No*.

There was something too meaningful in her eyes as they raked over my face, like a switch had been flipped, one that should not, *could not*, be turned on.

But she knew me too well, knew how to weaken me, what strategy to use to gut me the fastest.

Her mouth was my undoing, her lips my own personal heaven and hell. They were a weapon she used seldom but unrepentantly, and they were all the more potent for it.

I was a slave to those lips, a willing lamb to slaughter, and when she pressed them to mine, I was already past the point of all resistance.

I forgot my question, forgot hers, forgot everything but the simple joy of reveling in *her*—my weakness and my strength, my purpose and my distraction, my redemption and my undoing.

I couldn't even believe I was here with her, that she hadn't had me kicked out the second she found my drunken ass in her trailer. Instead she was straddling me naked, leaning over me as she kissed and kissed me, unbuttoning my shirt, pushing it aside to rub her naked breasts against my bare chest how she knew I loved.

She completely ignored the chain around my neck and the small objects that hung from it.

I was only relieved by that. She usually took exception to it.

But I would never take it off.

I returned her kiss with fierce abandon, not even trying to hold back.

When she spoke, it took a while for me to register her words, even as sharp as they were.

"What have you done to us, Dante?" she breathed into my mouth. "What have you *done*?"

I froze.

No. No. *No.* This could not happen.

Could not.

I was tense, ready for the next blow, the next unanswerable question, but it didn't come.

As though she thought she'd said enough, she didn't ask it.

Instead she kissed me again, her hands as busy as her tongue. She kneaded at my abs, working her wicked hands lower, undoing my slacks, freeing me.

She kept moving, poising herself over me, rubbing her wet sex against my cock in a way that she knew made me lose half my brain cells.

At least half.

She gave my lip one last drugging bite and pulled back to glance down at our bodies.

My head fell back, and I couldn't keep in an involuntary shudder.

I was half convinced she was just teasing me, that she'd leave me like this, high and dry (she'd done it before), but that was not what she did.

With excruciating slowness and utmost care, she impaled herself on me.

We didn't speak for a time, well, nothing coherent was

said, at least, just a lot of calling out names and speaking to God.

And begging. There was definitely some begging going on.

I'll let you guess which one of us that was.

I lay back on my elbows, fists clenched, and watched through heavy lids as she rode me, languidly and thoroughly, all the while wondering if this was just some wonderful, torturous dream.

I didn't touch her, didn't trust myself to put my hands on her and not just come instantly. I didn't want this to be quick.

I wanted it to last. It was a fact that there was nothing else I'd rather be doing, for as long as I could possibly get away with doing it.

My head fell back again, eyes closing as pleasure washed over me in acutely heavy waves. I was *so close*, but trying my damnedest not to embarrass myself.

I wasn't succeeding, about a thrust away from losing the battle, when her voice broke through to me.

"What have you done, Dante?" Her voice was as silky as it was deadly. "What lies have you told? Where do they even begin?"

Every muscle in my body tensed.

She leaned forward and kissed me. Her mouth and her movements had almost made me forget her questions, or at least had me back to ignoring them, when she spoke again. "What have you been keeping from me?" came out between kisses.

I froze and almost pushed her off me, almost fled. But there was no running from this, or her. Not anymore.

Also, she started moving again, in earnest now, working herself on my length with quick, jerky motions that were guaranteed to get me off and fast.

I groaned out a protest. She was distracting me from her words on purpose, using a very sound method to switch my attention, and at first, I fought it.

But not for long. Not for more than a few seconds, if I were honest.

She knew what she was doing.

I jackknifed up, bear-hugging her to me as I started to come, pistoning my hips against her, face buried in her neck, as I let myself go.

I was still jerking inside of her, mid ejaculation, when she whispered against my ear, her voice filled with gentle malice, "What secrets are you holding trapped in that manipulative brain of yours?"

It was a sobering enough question that it probably should have stopped me in my tracks, if it were possible.

It probably wasn't. I kept her crushed against me as I rubbed out every last twitch.

Even with a heavy dose of trepidation mixed in, it was glorious.

She had to wriggle against me for a time before I'd let her loose. When I finally did, she shoved her hands against my shoulders, pushing away from me, drawing me out of her with one long, decisive pull.

I couldn't help it, I tilted my head down to watch.

I shuddered as I noticed the evidence of our passion on her thighs.

It was a sight to behold, if you're animal enough to like that sort of thing.

I certainly am.

She moved away from me without another word, striding naked into the bathroom.

I collapsed back on the couch, feeling exhaustion creep over me. I didn't even have the wherewithal to be worried just then. I was nothing but spent.

It seemed I blinked and she was out of the bathroom and dressed again, looking like she hadn't just rocked my world on her lunch break.

I rallied myself enough to speak up when I realized she was just going to leave. "Wait," I said weakly, barely keeping my eyes open. "You didn't answer my question.

She paused, eyeing me with spectacular detachment. "Did you answer any of mine? Goodbye, Dante. Don't be here when I come back."

"Can you wake me up at the soonest possible moment?" I murmured at the empty trailer about a second before I passed out.

"Doubt thou the stars are fire, Doubt that the sun doth move. Doubt truth to be a liar, But never doubt I love."
~William Shakespeare

chapter fifteen

PAST

Scarlett

Weeks went by and there was no progress in the police investigation. No arrests were made.

I was too creeped out by Harris to pursue it, in fact, I actively avoided dealing with him, but with every day that passed, Dante became increasingly disturbed, and I became progressively more paranoid.

I dropped out of drama exactly three days after the attack. Gram's house was just too inviting for me. And of course, there was Gram herself, always there to greet me when I arrived. For the first time in my life, I felt like I had a home I was welcomed in, and I spent as much time there as I possibly could. I'd have dropped out of school without a qualm if I hadn't known it would've disappointed her.

Dante didn't like it. He threatened more than once to quit football in response to my change in schedule, but perversely I was the one that talked him out of it. We were co-dependent enough without inventing new reasons not to leave each other's sight.

A few weeks later, I was willing to rethink my position on the matter. He was fighting again, I could tell. More than he ever had before, in fact, coming home with more bruises than he could hide or football practice could account for.

I didn't have to ask. The guys must have been talking about me again, and I knew just the types of things they'd be saying. When girls with my reputation were attacked, it was a no-brainer, to my mind at least, that I'd be blamed for whatever the rumor mill was saying had happened. It'd likely been blown out of proportion, and I figured I was either being called a liar or a slut.

I didn't hear any of the rumors directly myself, but every new bruise on Dante's body told me the story as clear as though I were reading it on paper.

Just when I thought I couldn't love him more.

Detective Harris came to the house twice to talk to me, but he had no new information about the case, and as soon as he realized that Gram was as good as glued to my side, he quickly found a reason to leave.

"I do not like that man," Gram said, after the second visit. She was studying my face. "Darling, do me a favor, always insist that I be there when he needs to speak to you. Always."

I agreed happily, but Harris never came back to her house after that. Instead, he started pulling me out of my classes at school when he wanted to have a word. So much so, rumors started to go around that I was having an affair with 'the hot cop,' as he'd been fondly nicknamed by the girls at school.

It infuriated me, especially so since he never seemed to be doing anything to find the man that had attacked me. Instead, he wanted to have short, intense, *meaningless* conversations with me, always pretending it was 'official business.'

The third time he pulled me out of class, I was outright hostile toward him. "Any updates on finding the man that attacked me, or are you just here to ask about my *health* again?"

We were standing near my locker—he'd asked me to show him where it was—and he was looking around, barely paying me any mind at all.

I clenched my jaw. "And if you want to talk to me, I'm going to need to call Vivian Durant. She's insisted that I not be alone with you."

That got his attention, his head snapping toward me, eyes narrowing on my face. "What did you tell her? You remember what I said, don't you? Everything about this case is confidential. If you share any information, with *anyone*, you could get yourself into big trouble, *and* we will *never* catch this guy."

I bit my lip, it wanted so badly to tremble. *What did this man want from me?* I honestly didn't know. It seemed to me he enjoyed terrifying me, but I also knew I had some serious baggage where law enforcement was concerned. "W-w-why did you pull me out of class?"

"I told you, I want to see your locker. Go ahead and open it up for me."

I did, stepping back so he could look inside. "What are you looking for?" I asked him.

"How are you feeling?" he countered.

"Fine," I bit out.

"Breasts still tender? I see you can wear a bra again."

My shaking hands were in fists. "They're fine. What are you looking for?"

He was standing right in front of my open locker, not touching anything, just looking. "Clues. I'm a detective, you know."

"You sure don't act like one," just sort of slipped out.

I was immediately sorry. He didn't touch me, didn't lay one finger on me, but I felt physically intimidated nonetheless as he stepped into my personal space.

"Just because I'm police," he said very, very quietly, right into my face. "Doesn't mean I'm not a *man*. Doesn't mean I can't be *riled*, so I would show a little more respect, if I were you, Scarlett. Not only am I the only one who is willing to help you, no one else on the force would lift a *finger* if something were to happen to you. Do you understand? You've burned every bridge but this one."

I tried to take a step back, and that's when it happened.

Harris grabbed my arms to stop me, to keep me from moving away, and I swear I felt his presence before I saw or heard him, like electricity in the air. Rage on the wind.

"Get your fucking hands off her!"

My eyes shut tight. In relief. And horror. Because I was saved, and Dante was about to get himself arrested.

"This is none of your concern," Harris told Dante. "Go back to class, son."

Dante, my hero, my everything, was not intimidated by *anyone*, not even a cop, and he was *furious*. He was in the older man's face without hesitation, moving between us, shielding me at the same time he put himself into harm's way.

I was shuddering in relief.

And I thought I couldn't love him more.

Whatever happened, if Dante was here, he wouldn't let me be harmed. I knew it. Absolutely.

"What the fuck are you doing, putting your hands on her?" Dante raged, backing Harris into the locker. "Don't you dare ever fucking touch her again, you hear me?"

The other man was so surprised, I think, that for a moment he let the younger, unarmed high school kid back him into the lockers and then shove him hard in the chest.

"Dante, no," I cried right at the same time that Harris reached for his gun.

I couldn't keep it in, I screamed.

Dante almost, almost kept going for it, his hand covering the other man's, a ghost of movement but it was there. He was going for the cop's gun.

But there was some sanity left in him yet, because at the last second, he took a step back, hands going up.

"On the ground," Harris snarled, pointing his gun right into Dante's face.

I was sobbing as I took a step forward, and then another.

Harris caught the movement and pointed at me with his free hand. "Don't move another inch. Your boyfriend's in big trouble, and if you don't stay out of it, it could be the difference between handcuffs or a bullet, you understand?"

I backed off immediately.

People were starting to spill out into the halls by then—kids, teachers—all looking on in stunned disbelief, no one even talking.

"Get on the ground, now!" he screamed into Dante's face.

Dante glared at the other man, his expression utterly dauntless, but he complied.

I felt helpless as he cuffed Dante's hands behind his back and then dragged him to his feet. I found myself trailing after them as Harris began to lead him out.

"Stay here," Harris said curtly. "Go back to class."

"I'm fine," Dante told me, and though I couldn't see his face, he sounded composed, all things considered.

I watched them leave with a pounding heart, following behind, far enough back that Harris didn't take exception, but close enough to see them get into his car.

My mind was racing. I had no idea what I should do, so I did the only thing I could. I called Gram.

We were all surprised when Harris didn't arrest Dante. I was frantic in the interim as I coordinated with Gram to find out what had happened to Dante.

I was so convinced that they'd be at the police station that I left school, taking Dante's car to pick up Gram. We were literally pulling out of the driveway when Harris drove up in his brown sedan, Dante in the backseat.

Dante got out, and Harris drove away.

I stopped the car, put it in park, and got out. I ran and threw myself at Dante with such force that it made him sway precariously for a beat before he settled back solidly on his feet and wrapped his big arms around me.

"I'm fine, shh, I'm all right," he said into my hair, voice pitched loud enough to be heard over my sobs.

"D-d-did he hurt you?" I gasped him.

"No, he didn't lay a finger on me. Calm down, angel. Shh. You're okay. Calm down." He was stroking a hand over my hair, over and over, to soothe me.

Slowly but surely, it was working.

"What happened?" Gram asked him. She was, as always, the epitome of calm.

He gave her the short version of what had happened at school.

"But he didn't arrest you?" she asked when he finished.

"No. He just took me for a drive and then brought me here. And you know what? I don't think they're doing a damned thing to find the guy that attacked Scarlett. He straight up told me that they're not even close to making an arrest. And you know what else he said? They haven't even gone to look where we told them the guy hangs out. At this point the only way they'll even find him is if he goes to the station and turns *himself* in."

The more he revealed, the more agitated he became, until at the end he was raising his voice.

Gram held up a hand, and he quieted. "I'll start asking around about all of this—Harris, the case. I will get some answers, but I need you to stop getting into trouble. You're only making it worse, Dante."

"Harris was bothering me at school today," I defended him. "Dante only got into trouble helping me."

She studied us both, looking more ruffled than I'd ever seen her. "*Jesus*. What the *hell* is going on?"

That scared me more than anything. If Gram didn't know what to do, the cause seemed completely lost.

She took a few deep breaths and seemed to regain her composure. "Like I said, I'm going to get some answers."

I believed her and was comforted.

And I believe she would have, if she'd had more time, but everything came to a head just two days later.

I don't know just what Harris said to Dante, what seed he planted that troubled him so, but it took root quickly and flowered into this: Dante believed that the only way my attacker would be arrested was if he went to find him personally.

He left in the middle of third period, but I only found that out later. I didn't even know he had gone at the time.

When the news came, it was like a ripple moved through the school, information spreading like a furious gust of wind. I was not the most social, as usual, and so I wasn't the first to hear. I was blissfully ignorant for a few more minutes than the majority of the school, but when I heard the news, I was as shocked as everyone else was.

Dante had been arrested for killing my attacker.

"Never go to bed mad. Stay up and fight."
~Phyllis Diller

chapter sixteen

PRESENT

Dante

I woke up still on her sofa with a pounding headache and my cheek pillowed against a silky thigh. It was almost enough to make my hard-on win out over my hangover. Almost.

And fingers, gentle, familiar fingers, stroking through my hair, lightly rubbing my temples.

Was this real? Was I dreaming she was tending to my hangover as if she didn't hate me?

Was even my dream mind longing for her scraps? What could be more pathetic than that?

"Am I dreaming?" I mumbled into her skin.

"Do you usually dream about feeling like shit? Because you look like shit."

Almost was caving quickly to yes, please. "Hangover," I murmured into her skin, turning my head to nuzzle, one curious hand sliding up her bare leg, trying without any conscious help from my brain, to figure out what she was or wasn't wearing.

Pants, no. Panties, yes, though they weren't much of a deterrent, and she wasn't resisting me, thank God. I fingered her, and she shifted under my cheek, her thighs parting just the slightest bit.

It was enough.

I slid to the floor, going to my knees in front of her.

I made my way up her legs with my mouth, placing open-mouthed kisses against her thighs, spreading her legs wider as I moved higher, wedging my shoulders between. I licked the tender flesh of her groin with quick, wet flicks of my tongue, rolling my eyes up to watch her reaction.

She made a little noise, higher pitched than a groan, but more stifled than a mewl.

I licked long and slow, right in that perfect little strip of skin at the very top of her inner thigh.

She made the noise again. I sucked her flesh into my mouth, drawing hard, until she gripped my hair and cried out my name.

I smiled and went down on her, spreading her legs wide, pushing the tiny scrap of lace to the side, and kissing her, licking her, driving my tongue into her until I had her clawing mindlessly at my shoulders, just losing it, begging me to stop, to fuck her, to let up with my tongue.

But I couldn't stop, wouldn't stop. My entire life was out of my control, but this, her body, her pleasure, was *mine*.

She let me get her off, but the second she was done, she was up, moving away from me, agitated hands scraping her hair back from her face.

I was still wiping my mouth as I studied her. She was wearing the shirt she'd worn earlier but that was it. No bra, no shoes, makeup scrubbed clean.

"How long have I been out?" I asked her.

"A while," she answered, still out of breath but trying to hide it, one hand braced against the counter, the other on her hip. Her back was to me. "I'm done shooting for the day." She moved to the trailer's small coffee bar and I watched her silently, eating up her every move as she began to brew a cup.

When I realized she was making it for me, prepping it exactly how I took it, my heart did a slow, painful turn in my chest.

What the hell was going on? Why was she being so civil?

It undid me faster and more thoroughly than her hostility ever could have.

Perhaps that was why.

She reached up into one of the tiny overhead cabinets and fished something out.

I heard more than saw the rattling bottle of pills, because my eyes were preoccupied with every inch of skin she revealed as she reached up.

I shifted uncomfortably, and it was only as I did so that I realized my clothes were off. She must have stripped me while I slept, leaving me in nothing but my boxer briefs.

She brought me two ibuprofen and the just right cup of coffee. I thanked her, eyes devouring her face, but she wouldn't look at me, instead giving the barest nod and turning away again.

"You took my clothes off while I slept." It wasn't an accusation so much as a question.

"It was the wind," she said absently, sarcasm present even if the will for it was not. She was looking at the counter. At the gift I'd brought her. "What's that?" It wasn't a question so much as an accusation.

We'd always been good at balancing each other out.

"I don't know," I drawled. "I think the *wind* carried it in when it was blowing off my clothes."

I could only see a hint of her profile with the way she was turned, but I caught her ghost of a smile.

My chest ached at the sight. To say I missed her was a cruel understatement, like saying you'd miss your soul after you gave it away. After it was torn from you.

I was empty.

Flesh without blood.

I was not *whole* without her.

Never would be.

I wasn't a big enough fool to believe that could ever change.

I downed the pills and took a long swig of my coffee. All the while she didn't move, just staring at the box.

"Open it," I urged her. I had no idea if she would. At that moment she was an utter enigma to me.

I still couldn't figure out why she hadn't made me leave yet.

Well, I had an *idea*, a gnawing, sickening suspicion, but my fear of the notion made me instantly reject it. Denial is a powerful thing.

I tensed when I realized she was actually going to open the gift, leaning forward, resting my elbows on my knees.

She took the Louboutins out of the box without a

word, setting them side by side on the counter. "Highness Strass," she said reverently.

"Did you just address your shoes as Highness Strass?"

She shot me a look. "That's their name."

"You know the name of the shoe?"

She actually looked sheepish for a short, endearing moment. It was adorable. It made me want to kiss her silly. And fuck her mindless. But that was nothing new.

"What I mean is, I don't want them," she rallied. "Quit buying me shoes, you stalker."

"Well, you can throw them away, like the other pair, or do whatever you want with them, but I'm not taking them back, and I had to get you something. To congratulate you on landing the big part."

She was back to drooling over the shoes. "Why did you pick these ones, in particular?" She asked it with begrudging admiration in her voice.

I'd done well.

"I had help, from one of our department store stylists. I told her you were deep into shoe-porn, that you only get off on the hardcore stuff." I warmed as I saw that she had to bite back her smile. "And she recommended a few. These ones stood out to me the most."

With a sigh, she set them back in the box, turning to look at me. "What are you doing here?" Her voice was almost gentle with the finest edge of pain.

It was foreign on her, so unaccountably vulnerable, that it made me wince. "I told you earlier. I had a question for you. You didn't answer it."

She waved her hand in the air, dismissing the notion. "What I mean is, what are you doing in town?"

I stared at her, because she knew the answer to that. Still, if she wanted to play pretend, I could do that too. I was, in fact, excellent at it. "I'm here for work. Thought I'd stop by while I was in the neighborhood."

She folded her arms together until she was almost hugging herself and just stared at me.

Her face was tragic.

It was too much. It knocked the wind out of me.

I was undone with a glance. I couldn't even meet her eyes when she gazed at me like that. I looked down at my hands as an unmistakable wave of fear rocked through me.

Her expression told me everything and nothing, but one thing was for certain, she knew something she wasn't supposed to, and all of the rules had changed.

I felt unutterable guilt at the relief that washed over me. It was so powerful that for a moment it nearly drowned out the fear.

But only for a moment.

"Look at me," she coaxed softly. "Look at me and tell me *what you've done.*"

I fled. Found my clothes, pulled them on with clumsy, jerking movements, and got the hell out of there.

She never stirred, didn't turn to watch me, didn't say another word, though it didn't escape my notice that she was shaking like a leaf.

Hugging herself and trembling like she could barely hold herself together.

It was pure hell to walk away.

And absolutely necessary.

"Beauty, more than bitterness, makes the heart break."
~Sara Teasdale

chapter seventeen

PAST

Scarlett

I'd heard rumors, and over the years they'd grown more persistent. Whispers about Jethro Davis. It was commonly assumed that he was my father. Even my doubtful grandma had admitted a few years prior that he was the most likely candidate.

I'd never seen the man, but I hated the very idea that I could have a dad so close, in this very town, and he'd never even bothered to meet me.

Never once bothered to see what his daughter looked like. If she was all right.

Never bothered to make sure she didn't end up in a dumpster.

I preferred instead to fantasize that he was someone

glamorous, someone rich, maybe even famous, some man who didn't even know I existed, because if he did, nothing could have kept him away.

But then, one day, I ran into Jethro Davis.

The rumors I'd heard about him weren't only about him being my father. A lot of them were about the man himself. The things he did. He was a criminal. A drug dealer and some said worse, that a few people who'd crossed him hadn't lived long to regret it.

He'd served some time in prison. For what exactly, I couldn't say. Assault and battery, some said. Armed robbery, I'd also heard.

I was familiar with the story of my supposed father long before I ever set eyes on him, but when I did see him, at the grocery store, randomly, I knew who he was right away.

I was in the peanut butter aisle, grabbing a few things off Gram's grocery list. Her housekeeper usually did all of the shopping, but she'd recently come down with a bad case of the flu, so I'd taken over the duty.

I'm not sure why I was so sure right off the bat. The way he was studying me maybe or that combined with the tilt of his eyes, the stubborn line of his jaw. It wasn't his features so much as the way he moved them. There was a strong resemblance, but there also wasn't.

He was a gorgeous man. Just stunning, his face perfectly symmetrical, and it wasn't vanity, but I couldn't help seeing some of myself in him.

And all of my fantasies about some heroic father who would have wanted me had he known . . . flew right out of my head for good.

He seemed as startled to see me as I was him. "Hey, I know you," he drawled.

"No, you don't," I contradicted haughtily.

He sure as hell didn't know me. He'd *never* have the privilege, I swore to myself.

"I do too," he said, unfazed. "You're Scarlett Theroux. I hear all kinds of stuff about you. Quite the little charmer, I hear. Raising hell since you was li'l. Not much diff'rent than your mama."

He smiled. He was beautiful, but I hated his face on sight. "Not much diff'rent than your papa, either."

"Both of my parents are dead," I said, for lack of anything better. They were certainly dead to me.

He laughed. "Oh, you think so? I think you're full o'shit. You know damn well who I am, don't you?"

I glared at him, but I didn't answer.

"I'm your daddy. You knew that, right? You're prolly not too keen to hear that, but it's the truth. I can see the Davis blood in you, too. I hadn't heard about that. Folks only been tellin' me how you're the spittin' image of Renee. And I can see that. But I see me in you, too, no denyin' it.

"But I guess you don't care 'bout that, huh? You done all right for yourself, I hear, livin' up at old lady Durant's fancy mansion." I hated the way he spoke, slow, each word drawn out insinuatingly. Also, he sounded like a hick.

"What do you want?" I asked him. Clearly, if he'd actually wanted to be my dad, he wouldn't have waited for an accidental grocery store run-in to introduce himself.

He grinned, and I hated that it looked strangely familiar to me. "You're in high school, right? That can come in handy for me. You interested in making some money, girl?"

I started to leave without another word.

He stopped me with a grip on my elbow. "Now, now. It's *good* money. You wouldn't have to beg the Durants for charity no more. Don't you want a bit of cash of your own? I'd make sure it was all cake work. I'd just need some things, small packages, delivered to your classmates, yeah?"

"Get your hands off me, you piece of—" I snarled at him.

"Hey, now. It's Daddy to you."

Just when you don't think you can hate yourself any more—and then you find out you come from even worse white trash than you thought—yeah, that's where I was sitting.

His smile turned unpleasant. "Got a little attitude on you. I shouldn't be surprised. You know who else had one? Your mama. Didn't turn out too well for her, I hear."

That stopped me in my tracks. "What is that supposed to mean? Do you know where she is?"

He laughed and it was mocking. "Can't say I do, but I have heard things. Maybe if you were a little nicer to your old pa, I'd tell you some of the things I've heard about your mama."

I tugged my arm free of his hard grip. "What are you suggesting?"

"How about you come up to my house with me? I have a nice little plot of land, and seeing as you're part of the Davis clan, I think it's time you come have a look. When we're there, I'll tell you what I know about where Renee, your mama . . . ended up."

I was not nearly as dumb as he seemed to think. No way in hell was I going anywhere with him. Ever.

I opened my mouth to tell him that when I was interrupted.

"Jethro Davis, how about you leave this nice young lady alone before I find something to arrest you for? I'd guess I wouldn't have to look much farther than your pockets if I wanted to get you for possession, yeah?"

I shuddered. This day was getting worse and worse.

I'd just been saved from my lowlife father by the only person I could possibly want to see even less than him.

Jethro couldn't get away from me fast enough after that.

And then I was left with Detective Harris. He gave me his deceptive smile. "What a coincidence. How'r you holding up? That had to be a shock, what your—Is he still your boyfriend?—did to that homeless guy. I hear he's managed to find a way out of it, though. Congratulations. It's amazing what money can do, especially when you're dealing with a D.A. who's hoping to have a long political career ahead of her."

"It was self-defense," I said, voice and face hard. "Everyone has a right to defend themselves." I said this the same way I'd said it a hundred times before, with stony resolve. I was used to defending what Dante had done. I'd never stop defending it, because I knew he'd done it for me.

He smiled again. "I apologize. I was out of line there. I didn't mean to upset you. I was actually just trying to help you. I saw that creep bothering you and thought I should intervene. Jethro *was* bothering you, wasn't he?"

I nodded, thinking it was ironic that this piece of work saw Jethro as the creep, but I begrudgingly said, "Thank you," because Jethro *had* been bothering me.

"Anytime, Scarlett. You know I'm always here if you need me. *Always.*"

I didn't like the sound of that one bit. I tried to move

past him, but he stepped in my way. "Listen, you may not see it now, but I thought I should warn you: Dante *is* dangerous. Dangerous to others, dangerous to you."

I just stared at him, wondering what his intention was. By his face and voice, he seemed genuinely worried for me, but with him, I didn't trust it.

And his intention really didn't matter. Nothing on earth could make me afraid of Dante. He would die before he'd hurt me. He would die to keep me from being hurt. By anyone. This I knew.

"You think he defended you, I get it. You think it was, what? Manslaughter? Self-defense if you're being completely naive? But it was more, I promise you. He went into the woods looking for a man, and that man ended up dead. What is that, if not intent?"

I started shaking my head. He was wrong. I knew it for a fact. I'd looked into Dante's eyes while he told me what really happened. He'd gone looking for my attacker, intending to bring him to the police, since the police were doing *nothing*, but when he'd found him, the man had pulled a knife and attacked. They'd fought, Dante had tried to take the knife away, but instead, much to his horror, he'd ended up stabbing the man. He'd tried his best to get help, but my attacker had bled out before he could get the proper medical attention.

Dante had told me the story in painstaking detail and with utter sincerity, and I believed him unconditionally, even if I was one of few.

"If he loses his temper again, how can you know it won't be you that ends up on the wrong end of it?"

"He's taking anger management courses," I told Harris, not because I thought Dante really needed them, but because it seemed like something Harris should hear.

"You're not listening, Scarlett, or else you're not hearing me, but I want you to know that if you ever need me, I'm just a phone call away. You can come to me for anything."

His words felt insinuating to me, they always did, but I just nodded and moved past him. At least he wouldn't be bothering me anymore, not more than the random coincidence. My case was closed, thank God.

Harris let me leave, and I went straight to checkout. There was only one lane open, and I had the terrible luck of being directly behind Jethro.

He sent me a greasy smile as he paid for his beer and cigarettes with his EBT card.

Of course this was not allowed, but when you're a small town's biggest drug dealer, things like that tend to just go your way.

I glared at his back when he left. I sincerely hoped I never had to set eyes on him again.

Meeting Jethro had bothered me. It was disheartening and disturbing to realize that even I believed he was my biological dad. Before I'd always just been able to shrug off any relation altogether the rare times that it came up, because the idea had been as abstract as it was distasteful. I didn't want this man to be my dad and so he wasn't.

But not anymore. After that, I carried the weight of belonging to even more white trash heritage than I already claimed. It was a blow to my ego that I hadn't needed, to say the least. Not a day in my life had gone by when I hadn't known and been reminded that I was trash. More proof was just picking at a wound that was already bloody.

One other thing did come out of meeting him, though. A lesson. Or at least, a reminder: I was not a

Durant. Gram had accepted me into her heart, into her home. She fed me, clothed me. She provided me with everything I needed and more, from my phone to my haircuts.

She'd even tried to buy me a car, but I'd drawn the line there.

No, I'm not crazy. I just couldn't do it, couldn't defend taking such an extravagant gift, not without earning it. She had three extra cars. When I needed one, she always generously allowed me to borrow one. It was enough for me.

And as much as I wanted to tell all of the people that looked down on me to go fuck themselves, I did care how it looked, how *I* looked when it came to Gram and her kindness toward me.

If the world thought I was taking advantage of that, then hell, maybe I was, and so I tried my best not to.

So meeting Jethro Davis wasn't all bad. It made me realize that I needed to start earning my keep.

"I love you as certain dark things are to be loved,
in secret, between the shadow and the soul."
~Pablo Neruda

chapter eighteen

PRESENT

Scarlett

Filming was not going how I'd expected. It was a rollercoaster. All ups and downs, nothing in between.

A part of me hated it, and a part of me found it stimulating. At least I wasn't bored.

The acting was the only thing I wasn't conflicted about. I loved it, because *God* I was tired of being me. It felt good to slip into some other shoes.

But the rest was a jumbled mess that consisted of changed scripts, new lines, and repetitive reshoots.

Every scene felt like it had to be redone a dozen times. At least.

I thought that all of this traced back to one thing: the director. He was hard to please and harder to impress.

Stuart Whently was known for making A-list, character driven films that made the film academy swoon, and for being an eccentric, sometimes tyrannical, perfectionist.

When I thought of it that way, things weren't actually going so badly.

Still, it felt like I was somehow failing, and I had begun to miss my friends, who were gone four days or more a week, and hell, even my crappy old airline job, where at least I hadn't felt l was incompetent.

I had quit with relish over a month ago, never dreaming that I'd long to go back to it for even a *second*.

I'd never admit any of it aloud though, and even if I was doing a horrible job, I'd keep trying my best until I either got it right or got canned. It wasn't even a question.

"Is he always like this?" I asked one of the production assistants after Stuart had called an abrupt break and stormed off set. Again.

"Hmm?" she asked.

"What I mean is, is this how a movie production is supposed to go, or is this one just a colossal failure?" I hoped that wasn't the case, but I needed to know if it was.

I always, always preferred the truth.

That had her finally looking at me, pushing her glasses up high on her nose to study my face. "This project is as smooth as they get, to be honest. Usually filming with him is a *nightmare*."

I was shocked, relieved, and somehow annoyed. But at least it wasn't me.

Stuart was back within the hour, which was usually the pattern, and we set up again.

Two takes later, and good ol' Stu was back to ranting.

"It's a journey back from feeling alienated from the world," he said passionately, speaking directly to me.

Well, that I could relate to. The second part of it, at least.

"It is about personal growth, not an explosion of it, but a gradual unfolding, petal by petal, bit by bit. This scene is supposed to make you blossom. He's doing something for you that no one ever has before, showing you kindness, changing your perspective, on people, on men. You two are supposed to like each other!"

And that was the whole problem. I couldn't stand the lead actor. He was a Hollywood asshole of the first order.

I'd been excited when I heard who was chosen for the role.

David Watts had seemed the perfect pick. He was successful, a household name, great-looking, and because he was a hunk and he liked to post shirtless pictures of himself holding kittens on Instagram on a fairly regular basis, he brought his own rabid fan-base to every movie he made.

But how he sounded on paper was far from how he was to work with.

Stuart got right up in my personal space, as he was wont to do, distracting me from my train of annoyed thought, spectacled eyes studying me closely. "But you're not the problem, are you? You are her. You are this character. She is you. *You* are this movie. That is clear to me. So it's you we must begin to work around. What we need for this is chemistry. I'll ask you plain, can you think of any man you have chemistry with that's fit to play this role?"

I was floored, but pretty thrilled. He'd really fire David Watts? Is that what he meant?

I opened my mouth to respond, because hell, I'd find someone, but David interrupted with a grownup hissy fit.

Apparently he wanted this job, too.

David probably wasn't a terrible person. He was just out of touch with reality. And normalcy. Something I figured a lot of famous people suffered from. I'd have bet money from what I'd seen on set that he surrounded himself with people who only told him how awesome he was, that he was the most special snowflake of all of the special snowflakes.

People that never let him know when he was acting like an entitled douchebag.

He wasn't even a bad actor. He had a limited range, as most too good-looking men do, but what he played, he played well. He'd just decided to be a dick to me since the first day we'd met, and he couldn't hide it even when the cameras were rolling.

I was still a little bummed about it. I'd been excited to meet him, more excited when he wanted me to come over to his house to rehearse together.

About two hours and a few drinks later into that first meeting he'd asked me (way too bluntly and without an ounce of charm) if I wanted to fuck, and I'd politely turned him down.

Okay, polite maybe wasn't the word. I'd *tried* to be polite, but I'm sure my version of a polite no had come across more than a touch sarcastic. And likely mocking.

He hadn't taken the rejection well. I honestly didn't think he knew how to deal with it. So he turned it on me. Told everyone I was difficult to work with while taking exception to every word that came out of my mouth.

I ignored it and tried my best not to let it show that

I couldn't stand him when the cameras were rolling. I thought I succeeded.

David didn't even try. I don't know if he thought he could bully me into wanting to sleep with him, or if he was just that unprofessional.

One thing was for sure. Before today no one had dreamed there was a chance he could be fired.

"I don't want to fire you," Stuart told him when David had calmed enough to let someone else get a word in. "I don't *want* to. I just may *need* to. Scarlett is electric. She's magic. Incandescent. She *gives me life.* She's my muse, and she was made for this part, but as soon as I put you together, everything goes flat. *Flat*! I can't have it be flat, David. Tell me how I can keep from firing you."

That little speech, and fear of losing the role, seemed to help. David tried harder. Became more civil with the next take, like a light had been switched on. A big heaping of humble pie had been just what the doctor ordered.

What a spoiled brat.

When we finished another take it was to a spattering of applause and eccentric Stu blowing kisses into the air.

I was almost disappointed. I'd have loved to replace David with Anton or, hell, just about anyone, but if he was going to behave himself, I wouldn't be a butt about it.

We were taking a short break while we waited for setup on the next scene when my phone started ringing.

It was Bastian. I took a deep breath and answered.

"I can't find Dante," he began.

I closed my eyes, rubbing my temple with my free hand. "He's here," I told him.

"What do you mean by here?"

"Somewhere in town. Or at least he was a few days ago."

Bastian cursed. "Damnit, I should have guessed. If you see him again, tell him I need him to call me. He needs to pull it together."

"Do you really think that's a good idea?" I asked pointedly. If Dante knew I was talking to his brother, no matter the reason, I had no doubts it would send him into a jealous rage.

"I see your point," Bastian admittedly wryly. "Well, if you see him, will you figure out what he's doing there, where he's staying, and then let me know?"

"If I see him, yes, I will."

I stared at my phone long after the call had ended.

Would I see Dante again? Did I want to?

I was able to answer the first question much sooner than I'd imagined, as the next time I went to my trailer for a break, I found Dante sprawled out on my sofa. Again.

And he was stinking drunk. Again.

I didn't think it was the alcohol racing through his system, though, that made it so he couldn't meet my eyes.

He'd come here to see me, and he couldn't even look at me.

I'm not sure how that would have made me feel a few months ago, or even weeks, but with what I now knew, it made me feel wretched.

And angry. Confused and conflicted. Wounded and lost.

But also, it touched me deeply.

How long had he been living this double life, stuck in purgatory, trapped in a vicious web of lies, completely alone?

Protecting me from everything.

I, frankly, didn't even *want* to know. It is much easier to hate someone who you're certain has wronged you than it is to hate yourself.

And I was very afraid that if I knew just how far back his lies went, my self-hatred would know no bounds.

"Dante," I said, my voice so soft that it forced him to look at me, his entire drunken face registering a sort of endearing surprise, like he'd forgotten where he even was.

"You look like hell." That being said, he made hell look good. His hair was messy, more scruff on his jaw than usual. I was still wearing the evidence of that scruff on my thighs from his last visit, and no, that wasn't a complaint.

No suit for him today, instead he was wearing gray sweats and a zip-up hoodie that was open wide enough at the neck to expose his defined collarbone and the top of his muscular chest. And the *cursed* chain that he never took off. Also, there was enough bared skin that I suspected he wasn't wearing a shirt under. If he weren't drunk, I'd have assumed he just came from a workout. He was dressed for it, down to his running shoes.

"How do you keep getting past security?" I was mostly curious about it. I'd had to jump through hoops to get on set the first few times, they were so strict. How did he get so lucky?

"They think I'm your boyfriend."

"Why would they think that?" I asked him, but I knew the answer.

"Because I told them so. And I bribed them."

At least he was honest. For once.

"What are you doing here?" I asked him point blank.

His shaking hand pushed his hair impatiently back from his face. "I'm here for the same reason I always come back to you. I've come for scraps. Anything you'll give me. I've come because I *can't stay away.*" His voice was low and hoarse from the drink, but thick and dark with emotion. "I tried to. Don't you know that I'm always trying to stay away? It doesn't matter. It never works.

There was a time in the not so distant past that his words would have set me off, thrown me into a temper that would have left us both bloody.

But something had changed. Something that terrified and excited me both.

Something that utterly destroyed me.

Something that made me whole again.

I did not know how far all of his betrayals ran, how deep or shallow his lies, but I was starting to realize that in one respect, at least, it didn't matter.

Some part of my pathetic heart was going soft for him again.

"'Love' is the name for our pursuit of wholeness, for our desire to be complete."
~Plato

chapter nineteen

Without another word I went to make us both a cup of coffee. My hands were shaking badly, but either he didn't notice, or he was polite enough not to comment on it.

"Are you in town long?" I asked him as I offered him his cup.

He took it with a soft thank you, dragging a hand through his hair, eyes downcast. "I don't know. I don't know what the hell I'm doing anymore, Scarlett. That is a fact."

I stood over him, studying him. I'd forgotten how thick his eyelashes were, double-rowed and darker than his hair. I'd forgotten how well defined his lush top lip was, how broad his shoulders were, so muscular they flexed even when he made a movement as small as taking a drink of his coffee.

I'd forgotten that when he showed me the tiniest

glimmer of vulnerability, it made me go weak as a babe.

I'd *forced* myself forget so many things about him, and I wondered, hardly daring to even *hope*, if it could be different now.

Was there some chance that I could turn my bitter memories sweet again? Not all of them. *Of course not.* But perhaps some?

I still didn't know.

Everything had changed, but the future was more uncertain than ever.

I stroked a hand oh so softly over his hair, and his entire big body tensed as though bracing for a blow.

He had good instincts. "I know, Dante." My voice was quiet, but the tremulous intensity of it reverberated through the room. "I *know.*"

"I don't have the faintest notion what you're talking about." Slowly and carefully, he set his coffee down on the side table to his right.

"You're such a liar," I told him almost playfully, because *for once* I had the upper hand.

Finally, that had him looking up at me, meeting my eyes without flinching.

"Who have you been talking to?" The question came out careful, his tone measured. Deceptively harmless.

I wasn't fooled. His face was bland, still, except for his eyes. They were telling me a different story.

A story of rage and violence. Of his temper boiling, unchecked, just under the surface.

If I gave him a name, told him who had clued me in . . .

Heads would roll.

"That's the least relevant thing you could ask," I finally answered, an evasion, but one I knew would be effective.

"I don't agree. Who?" The bland veneer was slipping from his voice.

"I'll answer one of your questions, but not that one." My voice was almost teasing.

He licked his lips and it was an effort not to bend down and kiss him. "What do you mean?"

I was in dangerous territory now. My urge to heal him was becoming as strong as my need to harm him.

"The answer is yes," I uttered softly. It hurt my tattered heart to get the words out, but I could not seem to keep them in.

Confusion drew his brows together, his brilliant eyes studying my face. "Yes to what?"

"Yes. I do love you as much as I hate you."

Something happened to his face; it fell and lifted as a shudder wracked through him. "Jesus," he whispered, again and again as he grabbed me, burying his face in my stomach, his big arms wrapping around me.

My voice was grating, as brittle as breaking glass, as I added, "It is a near draw, the love and the hate, but it could tip either way. I'm *done* with the lies, Dante. I have some questions, and you are *going to answer them.*"

He didn't let go of me, didn't flee this time.

Progress.

"What do you know?" he asked carefully, voice muffled against my belly. His face was still pressed tightly to me.

I touched his head lightly with my fingertips.

My nails scraped roughly against his scalp as I gripped two good fistfuls of his hair, angling his head back, face up, forcing him to look up at my face.

He let me, blinking slowly up at me.

I bent down and pressed my mouth to his.

He'd been drinking beer, I could tell. The taste of it

was drugging on his breath, turned impossibly sweet. It brought back memories, good ones and bad, as all things did with Dante.

I lingered at the kiss. I was running short on time but I didn't hold back.

When I finally tore my mouth from his, we were both panting hard, but I found the breath to say, "You will come clean about this or you will *stay out of my life.*"

He didn't say anything, and I thrusted myself away from him, moving a safe distance out of his reach. "I assume you're staying somewhere in town?"

He just nodded, looking a little dazed.

"I have to get back on set, but we're not finished here. Why don't you text me the address where you're staying? I'll come see you when I'm done working for the day."

"I'll wait here until you're finished. We can drive together."

I chewed on my lip as I thought it out. "Fine. As long as you've sobered up enough by then to drive."

He grabbed his discarded cup of coffee, toasting it at me. "Got it."

Stuart felt we were on a roll that day, and so we ended up shooting hours longer than I'd even anticipated.

We'd worked so deep into the night that P.M. had passed into A.M. hours prior.

I figured Dante would have given up, would have left by the time I made it back to my trailer.

I figured wrong. He was there and awake. And hell, he was even sober.

Our eyes clashed for a few intense beats before I moved to the small bedroom in back, changing into street clothes.

"We talking here or at your place?" I asked him as I

came back out, grabbing my things. "Or my place?" I added.

"Mine," he answered instantly, rising from the sofa.

"What have you been doing in here for all this time? Meditating?"

He gave me a small smile for that. "I kept busy. Sobered up. Went for a run, made some phone calls."

I hadn't expected a semi-straight answer. Usually he matched sarcasm with sarcasm. "Who were you calling?" I didn't really think he'd answer if it was anything besides business, but it never hurt to ask.

"I was trying to figure out who's been talking to you."

I rubbed my hands together, a nervous tell. I made myself stop. "And did you?"

"No. I couldn't get anything concrete, so I've put some people on it. Unless, of course, you'd like to change your mind and tell me?"

I shook my head dismissively. "Not likely. And it doesn't matter. Truly. You should be more worried about what I know than who told it to me."

His mouth twisted bitterly. "Touché."

That shut us both up for a while. I left my car in the lot, going with him.

"How long is the drive?" I asked him.

"Not far," was all he said.

I didn't press the issue. I'd find out soon enough.

And I did. Sooner than I thought. As though he'd found a place just to be close to the set, it was a scant ten-minute drive from the lot to his lodgings.

"You're staying at a *house*?" I asked him as he parked. It was nice, not too huge, but heavily gated. It didn't seem like the type of place you could stay for just a few nights.

"Temporarily."

"If it's so temporary, why not just stay at a hotel?"

"I needed more privacy. I require gates. And tinted windows."

I digested that, and thought, just maybe, that I understood it.

He parked his car in the U-shaped drive, stopping just shy of the front door.

"You have the place all to yourself?" I asked, looking around.

"We do, yes. Do you like it?"

I shot him a look for that. "It doesn't matter if I like it. I just came here to talk. And then leave."

He firmed his jaw and nodded, looking away.

He let us into the house silently, waving me in.

I took a few steps into the entryway and stopped. The place was bigger than I'd thought from the outside. It was also fully furnished. Well-decorated, too, with lots of grays and whites. It felt more like a private residence than a short rental.

"Do you mind if I shower before we talk?"

I shrugged. "Whatever."

"Make yourself at home. The kitchen is stocked, if you're hungry."

I realized that I was. "Just point me in the right direction."

He showed me to the kitchen and left.

I had just dished out omelet number two when he joined me again.

I sent him one glance, then looked away again. He was in a fresh pair of sweatpants, these ones black, his muscular chest deliciously bare. His hair was still wet.

I wanted to lick him, head to toe. Twice. Slowly.

Instead, I asked, "You run out of shirts?"

"Yes. Feel free to take yours off, too, to make it less awkward."

I curved my lips down to keep them from curling up, which they'd naturally tried to do.

He wasn't allowed to charm me right now. The bastard.

I handed him his plate. I could have waited to ask if he was hungry, but I hadn't seen the point. From what I recalled, he never turned down food. Like ever.

"Thank you," he said.

We sat down at a round table in the breakfast nook. It was a friendly spot, surrounded by windows. If we were there when the sun rose in a few hours, we'd likely have a killer view.

I ate my omelet without a word, not looking at him. I had been collecting my thoughts for a while now, and I had too many questions.

I didn't even know where to start. And I was hesitant to. If he started lying or evading, or so help me God, *manipulating* me again, this thing would be dead in the water.

He finished his meal before I did, rising to take his plate to the sink then came back to sit across from me.

I felt him staring at me while I ate, but I didn't look up.

I finished about half of my omelet before I pushed my plate toward him. I'd prepared us both the same portion size, just kind of assuming he'd finish what I didn't.

Because he had a thousand times before. Jesus, even eating together was like walking through a field of landmines.

Put us together to do anything, and there was a memory behind it. A dozen. A hundred.

We had words with whole lives attached to them.

That was the burden of falling in love so young. Of letting yourself go so deep into another person. You owned too much of each other to ever really walk away.

And we had proven as much. Time and again.

I waited until he finished the second plate and rose to take it to the sink.

I got up and followed him. "Your mother's been blackmailing you." It wasn't a question.

I watched his back as I said the words, witnessed how he braced himself and shuddered like his whole world was crashing down around him.

Because it was.

He turned to look at me, and I read too much in the agony of his eyes. Knew too much from what they held. So many of my questions were answered from just that look, if I was honest with myself.

But denial is a powerful thing, and I wouldn't have minded clinging to it for just a little bit longer.

"Yes. *Yes.*" He said it with a sort of reverent lightness, as though some great weight had been lifted from him.

Because years of burdensome secrets had just been taken off his shoulders.

Jesus, *I was a fool.*

"Of course she has," he continued succinctly. *"Of course she has."*

"I know of only one duty, and that is to love."
~Albert Camus

chapter twenty

PRESENT

Dante

I was shocked at myself, at my reaction to her words.

I'd been avoiding this for so long, had gone through so much pain, suffered *so much* just to keep this from happening.

I'd never imagined in my wildest dreams that my knee-jerk reaction to having it all come crashing down on me would be a torrential downpour of *relief.* I was weak with it.

But also, *of course*, it was my worst nightmare. The very thing I had always dreaded.

Because what she would do now that she knew terrified me.

"This place doesn't feel like a temporary rental to me, Dante," she said, her voice somehow *normal.*

Oh, now she was changing the subject? It was infuriating, but I answered her anyway.

"I am considering making it a more permanent residence . . . My mother can't know about it, you understand." As I spoke, I turned fully to look at her.

She grinned, tilting her head to study me. An expression fell across her face, one I knew she didn't intend, of almost curious affection.

That look on her face was like a punch to the gut. So many feelings rushed at me when she studied me like that, like years had disappeared and we were back to some petty arguing that meant nothing in the long-term to us, some form of the old bickering that we used to enjoy when we still had complete faith that our bond to each other was unassailable.

This wasn't that, of course I knew that, but it was painfully pleasurable to pretend that it could be like that, even for only an evening.

"You plan to stay in L.A. . . . close to me . . . as long as your mother doesn't know about it." She tapped her chin as she spoke, looking thoughtful.

I made my face stay bland and neutral and just kept meeting her eyes, but it was no use.

She was onto me, and I couldn't have said if I was more acutely relieved, or utterly horrified by that.

"You don't know how much I know," she accused correctly. "You have no idea how to handle me because, *for once,* you're more in the dark than I am. How does it feel, lover?"

"Wretched." I gave her that one bitterly honest piece, because *God,* she deserved it. "As wretched as you could hope. Care to clue me in?"

"Of course not. You can guess, and worry, and stress

your deceitful black heart out. And while you're doing that, you can make me a drink. I assume you have a bottle of superior scotch around here somewhere."

I decided to take the order seriously, leading her from the kitchen to an adjoining sitting room. As she'd correctly guessed, I did have a fully stocked bar.

I fixed us both a drink. I didn't have to ask her what she wanted or how she wanted it. It was all too familiar to me.

"What are you planning to do?" I asked her, handing her a glass of scotch, straight up. "Are you going to confront anyone?"

She laughed, a sound of pure delight that reverberated through me, making my heart pound, reminding me that it was still a slave to her whims, damn her. "Who would I confront? And about what? What do I know, do you suppose? If I say I know everything, will you slip and tell me even more?"

I took strong exception to how much she was enjoying this. "This isn't a game."

Her smile died a short death, leaving behind the quiet rage that had never really left. "You think I don't know that?" Her voice was so full of icy bitterness that I could taste it in my own mouth. She could flay me alive with that tone, strip the skin from my bones. "You think this was ever *fun* for me? Being lied to? Being *manipulated*? But I won't be answering your questions anymore. You'll be answering mine."

I didn't argue with her. Instead, I toasted the air and finished my drink.

I think I'd have agreed to anything just then if it kept her from leaving.

If it meant she would keep coming back.

I'd reached my threshold on living without her. As dangerous as it was, as much as it made my chest cold with fear, I was done staying away from her.

And, *God help me,* I didn't have the will to live with the lies anymore.

"So if I agree to answer your questions," I began, sometime later, charging bravely through the pregnant silence, determined to negotiate with her.

Compromising had always, ironically, been one of our strengths.

Ironic because two more prideful, stubborn souls had never walked the earth.

I think, and had always assumed, that it only worked because we were so devoted to each other.

We'd grown up as godless, savage creatures, believing in nothing so much as each other, and somehow it had always been enough. When you can't imagine living without a person, of course you'll do what's necessary, concede when you have to, to keep the peace.

"You'll stay with me," I forged ahead. "We'll be together."

She didn't answer for a long time, instead just looking at me, her eyes hard and unyielding.

I studied her back, taking in her dear face like I could never have enough.

Because I never could.

I was always obsessed with her. It was one of the defining, consistent characteristics of my life. Obsessed not just with her perfections, but also with her flaws. Her stubborn pride even held a special place in my heart. It had ruined me as a person in so many ways, but God did it get to me. She took it to a level where, even when it was to your detriment, you almost had to admire it.

But I had reached my limit. She would be compromising today.

We had lapsed into a staring contest, one I was determined to win.

I would have this from her.

And so I did. She broke first, her hard eyes wavering, lids trembling for a heart-turning moment before they watered and she looked away.

"We've been at war for so long. How do we just let that go?" Her voice was tremulous from her loss. It wasn't easy for her to concede defeat. It never had been.

"We've been at war alright, but you just didn't see that we weren't supposed to be fighting each other. It was *wrong*, but it's over now. I'm not asking for everything at once. I understand the damage that's been done here *more than anyone*. I'm just asking you to try. Give me your time, every spare moment of it, and I'll give you some answers.

I had her. I saw it. In her clenched fists and quivering lips, I saw it.

I moved a step closer.

She braced but didn't move away.

I took another step. She closed her eyes as my fingers traced over her brow. Feather light, I stroked her temples, sliding my hands back to cup her head.

I gripped her hair with both hands and touched our foreheads together. "You'll stay with me," I repeated. "We'll be together."

I needed this to be very clear; a verbal confirmation. There could be no miscommunications. We'd had enough of those.

"And you'll tell me the truth?" she said in a vulnerable

voice that gutted me far quicker than a razor sharp one could have.

"Yes. Yes. I'll answer your questions. Your turn."

"I can't just let these things go. I can't just forgive. Not you, not me."

"I'm not asking you to," I explained. My tone was calm and reasonable, my heart pounding like a stampede. "I'm not that greedy or that delusional. I asked you to be with me. The rest can come later."

Her voice was barely audible in the quiet room, but piercing all the same. "Yes. I'll be with you." She sounded uncertain and dismayed, but I'd take it.

My eyes shut tight in acute relief, and I held her like that for a time, our foreheads touching, my fingers gently rubbing her scalp.

I felt I could have stayed that way indefinitely, I was so grateful for the connection.

But then she touched me, her hands reaching up, stroking lightly from my wrists down to my elbows and back again.

And that was it. Sweetness turned base.

Blood rushed through my body, my stomach clenching as lust kicked in, too overwhelming to deny.

It was an effort not to drag her down to the floor, or hell, push her to her knees.

I straightened instead, pulling away from her, and she opened her eyes. They flitted from my face down to my bare chest. I dragged a hand through my hair and watched the way every movement of my body caught her attention.

She licked her lips, and I twitched so hard that her gaze caught the movement darting farther down. She sucked in a deep breath that made her breasts shift, which caught my gaze. Her nipples were hard under her tight white cotton shirt. Without even willing it, my hand moved to her, thumb tracing over one of the hard little nubs.

She sent me one long, sultry look, and lowered to her knees.

"Jesus," I said. I steepled my hands at the crown of my head, eyes glued to her as she shrugged off her shirt, unclasped her bra, and slid it smoothly off.

She rubbed her face against me like a cat, using her nose to play with me through the sweats. It was adorable and one of the most arousing things I'd ever witnessed.

My stomach clenched as she opened my sweatpants, dragging them down, freeing my heavy length to bob against her lush pink lips.

Jesus.

She'd just sucked my tip into her mouth when I snapped out of my trance.

I tried twice before I found my voice. "Wait. Stop."

Me turning down head from Scarlett.

That had to be a first.

But I needed something else just then, and the urge was so realized, so *complete* that I never even considered denying it. When I spoke, my voice was hoarse with all the words I couldn't find for a need so powerful it left me shaken. "I need to be inside of you."

She laid her cheek against me, rolling her eyes up to look at mine.

"Let's go to the bedroom," I said thickly.

She didn't agree or disagree, so I pulled her up, lifting her under the arms and propping her on her feet. I couldn't keep my hands to myself. I palmed her breasts and watched her jaw go slack.

Fuck. I let her go, taking a step away as I pushed my stiff length back into my pants. "Bedroom. I want you in the bedroom."

I turned, heading down the hallway, through the entryway, and up the double staircase. I headed for the east wing of the house, aware every step that a topless Scarlett followed.

"This place is bigger than I thought," she observed, her tone neutral.

"Do you like it?" I hoped so. I'd purchased it with her personal preferences in mind. Because it was for her.

"Sure."

At least it wasn't a no.

My mouth twisted wryly as I showed her our bedroom. The house was for her. The bedroom for me.

"Subtle," she said wryly. The ceiling over the bed and every wall that wasn't a window was mirrored.

What can I say? I like to watch.

"It's the first time we've had a house to ourselves. I might have gone a little overboard." Proving my own point, my eyes were on her in the mirror as I spoke.

She met my gaze, hers enigmatic. "You planned this all along."

I shrugged. It was too complicated to explain, the efforts I had gone to based on the most meager thread of hope. And I was not in the mood to talk.

We were of a like mind, apparently, because she started peeling off her jeans without another word.

I shoved out of my sweats, my eyes glued to her, raking over her, devouring every inch of skin she bared.

When she was bare, I was on her, pushing her to the bed, straddling her, pressing my chest to hers, our warm flesh rubbing together, creating more friction than I needed to ignite.

I cupped her face in both hands and kissed her, shifting on top of her, wedging myself between her legs. I pulled back to watch her face as I breached her, near mindless with need.

Abruptly and unexpectedly, she began to struggle, pushing me off her. I moved back with a jerk, too stunned to protest.

"Not like that," she said, flushing. She sat up, not looking me in the eye. "Not face to face. Not right now."

It stung, but I told myself it was fine. She had given me so much in such a short time. It was a miracle that she was even here.

Clearly, more time was needed for certain intimacies. But if I worked on her long enough, she wouldn't hold back. It was inevitable. Left to our own devices, we would give each other everything, because that was the order of the universe.

I truly believed that.

I brushed off the sting and accommodated her. I was too far gone to split hairs, my mind in a dark and primitive place that didn't particularly care about anything except getting balls deep inside of her and rutting like an animal.

She showed me just what she wanted by moving to a large chaise lounge that dominated the corner of the room closest to the shoe closet I hadn't yet shown her. She climbed onto the cream-colored piece of furniture, getting on hands and knees, positioned right on the edge.

I didn't need to be told twice. I was covering her back, arms reaching around to palm her breasts, my tip butting up against her entrance between one thumping heartbeat and the next.

I shut my eyes with that first drugging thrust. She was wet, pliant, so I didn't hold back, jamming in to the hilt without preamble. The noise that escaped me right as her wet heat covered the base of my shaft was more animal than human. I was not a thinking being in that moment.

I was mindless. Her *slave*.

I watched us in the mirrors, watched myself going in and out of her, watched my cock squeezing in and dragging out slowly, then faster, frenzied. As soon as she began to get loud, close to her release, I slowed the rhythm again.

She was braced on all fours, her back arched, but her head was turned with mine, watching our bodies, never meeting my eyes no matter how long I stared at hers, trying to catch her gaze.

Again, it stung, but it was a battle for another day.

I watched her face while my body pumped into hers, watched her watching where we joined, and that did it. I'd wanted to last longer, wanted to savor more, but it was hopeless. I should have been amazed with myself for lasting as long as I had. The first touch of her nose nuzzling my shaft back in the living room had nearly had me coming in my pants.

I kissed her nape while I emptied inside of her, savoring with complete pleasure that moment of total abandon where I lost myself in her, my mind blown to bits.

I was still coming, spurting after-effects deep in her womb, when I lifted my head to watch her slack-jawed release, caught the way her eyes glazed over as the skin-tingling rush of her orgasm overtook her.

It was breathtaking. A heaven worth going through hell for. I'd never thought otherwise.

And the best part of all. I got to have her again. And again.

And I did. I was greedy with it. Insatiable. Voracious.

She brought me to life. I had her as many times as I could before she cried uncle.

There was never an end to this need she created inside of me. This endless chasm of want in my blood for her. Never had been. Never would be.

"I wanted the whole world or nothing."
~Charles Bukowski

chapter twenty-one

PAST

Scarlett

Gram was not happy about my decision to get a job.

Dante less so. He was irate, predictably belligerent about it. He threw such a fit initially that Gram ordered him to go for a run.

When we were alone, she tried several different tactics to get me to change my mind. She was a formidable woman, not used to hearing no. And when she did hear the word, she didn't even consider accepting it. It was nothing but a challenge to her.

It was the closest we'd come to really butting heads. That alone almost made me cave.

"Darling," she said with her most charming smile. "We only just got you here. I was looking forward to your company."

It was the principle of the thing. I would not, could not, end up like my parents, like my grandmother.

"I've made up my mind," I told her stubbornly. "It's not a big deal. Just a few hours on school nights, a few more on weekends. Now that I've quit drama, I have plenty of free time."

She tried a different tactic. I knew she would. "I wouldn't get your hopes up. It's the wrong season for part-time jobs. I guarantee no one is hiring."

I swallowed hard. "I already have one. The manager of the 5 and Diner hired me on the spot. I start on Monday."

Her eyes narrowed on me. "It's quite unnecessary. Why on earth would you need a job? Any need you have, I'm happy to provide for. Just tell me what it is you're earning money for. I'll buy it for you, darling!"

I gave her brutal honesty. Not because I wanted to and not because I wasn't grateful. It was a matter of self-worth. If I was ever going to get some, I knew I had to earn it. "I can't be a Durant charity case, not more than I can help. At least if I get a job I'm *trying* to take care of myself."

She gave me the coldest look I'd ever seen her aim my way. It made me shiver and instantly want to take back whatever I'd said that put that look on her face.

She was a force of nature like that. What she felt, you felt. If she was happy, the world knew joy. When she was angry . . . yeah, you felt that too.

And when she was disappointed in you, you felt like absolute shit.

"I'm sorry that you thought this was charity," she said with haughty chill. "You thought I felt some sense of duty toward you? And here I thought I was doing it out of love. Silly me." Her tone was scathing. A vacuum of disdain, it sucked all warmth from the room. Took my stubborn pride and left me feeling ashamed and alone.

I was out of my league. A trashcan girl could not hope to go head to head against a queen.

I shook it off, shed the feeling. I would not back down on this, not even against Gram. "I-I-I-I'm s-s-s-s-sorry it c-c-c-came out that that way. I'm not u-u-u-ungrateful. B-b-b-but I'm k-k-k-keeping the j-job."

The stutter did her in. Her hard expression went soft, and she let out a soft, "Oh, my darling girl. Oh, I'm sorry. I lost my temper. You see now where Dante gets it. I won't stop you from having this job, if you really think it will make you happier. I just worry about you."

I wasn't sure if I was relieved or completely humiliated that I'd won because of pity.

But I took it all the same.

Gram was one obstacle, Dante another.

Over the years, we'd learned to pick our battles with each other. What that meant was basically whoever cared more won, whoever cared less compromised.

I just assumed I'd be winning this one. I didn't count on him freaking out, his hellish temper coming out to play.

"No," he said to me first thing as he came back from his run. He was sweaty and agitated. He looked good enough to eat.

But it was the wrong approach.

"I already have the job. I was hired to wait tables. You're just going to have to get used the idea."

"No. I'm putting my foot down about this one."

A fight it was. "Excuse me?"

"You heard me."

Hello, temper. It's me, Scarlett. What are we going to do about this bossy son of a bitch?

Likely nothing productive. Still, we'd try.

"What the hell is your problem? And when did you get the idea you could tell me what to do?"

"Why the hell do you want a job? If you need something, just tell Gram."

I rolled my eyes, making sure he saw it. "Spoken like a true trust fund baby. I need to start making my own money."

"Why?"

"Why do you care?"

He was right in my face, leaning down to me.

I met him glare for glare.

"Why do you always have to push it? I don't *sleep at night*, worrying about you since the attack. And now you want to go off on your own, for hours a day, and for what?"

That softened me a bit. "He's dead, Dante. He can't bother me or anyone else ever again."

"And what about that fucking cop? If he gets wind of you working as a waitress, he'll bother you every day."

I swallowed the lump in my throat. Now there he had a point. "I'm sorry you're worried, but I'm not quitting. I can't live my life in fear of what ifs, and I can't be a Durant charity case for the rest of it either. I need to be more independent."

"*What*? What the hell is that supposed mean?"

"It means I'm a loser. I don't do anything. I don't contribute. I'm living here, in a mansion, and I've done nothing to earn it."

"That's bullshit. You're a high school student. That's your job right now."

That was laughable. I was a C student on a good day, when I was actually trying.

Most days I didn't even try. My mind tended to wander as soon as a teacher started talking.

"I don't deserve any of this, Dante. I don't deserve to be here."

"Deserve? What does that even mean? And if you don't deserve to be here, I don't either."

It was so outrageous I almost felt slighted by it. Insulted. "*Please.* Look at you, with your perfect GPA, your scholarships, your college applications, your SAT scores, your popularity, your football, your perfect *everything*. You belong here, in a house like this, in a life like this. The only thing about you that doesn't fit in here is that, for some reason, you want to be with *me*."

That got to him. I'd been bringing up a sore spot of mine, but I saw I'd rubbed us both wrong. His voice when he spoke was derisive. Offended. "*None* of that's for me. You think I enjoy any of it? And do you think I have a choice? Those things are the bare *minimum* that's expected of me, the Durant heir, and even that is not enough. And you're not a fucking Durant charity case. You might as well be a Durant. You will be someday, because you're never leaving me. Not happening."

That did something to me, played havoc with my heartstrings, made me become more agitated and go soft. It was nothing so much as a hostile, backhanded proposal of marriage, but sucker that I was, it still made me melt.

I was flushing as I tried to get back on topic. "I'm keeping the job."

His lips curled. He looked like he wanted to punch a wall. "Fine," he bit out. "But I'll drive you to and from."

I didn't argue the logistics of it with him. I'd won. It was enough. I didn't need to rub it in his face.

All that fussing aside, talking about having a job and the reality of it were two different things. After four days waiting tables, I wanted to quit. Pure stubbornness was all that kept me from it.

People were rude, men were gross, and the manager was a lech.

It was an old-fashioned diner with a pretty simple menu, but it seemed like I did nothing but screw orders up for at least the first week.

And worse, much worse than any of that, five days into the job Harris found me.

He didn't do anything I could take real exception to at first. He just occupied a booth in the corner, ordered cup after cup of coffee, pretended to work on a laptop, and watched me.

For hours.

I tried my best to serve and then ignore him, but the barest amount of small talk was required for the job, even for him.

"Do you bring your work here often?" I asked him begrudgingly the first day he did this.

He smiled warmly. "Every day."

Oh joy.

I asked my manager, Brett, about that at the end of the shift. He was an overweight, middle-aged man that I was 100% sure had hired me because he thought I was attractive and he liked having eye candy around.

As always when he spoke to me, he addressed my breasts instead of my face. "I think he's been in once or twice. Be nice to him. Don't charge him for coffee. Police discount."

I tried not to roll my eyes, and complied.

"Do you ever eat?" I asked Harris on his third day of stalking me out in the open.

He sat back in his seat, biting his lip. Something new had entered his eyes. Something I did not like. "That an invitation? You want to grab a bite to eat with me after your shift?"

I blushed, *blushed* like an innocent fool. I could tell he got off on it, and I wanted to kick myself. "I have a boyfriend," I muttered and hurried away.

He never did more than watch me. He never had the opportunity. Dante was true to his word, he dropped me off and picked me up every single shift. I was more thankful for it than I'd been anticipating.

After the first day of Harris eye-fucking me for three hours, he was there when Dante showed up to get me. The two men had a volatile stare down but that was it. Harris made sure to leave before Dante showed up again. He was oily slick.

It put me in a bad position. Harris wasn't doing anything, so there were no actions I could take to stop him.

I told myself that I was bothered by him because I allowed myself to be bothered.

I wanted to tell Dante about him, but how could I? It would prove his point, and besides and above that, there was not a damn thing he could do about it.

There were a few times Harris stepped over the line, but even then it was a tenuous thing, and in a game of his word against mine, mine meant shit to anyone that could've done something about it.

I was a few weeks into this. I was at that point where I hated it, but I wasn't done fighting for it; my cursed stubbornness at its most counterproductive.

Harris was doing his usual routine, inhaling bad coffee and unabashedly watching me.

It was a particularly dead day, and the slowest part at that. There was a half hour window between the after school rush and the late dinner crowd where we rarely had more than three customers sitting at a time. On this day there was only one.

My stalker cop. I was refreshing his coffee when he said, voice low and dirty, "You sucked your boyfriend's dick today, didn't you? I can tell. Your lips are swollen. Was it this morning? You're living with him, right? Did you wake him up with your mouth around his cock?"

I'd frozen at the first sentence. Literally. I'd been pouring his coffee and I just kept pouring, overfilling the cup until it ran in a slow dribble onto the table.

I was mortified, face flushing in embarrassment and building temper. And he wasn't finished.

"Or was it in the car on the way over? Did he pull over to the side of the road and give you a throat-full right before he dropped you off for your shift?"

That made me blush harder, because it wasn't far off from the truth.

Had he been following us, or was it really that obvious?

"You're disgusting," I told him with heartfelt venom.

"Careful. Remember that you don't want to rile me."

I stormed away and refused to serve him for the rest of the shift. I just let him sit there, glaring at me.

Later, when I'd collected my composure and calmed my rage enough to talk about it, I told on him to my manager.

It fell on deaf ears. Or rather, ears that could not have cared less.

"Don't piss him off. The last thing I want is trouble from the police," was all he said.

Two strikes, I told myself. One more and I was quitting.

"Being deeply loved by someone gives you strength, while loving someone deeply gives you courage."
~Lao Tzu

chapter twenty-two

PRESENT

Dante

Scarlett woke up moody and cross after about four hours of sleep. She had to be on set again. I'd selfishly deprived her of sleep and she let me know it.

When I tried to shower with her, she locked me out of the bathroom.

I was repentant . . . to a point. I was sorry she was exhausted, but I also knew it'd been unavoidable. She was lucky to have gotten any sleep at all.

I was driving her to the studio before she spoke the thing on both of our minds.

"What does Adelaide have on you? Tell me."

I tried not to let my face so much as twitch. "You want to do this now? On your way into a long day of work?"

She didn't answer, which was answer enough. This role was important to her. Even at her most self-sabotaging, she wasn't going to screw it up. And aside from the previous night's unavoidable, sleep-depriving gluttony, I wouldn't be screwing it up for her, either.

"Tonight," she stated stonily, a faint but unmistakable hint of a threat in her voice.

And I knew what the threat was. Of course I did. I needed to talk, or poof, she was gone.

"Tonight," I agreed. "Are your roommates still on a trip?"

"Yes. They come back late tomorrow."

This next part I didn't like. It went against the grain of every instinct I had. But I'd rarely balked at doing what needed to be done. "When they're home, you sleep at your apartment." My tone was careful. I was going for neutral, but it came out more than a touch pained.

I felt her staring at me. Her eyes were burning a hole into the side of my face.

I kept my gaze resolutely on the road.

"Okay," she said simply.

She wasn't even going to ask? I hated that. Hated that she might not really care, that somehow she could go even one more night without me and not need a reason *why*.

I'd spent many, many nights without her, but I'd always, *always*, had my reasons and known them too well.

But if she was going to let it drop, I had to let her. I had so many blows to deliver. I needed to pull punches whenever, wherever, *however* I could.

Maybe if I could space out the damage it would do less lasting harm to her.

One could hope. I was less a man for wishing and

more a creature of action, but I'd take anything I could get.

The drop-off didn't go well. She tried to dart out of the car without a goodbye, but I stayed her with a firm grip on her wrist.

"A kiss," I told her solemnly. We would get back on track. We had to. I'd been through hell and back, had lost faith in everything except for this, her and me, simply because I had *refused,* despite every awful thing working against us, to let it go.

Sometimes faith is a choice.

We *would* get back on track.

She was as far from me as she could get in the restrictive confines of the vehicle.

It was a small car though, a Jaguar F-Type, so we were still pretty damned close.

"Scarlett, just a kiss. I'll behave myself, I promise."

She watched me warily. "I can't, Dante. I don't have any time. I need to keep my game face on here. This role is important to me.

I knew, absolutely knew, that she was just making excuses. It hurt, but I'd been hurt worse.

I told myself that it wouldn't always be this way.

"Just a kiss on the cheek, then, and then we'll say goodbye," I cajoled.

She was worrying at her lip, looking at me like I might bite (because she knew me), but she slowly nodded and leaned a bit closer.

I met her more than halfway, placing a chaste, loving kiss on her cheek, then her forehead, then her other cheek.

Her breath was coming out in little pants, her eyes closed, lips parted.

So much for chaste.

I rubbed our lips together, tongue darting to lick hers tentatively, and then deeper, stroking into her mouth, my hands going to cup her face.

She moaned, deep in her chest, a sound of abject need, and started sucking on my tongue.

I pulled back with a gasp.

Her face was stunned for a moment but it quickly turned into a glare.

I almost smiled. "See you tonight."

"Bastard."

She got home late, and I was waiting up for her. Even if I could have put it off another day, I wasn't sure I wanted to, at this point. I was ready to come clean, to get it all out in the open, at last.

God, it was a long time coming.

Scarlett didn't draw it out. We'd barely cleared the bedroom door when she said, "What does she have on you? Tell me."

I stopped mid-stride, turning to her. She'd gone by her apartment before she'd come over and packed an overnight bag. I'd carried it upstairs for her and still had it clutched in my right hand.

I dropped it on the floor, just staring at her for a minute. Where to even begin?

I felt my head shake. A slow, precise movement. A little to the right, a little to the left.

It was enough. So simple but so telling.

Her face froze. "That," she said dully. "Of course. For how long?"

"You know," I said.

I watched as comprehension struck. It was a terrible thing.

The look in her eyes would haunt me. To the end of my days. Haunted.

Like everything with us, the hurt cut both ways.

"She made you break up with me." She said it like she didn't quite believe it.

You'd think the truth would be less harmful than the lies I'd told her. But sometimes the truth is the hardest thing to stomach, especially if you knew that some part of you should have seen it all along.

"Of course." Two words. Straightforward. Brutal in their simplicity.

She jerked like she'd been struck, her blinking eyes searching the room frantically, looking anywhere but at me.

"When you made that phone call," she paused, "both of those phone calls," she corrected herself. "She was with you, wasn't she?" Her voice broke on the question, her tone so raw it made my chest ache and my eyes sting.

But I answered her. "Of course."

And there it was.

She staggered where she stood. I was over in a beat, going to her, but I was a second too late. She had collapsed to the floor.

I'd only ever seen her once like this, bowed in on herself. Broken, bent, boneless in her pain. A pile on the floor.

Completely defeated. Destroyed.

Even with the way I'd known, because I *had absolutely known*, that I'd broken her heart, the pain of it had never made her shoulders less straight. Her pride, which was both the bane of my existence and one of the things that'd saved us both, had only ever left her one time before.

And now.

I scooped her up in my arms and carried her to bed. She was shaking and crying. The sobs quiet but powerful, rocking her entire body in waves until she was convulsing against me.

I'd hurt her, and myself more. I'd had to lie, *had to*, but I wished I could make her believe one truth: Her pain was always worse for me than my own.

She was inconsolable, sobbing in my arms like her heart was breaking all over again.

Eventually she spoke, haltingly and in near incoherent fragments. "The things we've done to each other. . . . The things we've done to *ourselves* . . . You don't know . . ."

"It's all in the past," I murmured into her forehead. I was running my hand over her head, over and over, petting her. It was an old familiar gesture, the way I always used to comfort her before our lives had gone to shit. "We can put it in the past and leave it there. We can move on. We will find a way to move on," I told her, the words ringing desperate because I was trying to convince myself, as well.

"You don't know," she sobbed brokenly. *"You don't know."*

I shut my eyes, old, familiar pain washing over me. My voice was thick with emotion when finally I said, "I do know. We both do now. All that's left is to move forward."

She started shaking her head and didn't stop. "No. No. You don't know. *You* don't know."

"What don't I know, angel? Tell me. I'll try to fix it, whatever it is."

But she wouldn't say. She was done talking and back to weeping. She was so upset she'd bitten her lips bloody. She didn't seem to notice, her eyes shut tight, but I did.

It was another thing I'd only seen her do one time before.

Quietly and firmly, with my fingers, I made her stop.

"Shh. Shh. It's okay," I soothed her, blotting at her lips with my shirt.

All the while, my heart was breaking all over again.

She didn't ask me any more questions that night, and I was relieved.

We'd both reached our threshold on suffering for the moment.

I hoped that the worst was past us, but I've never had much luck with hope.

"Life is hard. After all, it kills you."
~Katharine Hepburn

chapter twenty-three

PAST

Scarlett

"Do you know the kind of trouble that old bitch has gotten me into? Do you even *care* that you're messing with my career? All I've ever done is care about you and try to do right by you, and this is how you repay me?" Harris spoke to me in a low, mean voice, pitched quiet enough that his words didn't carry beyond his usual stalking booth in the diner.

That was the first time I started to get a real sense that he was delusional. He seemed to have some idea in his head of what our relationship was, and it was not even remotely close to reality.

"I don't know what you're talking about," I said stoically. I started to move away.

"Vivian Durant. She's been prying into my actions, questioning my methods. She went over my head, to my superiors, and, because she's filthy rich, they're listening to her."

Finally an encouraging development. It made me feel brave enough to say, "Good. Maybe you should stop bothering me every day. Maybe you should give up on stalking teenage girls altogether if you don't want to get into trouble for it."

I dodged away when I saw the look on his face. If we'd been alone with him looking at me like that . . . I'd have been very concerned for my safety.

Harris stopped coming to the diner after that.

I thought that was the end of it. I really did. I stopped worrying about him, stopped dreading any possible run-ins, stopped letting fear rule my actions.

Gram had scared him off and that was that. Yay for Gram.

I put him out of my mind.

But Harris was only biding his time. He was patient, and determined, and he held all of the power.

He showed up at school one day. He had no trouble pulling me out of class. All it took was a brief conversation with my English teacher and that was it.

"Scarlett," Mrs. Cowen called. "Detective Harris would like a word."

The girl next to me muttered, "The hot cop is here for you? Lucky girl."

I walked out into the hallway, turning to look at Harris. I folded my arms across my chest, stance belligerent. Expression belligerent. Attitude belligerent.

He killed that little bit of defiance soon enough. "Your boyfriend is finally being charged for that murder.

A warrant's been issued and some officers are planning to pick him up at football practice."

I felt ill. Literally. I thought I might throw up. I'd been so sure he was in the clear, that it was completely behind us, and now this . . . "Why are you telling me this?" I asked Harris carefully. His motives, as usual, were baffling to me.

"I think you can help him. Come into the station. Give a new statement. We can go over every word that creep said to you. You remember all of those unsolved, violent rape cases in the county, the disappearances? I think your attacker was our guy. Help me fill in some blanks. The more dangerous that bum looks, the more innocent your boyfriend will be."

I was wringing my hands, looking at him uncertainly. I really didn't want to go anywhere with Harris, but I wanted to help Dante more. I felt myself caving.

"I know it's a pain the ass," Harris said with a friendly smile, "but it won't take long, and it might make all of the difference. At least you get to ditch school for it."

I agreed to go to the station with him.

On the way out of school, we saw only one person as we walked through the halls to the exit.

Tiffany was at her locker, fishing something out. She stopped and watched us as we passed her.

Harris was walking just in front of me, but I slowed and let him get farther ahead as we came even with her.

"If you see Dante, will you tell him that Harris took me out of school? Tell him I need to talk to him as soon as possible." I said the words in a quick jumble, not wanting Harris to hear.

Tiffany nodded solemnly, looking back and forth

between my earnest face and Harris's retreating back. "Will do," she said. She looked sincere.

It was the most civil exchange we ever had. And the most damaging.

I hurried to catch up to Harris before he realized I'd stopped to talk.

I didn't trust him, but apparently, I trusted him too much.

In my defense, I did not think he would do or could do what he did in broad daylight.

But I did get into his car without a fight.

"*I started looking for you, not knowing how blind that was. Lovers don't finally meet somewhere. They're in each other all along.*"
~Rumi

chapter twenty-four

PRESENT

Scarlett

I woke up feeling rested and almost . . . peaceful. Crying yourself to sleep apparently made for a good night's rest.

It didn't hurt that my head was pillowed tenderly against a familiar chest. That I could hear the deep, throbbing beat of Dante's heart. It was so comforting that I had myself half convinced I was still sleeping.

It was one thing to wake up with him, another to be comforted by it.

What strange new world was this?

I couldn't believe he was real, that *this* was. That after all of the war we could have a moment of real peace.

Or that we were looking at trying to carve out some kind of a future together.

But was this even that? Or was this just another temporary reprieve?

I didn't know and I didn't want to think about it. Instead, I allowed myself a moment, a few, a dozen, a hundred, to revel in the arms of the only man who would ever own my heart.

His bare torso was warm, firm, and very real, but I ran my hands over him like he might disappear.

I could touch him now, and not as a way to hurt or wound. My hand on his chest spoke of the ownership I had been denying myself for five rough years.

Five hopeless years. Five hateful years. Five lost years.

"Morning, angel." His voice came out of his chest in a touchable rumble that spoke of deep affection. He kissed the top of my head, his familiar hand stroking over my hair.

I shut my eyes, letting myself enjoy it, letting myself acknowledge just how much I *needed* it.

This would take some getting used to. I was still afraid to even hope I might get the chance.

"Mm," I mumbled into his chest. It didn't mean anything, just a general sound of contentment.

He shifted me onto my back, propping up on one elbow close to my side.

I touched his face. Part of my mind was still in that fuzzy place between sleep and full cognizance. "Are you real?" I whispered it like I was afraid someone else might hear the silly question.

He grinned, shifting closer. His free hand grabbed one of mine, bringing it to his lips. He placed a soft, open-mouthed kiss on my palm. His eyes smiled as he dragged the hand down, cupping it over his very happy morning erection. "Is that real enough for you?"

I glared at him.

He threw his head back and laughed.

His laugh was wonderful, touchable. I set my hand to his throat just to feel closer to it.

His laughing eyes came back to mine, and his face sobered in one quick fall. He touched my cheek. "Jesus. That look. What are you trying to do to me here?"

I let my eyes answer that question. With a groan, he leaned down and kissed me. It was a tentative contact at first, his talented lips feeling at mine with utmost care, his own way of validating that *I* was real.

It was almost sweet and finished too quickly.

He started to pull back, but I stopped him by grabbing his face, crushing his mouth to mine.

The need came sudden and dark. I had to have him. Had to. On me, in me.

I craved that most intimate connection, him in the deepest part of me, with ravenous simplicity.

When he pulled back again I let him, my breath coming short. "Now." It was a plea, an order, a curse— all in one.

"Well, if you insist," he muttered. He was such a fake. He'd lost his senses several thumping heartbeats earlier and we both knew it.

He descended on me again, mouth on my jaw, kissing down to my neck, over my collarbone, moving down.

He peeled off my oversized cat T-shirt, lips coming back to my bare skin.

When he sucked my nipples, my back arched off the bed, my toes curling in delight. I was so primed that I thought he might bring me over with that contact alone, but he didn't linger there long, moving inexorably lower, and lower, nuzzling between my legs, eating me out like I was a feast and he was starved.

That made two of us.

When he'd—put a fork in me, done—finished me, he laid his cheek against my inner thigh, his drowning blue eyes aimed up the line of my body at mine, and managed to look winsome.

I shut my eyes and stroked his hair. I was having a battle with myself, feeling too emotional, wanting to tamp it down, to reprimand the part of me that *lived* for this, that thought my entire reason for existing was wrapped up in it.

In the end, emotion won, aided by sensation. He was licking his way up my stomach, nuzzling, kissing, touching everything with his fingertips like he would memorize me, though I knew he'd burned every detail of me into his brain a very long time ago.

This was just a refresher course.

By the time his mouth made its way to mine I was near incoherent with need again.

He raised his upper body over me, bracing with his arms, his lower body pressed against me, staring down at me.

The look on his face then was hard to describe.

His blue eyes were filled with a dark light. There was desire, yes, hunger, of a certainty, but also there was disbelief, reverence, hope. Fear. So much fear.

But above all, there was need. It was like the sun, so brilliant it was blinding.

I wondered what he saw in my eyes at that moment, if my desperation was as transparent as his. God, I hoped not. It was too much just having to witness his. Overkill.

He took me with ferocious delight, reveling in me, our hands clutching, every finger entwined.

He drove in and out of me with fast, solid strokes, kissing me, then pulling back, his eyes delving into my soul as his body plundered mine, then kissing me. Again and again.

In spite of my better judgment, if I had such a thing, I didn't hold back any more than he did, taking fervent joy in every touch, every contact.

Every possession—physical, spiritual.

When I came, it was with our eyes locked and his name on my lips like an invocation.

My name on his lips was more like a prayer.

I thought I was finished, vanquished, filled up, satiated, but he was far from done with me.

He was indefatigable. Insatiable. A tireless machine.

This had been the nature of our separation. It was always a flood or a drought for us. I wondered if we'd ever get past that.

Certainly not today.

We had ourselves a lazy morning. I was off until the next evening, and Dante's schedule seemed to be completely aimless.

Eventually we had to eat. He was the first one to scrounge up the energy to rise from the bed.

My smitten eyes were all over him. He was naked, prowling the room on his way to the closet.

I just lay there, enjoying the view. The symmetry and grace of his body would never get old for me.

It took a bit of effort on his part, but he did talk me out of bed.

It was a strange turn. Usually he only ever talked me into it.

We had croissants and coffee outside in the sun. The house had a heavy amount of decking, all of it private.

We ate silently for a time, and I studied him to my heart's content.

It wasn't always noticeable, the strange mixture of color in his eyes. But as the late morning sun hit them, the blue came alive like a flame, and another color, a rogue little circle of gold around his iris, was revealed. There were three colors if you looked closely. That strange gold around the middle, an almost pale aquamarine that bled into a darker blue at the outer edges. They reminded me of where sea met sand, but they were deep. Drowning deep ocean blue.

God, I was a sucker for his eyes.

I realized right then just how much I'd missed such a simple thing as looking at him without restraint. Without artifice. Without hiding what I was feeling as much as I possibly could.

"What are you staring at?" he asked, clearly amused.

"Your eyes. Your beautiful eyes." Tears were running down my face. God, he turned me into a sap. I hated it as much as I loved it.

With a helpless, exasperated little moan, he pulled me out of my chair and onto his lap. He started stroking my hair, his mouth at my cheekbone, lips tracing the tears, and murmuring, "Oh, angel," over and over.

After some time I found my composure again, and we went back to acting like things were normal and okay, because we were both starving enough to eat that lie.

"I know why you love to act," Dante told me. He was distracting me from heavy with light.

"I crave the escape. I long for it."

He nodded. He had known. "Who do you want to be right now?"

"Right now? Myself." It was sad how floored I was by that. And a little exasperating how every subject seemed to be an emotional landmine if you spent any time at all treading over it.

I had more questions for him, of course I did, but I had no urge to ask them. More truths could come later. I needed to keep some of my fiction for a time.

There's only so much a heart can take.

Also, the deeper I delved with him, the more inevitable it would be that he began to do some delving of his own, and I did not want that. It went beyond want. I could not take it.

"You have to find a cover story for where you're at when you're with me," he told me later that night.

That was easy. "Anton will be my cover."

I watched as his face went stiff, something dreadful and cruel crawling across it.

Jealousy, of course.

I watched his lips purse. I swear the more mean his mouth twisted the handsomer he was. It was out of hand. I squirmed in my seat.

"Not him," he said, tone hard. "You'll break it off with him, of course. I don't want you to stay tied to him for any reason, not even as an excuse."

"There was nothing going on between me and Anton. Never has been." I saw his face. "I was messing with you. Again." I caught his expression. "I don't know how you can be surprised. I'm not going to say it's your fault that I did it, but you made it too easy. Irresistible for me. And do you have any clue how angry I was?"

"That hurt," he said simply.

"Yes, it did," I agreed, just as simply. "And Anton's perfect as a cover, if I need one. No one ever wants to believe that we really are just friends."

His mouth twisted bitterly. "That's understandable. You are a very *convincing* couple.

"I told you, we are strictly friends."

"You think that doesn't make me jealous, too? I see how close you are."

"Would you rather I not have had anybody when I didn't have you? Did you want me to be alone?"

I saw I'd gone too far, as I tended to. I corrected the behavior with a quick and necessary subject change. "What do I need the cover for, anyway? Is your mother having me followed?"

"Worse and better."

I cocked my head to the side. "How so?"

"You've been living with one of her spies."

"Excuse me?" I asked him slowly, carefully, as though the way it came out might affect the answer.

"My mother has had someone close to you for quite some time. She knows things that only one of your roommates could know. So we have to be very careful. All of your living habits are being reported to her. That's why you still have to stay there some nights. Why you have to have a cover for the nights that you spend with me. It could be worse. At least they're all gone half the week with work."

It could be worse? I gave him a look of accusing bafflement. "One of my closest friends has been betraying me to your mother?"

He sucked in a breath, punched it out, and said, "Yes, I'm afraid so. Any clue which one it might be?"

I shook my head. I only knew one thing. No matter which one it was, if he was right, it would hurt like hell when I figured it out.

And in the meantime, there was the hurt of doubting

three women who had each come to mean the world to me in their own ways.

Farrah, who made me laugh every day, rain or shine. Demi, who made my heart lighter and less cynical. Or Leona, who had taught me what it meant to have girlfriends, to need them, to know the power of being supported by other women.

It was only after a while that I realized Dante and I had been staring at each other. His expression mirrored mine exactly, a moment of perfect understanding, that I'd only ever had with him, where I realized that we were taking the same information and doing the same pragmatic thing with it, processing it identically.

His mouth twisted up bitterly, but his eyes were affectionate on me, and I realized he'd just come to the same conclusion.

It was just another thing I'd made myself forget: The way we dissected life, with a razor-sharp cynicism that held just the perfect amount of shining optimism peppered in. Who else could ever love that about me the way he did?

What was a partner, if not someone who made you feel less alone in the universe? Someone who validated your existence just by understanding you completely and loving you anyway?

Jesus, I was in trouble.

"Just be careful," he finally said. "You can't let any of them know that you suspect them. You have to behave as if each one is the culprit."

I hated that, *hated* it, but I knew he was right. It was too much to risk if he was that certain one of them was spying on me.

"We'll know who it is soon enough," he continued.

"If they're on my mother's payroll to spy on you, they'll be quitting the airline job soon. Adelaide wouldn't be satisfied with a part-timer."

"It can't be Leona," I said finally. "She and I go too far back."

"I'd say she's the least likely, but better to be safe. Like I said, we'll know soon enough."

"Love is born into every human being: it calls back the halves of our original nature together; it tries to make one out of two and heal the wound of human nature."
~Plato

chapter twenty-five

"I'm home," I called out as I closed the massive front door behind me. My voice seemed to echo through an empty house.

It was surreal to be doing this, to be coming home to Dante. If you'd asked me just weeks ago if there was a possibility that I'd be shacking up with the bastard, I would have never even entertained the notion.

I hadn't seen him for more than brief stretches, stolen moments, for the past three days. My roommates had been off work, and that, combined with fourteen hours of shooting each day, meant there'd been almost no spare time.

I missed him like it'd been months, not days.

My friends were off on another trip, and I rushed to him the first possible second I could.

It was truly getting out of hand.

"Dante?" I called out loudly, thinking for a brief moment that he wasn't there.

But he emerged a few seconds later, from a hallway to the right that I hadn't even noticed before. I really needed to get a tour of the place.

I eyed him. He was shirtless, wearing nothing but a pair of athletic shorts and running shoes. He was holding both of his hands behind his back in a strange way, but I didn't notice the strangeness so much as the way it made his glistening muscles jump and skitter under his deliciously tanned skin. "You've been out running," I observed.

He bit his lip and nodded. He looked like he was trying to hold in a laugh.

It made my heart feel light to see that smile. God, how had I survived even one day without it?

"Do you not have a job of some sort?" I asked him. Last I'd heard he (predictably) worked for the Durant department store chain. He was the heir apparent to the family fortune and one of the bigger shareholders. He was filthy rich, so I supposed he could just spend his days playing around, but even in college, he'd always worked for and with his family.

"I'm taking some time off. Leo is giving me shit for it, but I don't give a damn. I'll go back soon enough."

"And you'll be able to do it . . . from L.A.?"

"Yes. But enough about that. Aren't you curious about your surprise?"

I'd completely forgotten. He'd said something about a surprise the day before. I gave him a probing look. So that's why he had his hands behind his back. He was holding something. "You know I hate surprises, right?" In my life, they had rarely been a good thing.

"I know you do, but I guarantee you'll like this one."

"It must be shoe-porn then." Shoes were always a good surprise.

He laughed, eyes twinkling at me.

My heart did a slow turn in my suddenly warm chest.

His laugh was like the first cup of coffee in the morning—warm and rich and exactly what I needed, exactly when I needed it. And God, did I need it.

"Even better," he said.

"Not possible."

With an irresistible, irrepressible grin, he pulled his hands out from behind his back.

In one of them was a little white ball of fluff that nearly passed for an oversized cotton ball.

"Meet Diablo," Dante told me.

My hands covered my mouth in that, 'omg I'm a girl and I am having an emotional overload moment' pose."

But I couldn't seem to help it. He'd gotten me a kitten. It was so perfect, and thoughtful, and reminiscent of old times that my eyes teared up as I scooped the little treasure out of his hand, cradling it to my chest.

Beautiful blue eyes blinked up at me. I'd thought the kitten was white, but it was really a sandy color, with gray on its nose, ears, and paws.

I sat abruptly on the floor, crossing my legs, holding the cat with one hand so I could stroke it with the other.

When I had it purring, I beamed up at Dante. "How did you know?"

His eyes were soft enough to melt me. "That you love cats? You always did. And all of the cat T-shirts gave me the idea."

"Is it a boy or a girl?" I asked him. I was lying on the ground now, playing with its paws.

"Girl."

"A girl named Diablo?"

"*You're* questioning that a girl could be the devil? That is rich."

I hid my smile in Diablo's fluff. The man had a point.

I had a three-day break from shooting the film. I brought Amos over, and we played house with childish abandon, doting on our new kitten like she was our child.

We were at a dangerous place then, he and I, where though I'd forgotten nothing—not a one of his sins and certainly not one of mine—they weren't crushing my mood into blackness as they usually did, as it was their job to do when he was this deep into my head.

"We're becoming one of those couples that we would make fun of," I told him the second day. We were in the backyard, making pet videos of all of the adorable interactions between Amos and Diablo.

"Joke's on you," Dante said with a soft smile. "We always were."

The time with Dante was good for me in a lot of fundamental ways. That was a fact. But always, running under our time together, over it, through it, was a bittersweet current of fear. This was not permanent. This was stolen time.

I'd steal it again, take and take, everything I could, because it was right. We were right together. He'd said it best—apart we were not ourselves. We only ever made sense together.

But no length of stolen time, no amount of righteousness, could change the past or the future.

"What's the plan here?" I asked him on the third day. It had started as a small weight, but as these things went, it became bigger the longer I didn't address it. "Are we just going to *hide* from Adelaide forever?"

We were in the kitchen, cleaning up after dinner. He

turned to look at me head on as he replied, "For now, yes. For however long is necessary. I'm working with Bastian on trying to get some dirt on her, some leverage for counter-blackmail—"

I smirked at the counter-blackmail. It was so Durant it hurt, the manipulative bastards.

"But until we have something that will ruin her beyond a shadow of a doubt, she's always going to have the upper hand. That is a fact."

It all felt so hopeless all of a sudden that I couldn't keep it in. "You know we're being foolish. Nothing has changed, not really. You and I are still hopeless. I should just stay away from you. If I were smart, I would."

That set him off, nostrils flaring, eyes flashing. He stepped right into my personal space, so I had to look up to meet his eyes. I'd done it now. "Oh yes. Your incredible *restraint*. Don't remind me. You think I need to be *reminded*? That restraint breathes down my neck every minute of every day. You could stay the hell away from me indefinitely; I'm well aware. But what if I can't let you? What if I'm sick *to death* of trying?"

My heart was pounding, eyes devouring his passionate expression. Sometimes I felt I could feed on his rage alone. It was sick and twisted and irresistible. "Sooner or later, we all have to pay for our sins," I said softly.

He shook his head, "No. That's not where this is heading. *No*. I won't allow it."

He said it like he meant it, with absolute inflexibility. I tried to find comfort in that.

"What matters most is how well you walk through the fire."
~Charles Bukowski

chapter twenty-six

PAST

Scarlett

Harris didn't take me to the station.

He took me back to my grandma's trailer, which he knew would be vacant.

He dragged me kicking and screaming inside.

It was like a switch in my brain that I couldn't turn off. I'd fight him until he decided I was more trouble than I was worth.

I'd fight him until he killed me.

I scratched him until he bled. On the arms, on his face. I went for his eyes and almost got one.

I bit him on the neck and wouldn't let go. I tasted blood and wondered if I was close to his jugular. I ripped chunks of his flesh out with my teeth, but it still didn't slow him.

Finally he clocked me on the back of the head, and the world went black.

I came to tied spread eagle on my bed. I was naked.

The first thing I saw was my bedside clock.

11:23.

It's only 11:23, I thought. *Not even an entire period has passed since he took me from school.* It seemed impossible that it was still so early.

I kept my eyes glued to that clock for four solid hours. The ropes were so tight that I couldn't shift even an inch to fight him.

I've never been good at escaping into my own mind, at finding any sort of distance from the things that torment me. But I tried. I tried to reach for some kind of solace somewhere in my being.

And found none.

For the first bit, I held onto a tiny grain of hope—maybe it wouldn't go that far.

Maybe he wouldn't take it that next step. Or the next. Or the next.

And, most wretched and unfair of all—perhaps Dante will come bursting through the door at any moment—somehow he'll sense what's happening to me—that his angel is being damaged *beyond all repair.*

Somehow he'll rescue me.

By the first half hour, my eyes still glued to that clock, I gave up all hope of that.

I'm not sure why the words came to my brain then, but they did. Gram had once told me that God answers all prayers.

I worshipped Gram, but I had not agreed. In fact, I was skeptical of God in general.

But just then, I was desperate enough to try. I prayed. With an anguished heart, I prayed.

Maybe God does answer all prayers, I really can't say, but if he does, sometimes the answer is no, I won't help you out of this.

And so it was. No one helped me. No one stopped it. No force of nature lessened the horror or the pain of it. No act of God cut it short. It went on until Harris was finished, and I'd lost what little faith I had that there could be some benevolent force watching over me.

And all throughout, I wouldn't look at him, though he wanted me to. Ordered me to.

He started slapping me when I refused, then pinching me, twisting my flesh, biting me hard.

He changed tactics and pleaded for me to look at him. I still wouldn't do it.

He started punching me in the stomach.

I still wouldn't look at him, and I swore I wouldn't cry for him either, but tears had been seeping steadily down my face since he'd first begun.

Still, I wouldn't sob for him, and I wouldn't beg him either.

He started screaming in my face. "Look at me. Look at me." Over and over.

No matter what he did, no matter how angry it made him, I would not look at him. I kept my eyes on that clock.

I didn't fear punishment. What was worse than what he was already doing?

He could beat me. He could kill me. Somewhere around hour number two, in fact, I wanted him to.

At hour three, I *begged* him to.

"Don't be silly," he panted into my ear, back on top of me again. "I'm nowhere near finished with you. Trust me, you'll learn to like this."

I stopped begging and tried to think of something, anything else, but I quickly stopped. I didn't want to taint any of my good memories with this, and the nightmare I was trapped in now was bad enough without adding to it.

When he was done with me, for some reason I cannot *fathom*, and I go back to it often, he untied me.

I tried to get my bruised, overused body to sit up, had started to, but he quickly joined me in bed, yanking me to him, wrapping his limbs around me so tightly that I couldn't move.

"Shh, go to sleep, dear girl," he told me, and promptly passed out.

As soon as his body went limp, I slipped from the bed.

I tried to move quietly from the room, but I was trembling so powerfully that I was sure the sound of it would wake him up with every limping step I took.

I saw his gun, but it was close by the bed, close to him, and I couldn't make myself move toward him. I struggled for a minute, trying to, but I could not do it. I could only make myself move *away* from him.

Once I was out of the room, my body just started to work of its own accord. It moved fast, fluidly, ignoring all of my soreness, ignoring the fact that my spirit felt broken, and I still wanted to die.

I went mindlessly to my grandma's room.

Feeling completely blank, I took the gun from her nightstand, checked the clip, and glided quietly back to my room.

He'd shifted in his sleep, turned so his back was to the bedroom door.

I didn't linger. I didn't stare at his sleeping form. I did not contemplate.

I don't remember making a decision. I just remember clearing the door, raising the gun, aiming it, and emptying the entire clip into his back.

"Love consists in this, that two solitudes protect and touch and greet each other."
~Rainer Maria Rilke

chapter twenty-seven

I don't know if I fainted, dozed, or blacked out, but what brought me back was a consistent, warm drip, drip, drip of fluid onto my chest.

I was huddled outside of my old bedroom. I'd shut myself out.

I didn't look down at my body. I was numb in a way, but still coherent enough to know that I wasn't ready to see the damage. Wasn't ready to face it.

My jaw was slack, and so my first assumption was that I'd been drooling on myself, but as the drip, drip, drip continued, I realized there was too much of it, whatever it was, for that.

Had I thrown up on myself? I wondered. It seemed as likely as anything. My mouth tasted foul enough for it, acid burning in my throat.

I kept my eyes trained straight ahead, at the stained yellow wall in front of me as I took a shaking hand and wiped my chin. I held it up all the way to eye level, not lowering my gaze even an inch to see what it was.

Red. So much red, but as I saw it I was not completely surprised. I felt at my lips, and to this day I wonder, I honestly have no recollection, which one of us had ravaged them, bit them bloody, that monster in his depravity, or me, in my anguish?

What do I do now? I thought. *Call the police?* Bitterness filled me at the thought.

Someone was pounding on the front door. I went from numb to trembling again.

But then I heard a frantic Dante calling, "Scarlett! Are you in there? Scarlett!"

I broke. Into a million pieces. In relief. In renewed horror.

I started sobbing and made my unsteady way to the door, fumbling with the lock in my rush to let him in.

Some part of me had shut off, slipped inward, gone dead, perhaps, for the duration of the nightmare.

It took seeing Dante's face to bring me back, to realize, and start to deal with the horror of what had happened to me.

A dozen expressions flitted across his face as he took me in. First shock, then horror, then anguish as he started to connect the dots.

I looked down at myself. I was naked, which I'd as good as forgotten, but that wasn't the worst of it.

Bruises were already mottling my torso, my wrists and ankles raw, open wounds from struggling against the ropes.

And there was blood, a lot of it, all over my thighs.

I crumpled with a sob.

With a low sob of his own, he caught me.

He didn't ask me anything at first, just held me, stroked

me, carried me inside, sat down on the couch and tried, around his own helpless sobs, to calm me down.

And when I'd quieted, and was just lying against him, hoping that I never had to leave his arms ever again for my whole miserable life, he asked me only one thing.

"Where is he?" His quiet voice bled like murder into the air.

Of course he'd connected the dots as soon as he'd seen the state I was in. Harris's car was right outside.

I started trembling anew. I shut my eyes and leaned heavily into him. I couldn't bring myself to answer him, and after a time he tried to stand, but I clung to him and cried.

It had sunk in. What had happened to me.

But more than that. What I'd done.

Who I was and what I'd done.

Eventually he had to pick me up and take me with him. I didn't make it easy for him to search my grandma's house, but at least there wasn't much to search.

It took him extra time to get my door open while still holding me clutched to his chest, but he managed.

I didn't look, but his reaction was far calmer than I'd expected.

His breathing barely changed as he took in the cop I'd killed.

"I'm going to jail," I said wretchedly.

"Shh, angel, shh," he said into my temple. "It was self-defense."

I shook my head. "He was sleeping when I shot him. He'd already finished with me. I wasn't thinking. I shot him in the *back*. Don't you see what's going to happen? With all the trouble I've been in? All the fights? All the reports from times when I've lost my temper? The cops hated me when I was a *victim*. What do you think they're going to do now that I've *killed* one of them?"

"He was a rapist," Dante said dully, but I could tell that what I was saying was starting to sink in. "He *deserved* it."

"They won't think so. What do you think they're going to do to me now when I've killed one of them, and then *I accuse him of being a rapist?*"

"He *was a rapist,*" Dante repeated, an absolute concentrate of hatred in the words. "I'm so sorry, angel." He was crying now. "So sorry. I didn't know. I didn't know this was happening. I had no idea. I've been looking for you for hours, but I was looking in the *wrong* place." He was breaking down now, sobbing, screaming, "I'd have killed him myself, I swear it."

It was funny how I only realized later that he never asked me if I was okay, and how that had comforted me. Because he knew me too well to ask such a *stupid* question.

Of course I wasn't okay. Of course I wasn't fine.

I'd been defiled, degraded, debased beyond all repair. I was covered in that monster's filth. Sticky with it.

I was wretched. Unhinged. Suicidal.

"I don't know what to do," I sobbed. "I don't want to go to jail."

"They can't put you in jail for this," he argued, but he sounded less and less convinced.

"I wasn't thinking right, Dante. My mind was just . . . gone. I shot him *in the back*. Emptied a full clip into him. Do you really think this is going to go my way?"

He was silent as his mind worked, and eventually I could see he came to the same conclusion as I had, but his next words floored me. "I'll say I did it. I'll say I caught him raping you and shot him in the back."

I started to struggle in his hold.

"No, no, no," I spat. "You think I'd let you go to jail for me? After you already killed someone for me, you think I'd do that? And with your record, do you think it could end *any other way?*"

"Don't be like that. I can take this hit. Gram will get me the best lawyer out there. It'll be fine."

I kept shaking my head. "No. *Never.* I'll confess myself before this ever goes on you. I fucking *swear* it. I won't let you take this on yourself."

He took a few deep breaths. He was thinking, I could tell, his mind racing, trying to figure out what to do.

"Does anyone know he brought you here?" he asked finally.

"I don't think so. People saw him take me out of school, but not to come here. He lured me into his car by saying he needed to talk to me at the station."

"He planned this," Dante said slowly, the pain in his voice excruciating to me. "He planned out a rape, and he's a cop. What are the odds he didn't cover his own tracks? What are the odds there is a *soul* on this earth that knows he was bringing you here?"

I studied him, feeling hope for the first time at what I saw. "What should we do?" I asked him.

He looked down at me, bent, and gave me a very careful kiss. "You don't have to do anything, angel. I'll take care of it. Do you think you can shower by yourself?"

It was pathetic, but I shook my head. I didn't think I could walk across the room by myself.

"Okay. That's just fine. I'll help you. We'll get this sorted out, I promise. No one's going to hurt you again.

And no one is going to take your freedom. I *swear* it."

I believed him, had absolute faith in everything he'd said.

He showered with me. He was very tentative, after what I'd been through, to get naked in front of me, so he showered with his boxers still on.

I couldn't even wash myself. I made him do it. He was excruciatingly tender as he lathered me up, head to toe, rinsed me off, then did it again.

We both cried like babies, in great, heaving, helpless sobs, when he washed the blood off my thighs.

Only after he was done with his soft ministrations did I take the loofah from him and scrub myself *raw*.

I was abrading my skin with such gusto that he quietly begged me to stop, and somehow something in the tone of his voice was convincing enough to actually get me to.

Otherwise I swear I'd have just kept rubbing until my skin was gone.

It was cowardly and weak, but after he'd washed me, and dressed me, he took me out of the trailer and carried me up the hill. And I let him.

"Aren't we going to . . . ?" I asked him.

"I'm going to get you settled in your room at Gram's. You need to rest and not worry about any other thing than that, do you understand?"

I nodded weakly. We were on his mother's property by then. It was closer than Gram's, and we always cut across it when we made the walk.

"Will you stay with me tonight?" I asked him. I didn't want to sleep alone.

"Of course. I won't leave your side after I . . . take care of things."

I went a little numb, and somehow it was easy to just

not think about it, the things he'd have to do, the things I'd already done.

We'd barely crossed the property line between his mother's and his grandma's when it all hit me again and I started sobbing into his chest.

He sat down on the ground and sobbed with me, chanting, "I'm so sorry, I'm so sorry, I'm so sorry."

"It's not your fault," I finally managed to get out.

"I can't believe this happened to you. I can't believe I didn't save you in time." His voice broke on the words, and I'd never heard him sound more lost.

He brought me straight to my room, left me briefly, and came back with sleeping pills he'd gotten from Gram.

I stared at him.

"Please. For me. Take them. I can't leave you until you're sleeping. I *can't*."

I took them.

When I came to, it was dark out, but my bedside lamp was on.

Dante had pulled a chair up and was sitting at my side. He was staring straight ahead.

I shivered at the look in his eyes.

That caught his attention and his gaze cleared—black nightmares turning to concern as he studied my face.

"What can I do?" he asked me.

Again, he didn't ask me if I was okay.

"Hold me," I said, and started crying again, the worst kind of tears, because they were only for me, purest self-pity.

He crawled into bed with me fully clothed and wrapped himself around me.

"Did you . . .?" I finally asked him.

"Everything is handled. If the police ever ask you about it, and they likely will at some point, you need to plead complete ignorance. They'll catch on that you might have been the last one to see him, because he took you out of school, but you tell them that he asked you a few questions and dropped you off at Gram's, okay? He dropped you off at Gram's at around eleven a.m. Gram will corroborate your story. He left you here at eleven and you know *nothing* else about it."

"Okay. Does Gram know . . .?"

"Gram knows everything. I needed her help, and she's your alibi. Also, we needed a very discreet doctor to examine you, and I didn't know any myself."

I coiled in on myself. "A doctor to examine me?" It sounded awful.

"You were hurt. Badly. A doctor examined you while you were still out. We thought that would be less traumatic . . . after everything." He nearly choked on the word everything. "A close family friend did a house call for Gram; someone she swears can be trusted."

He sat up and grabbed a little cup from the nightstand. "He left you some pills to take. He said the sooner you take them the better."

I looked in the little cup. There were a lot of pills. I didn't even ask what they were. I just downed them, then took a long drink of water from the glass Dante handed me.

We lay back down.

"Is Gram upset with us?" I asked him in a very small voice. She must have been so disappointed. Here she'd taken me in and now she had to deal with this mess.

He went stiff around me. "Of course not. You thought she'd be upset with you?"

I shrugged a shoulder. "I killed a cop. I made you, I don't even know what, get rid of the body? I'm nothing but trouble."

"Stop it. None of this was you. She's sad about it, very sad." The way he said, the way his voice cracked on the words, made it clear she wasn't the only one that was sad. "But of course she doesn't blame you."

"Do you think they'll ever find the body?" I asked him.

He was silent for a long time then, "I don't, and I don't think you need to know anything else about it. It's taken care of, okay? You trust me, right?"

I did. Completely and utterly.

"Love doesn't make the world go round. Love is what makes the ride worthwhile."
~Franklin P. Jones

chapter twenty-eight

PRESENT

Scarlett

I was wearing nothing but some pasties up top and a bare strip down south, simulating sex with a guy I wouldn't have let so much as kiss my feet if a camera wasn't rolling. Meanwhile somewhere deep down I was questioning my career choices.

I tried to get lost in the role, to put just the right touch of vulnerable passion into my expression.

I was always the epitome of nonchalant about the racy scenes, the nudity, all of it.

Because I was determined to be a professional, particularly about this.

Some of it was pure brassy nerve, the part of me always making up for the fact that I had been a victim once. Overcompensation as I tried to convince myself that I never would be again.

Deep seated and hidden just as well was how this elicited something ugly in me, how letting someone I hadn't chosen and did not want put their hands on me made me feel unclean. Sticky with an old filth that would not wash off.

There was even a physical pain that it triggered, a sharp stab, almost like a menstrual cramp but more acute and lower, that only came up when I kicked this particular internal hornet's nest. I'd never, never say it, though, or show it. I was determined to be a pro to the end, especially about this.

And I'd been good. Great. Compared to my co-star, I'd been a hell of a professional, but it was too much. Currently he was poised over me, grinding his relentless erection into my hip for about the thousandth time.

Suddenly I couldn't take it. Couldn't be tough and nonchalant about it for one more second.

I shoved at David, pushing him off me. "There's seriously nothing we can do about the erection he keeps grinding on me?" I addressed Stu.

"You know, most women would *love* this," David told me, tone deeply offended, like that would somehow change my mind.

I rolled my eyes. Those women didn't know this douchebag in real life. It was amazing how unattractive a mind could be even it fit was wrapped in a sexy as hell shell.

We'd been at it for going on fourteen hours. Take after take, with small breaks that didn't let us get far from set.

I was tired. The night before had been my first at Dante's house in four days. We hadn't slept much.

No rest for the wicked.

But it was more than lack of sleep that had me upset enough to pull a diva moment. I'd been dreading this scene, this interaction, from the get-go, and the fact that it was all worse than I'd been anticipating was not helping.

Stu called cut and came to stand by the bed. I sat up, one of the assistants brought me a robe, and I thanked him while shrugging it on. My eyes were on my director all the while. I was expecting to get an earful.

He looked back and forth between David and me several times, pursing his mouth. "This isn't working. I just assumed it would. I figured when I casted you two." He waved a hand, vaguely indicating our bodies. "I just figured playing up the sex would be a no-brainer. But I don't like it. I think we should do something with subtlety."

I was so relieved that I wanted to cry, but I hid it, just nodding agreement.

He wound up rewriting the entire scene. It ended with me taking my top off and fading to black. I was reassured that all he planned to show was some heavy side boob.

I actually had no problem with nudity. I just didn't. It was the touching while nude that I couldn't get past, or at least not easily.

The next time Stu called a break I found Dante in my trailer.

He was lounging on the sofa, phone to his ear.

He wasn't one to sit idle, so he'd started working again the week before.

He smiled when he saw me, holding up his index finger.

I just nodded and went for coffee. I listened almost absentmindedly to his side of the conversation and when I realized he was dealing not with day-to-day Durant Department store business, but with Gram's much beloved charity, I went warmer inside, the day suddenly felt less dark. Of course he would do that. Continue her work. Make her proud.

I was stirring the sugar into my cup when Dante pressed up behind me. He was still on the phone, and I hadn't realized he was moving close.

I jumped about a foot.

He slipped his free hand into my robe, running his palm over my breast. The pasty seemed to give him pause, and he fingered it briefly before he felt his way to the other one. That got a quicker check before his hand snaked down, feeling between my legs.

I shrugged him off, moving away. I didn't want him to touch me before I'd showered the feel of douchebag David away.

I went into the bathroom and locked the door.

I washed myself repeatedly, but I still didn't feel clean. When I finally emerged, he was done with his call. He got one look at my face and he seemed to know.

I felt like a child as he cradled me on his lap and tried to comfort me, but this was just the way of us. We'd always been too much to each other, filled too many roles. We didn't know another way.

"No part, no career, is worth doing this to yourself," he finally said.

"I'll be fine," I protested.

"And what about me?"

I pulled away, tipping my head back to look at him. "What about you? Can *you* handle this?"

"I'm dealing with it. I know you've wanted this since you were fourteen, and the last thing I'm going to do is stand in your way. I'm not going to lie, I hate this part of it. The idea of anyone seeing you . . . of your co-star touching you. It all makes me insane. But I can't stand in your way. This is your dream and I'll support it, even the parts that I can't stand."

"The worst is over," I reassured him. I understood the jealousy, the possessiveness. I could hardly fault him for it. I wasn't sure what I'd do if Dante's job consisted of touching other women for any reason.

It was a touchy subject all around.

"You were working on Gram's charity when I walked in, weren't you?" I asked him, though I knew the answer.

"Yes. I've always been involved in The Vivian Durant Project, but I'm particularly invested now that you've made me sink your entire inheritance into the endeavor. I plan to see that money work miracles."

I froze. "What the hell are you talking about? I don't have an inheritance."

He sighed loud enough to jostle me against his chest. It was part resignation, part exasperation. "Well, Gram left you eight million dollars, and you told me to give it to her charity. I figured since you never even let me finish talking about it that you meant what you said, so I damn well did it."

I was blinking, trying not to cry, trying not to fall apart. "She really did that? She left that to me?"

He made a noise in his throat that rumbled through him hard enough that I could feel every intense reverberation, his hand stroking over my hair, over and over. "Of course she did, angel. She thought of you as family. It was in her will for years before she passed. By the way, I have about a hundred papers for you to sign when you feel up to it."

Joy, yes joy, fluttered through me. Not because of the money. I'd meant it when I said I didn't want it, that I wanted it donated. No, again, I wasn't crazy, and prior to my recent starring role I'd been pretty close to broke, but I could not take money I had not earned, money that came from losing her. I wanted every cent to go to the charity she'd been so involved and passionate about, but the idea of it, the gesture, meant everything to me. She really had thought of me like family. So much so, she'd stood by the sentiment to the very end.

"Did Adelaide get her house?" I asked. A part of me didn't want to know. I was positive that Gram wouldn't have left it to her, but I also knew that Adelaide had her ways. I figured she'd have strong-armed Leo for it by now.

"Hm," Dante said. It was half-laugh, half-snort. "Not quite. Gram left her *nothing*, not a cent. The rest of us expected it, but Adelaide was furious. She's still on a warpath. It's been ugly."

I whistled. I could not even imagine. Adelaide was wrathful when it came to even the smallest slight. She'd once terrorized a woman into moving out of town just because she didn't like where she'd been seated at a wedding.

Being left out of the will for a payout she'd expected her entire adult life . . . it frightened me a bit just to contemplate the destruction she must have wreaked.

"My God, that is some justice," I said reverently, my mind on how much I still worshipped Gram.

"Time will tell if it will stick, though Leo *has* been holding his own more than usual."

"Let me know how it turns out."

"Oh, I will. Believe me, I will."

My phone dinged a text at me, and I checked it, assuming it was an alert to get back on set.

It was not. It was a message from Farrah.

I showed it to Dante.

FARRAH/SEXYASSBITCH: I just put in my two weeks at the airline. I'm over it. It's no fun without you. Shopping day soon! xoxo

"Well, I guess we have our spy." His tone was resigned but almost pleased. He was relieved to finally know.

I wasn't sure what to feel.

"Being in love shows a person who he should be."
~Anton Chekhov

chapter twenty-nine

PAST

Scarlett

I thought I was fine at first. I pretended—even convinced myself— that I'd bounced right back, returning to school as soon as I could, acting as though nothing had happened, talking about it to no one, not even the people I *could* talk about it with.

But I was not fine. Every day I got up, it felt harder. It was a struggle to shower, to put on clothes, to eat, to do anything but sleep, or lie in bed and wish I were sleeping.

Wish for something more permanent.

It affected me in strange ways. My stutter disappeared almost completely. I had almost no problem ignoring insults from the usual bullies. That sort of thing just rolled off me.

I started trying harder in school. Not because I liked it, or because I felt better, but because I wanted to finish and leave. Dante would be heading east for college the following year, and I was planning to go with him.

The rest of the school year felt like it passed in a thick, gray fog, but pass it did, and at the end somehow I rallied enough to actually graduate.

Dante left for college just two weeks into the summer. He had a nice apartment already set up for him for his freshman year at Harvard.

I went with him because I could not conceive of doing anything else.

It felt wrong right away. He was instantly busy, and I felt aimless, listless, shiftless. Pointless. I had nothing to do. When he was home with me, which wasn't often, he was tirelessly studying, whereas I was just watching TV, or reading book after book, feeling useless.

And worse, I was afraid when I was alone. Irrational fear. Debilitating. If I let the fear rule me, I'd have never left his side.

But I couldn't do that. Pure stubborn pride prevented it. And an instinct to do more than survive. I needed to thrive again.

And in order to thrive, I needed to find my own identity. My own life. My own purpose.

I started with something normal. As small of a change as I could stand. I got a job. Another waitressing gig. Dante hated it but he'd have done anything, agreed to just about anything by then just to cheer me up.

He was attentive. And he was loving. Possibly more so than ever.

It took a very long time before I wanted his touch for anything aside from affection and comfort, and he never showed one sign of losing his patience about it.

To the end of my days, I'll appreciate that.

He never even brought it up. When we talked about it, it was because I was worrying over it.

And even then he found the words, just the right ones, that I needed to hear.

The only ones that helped.

"This is not about me," he told me tenderly, "and what my body asks from yours. This is about you and what you need. I *need* to be what you need. That's all that matters right now. The rest will come later. We have time. All that you require. We have it. And when you're ready, I'll be here. Every second of every day. That'll never stop."

"Hear no evil, speak no evil, and you won't be invited to cocktail parties."
~Oscar Wilde

chapter thirty

PRESENT

Scarlett

"You're seeing somebody, aren't you?" Farrah asked me, not for the first time.

We were shopping (her idea), and it was her first official day of unemployment. "How are you planning to make rent?" I responded, trying not to feel as hostile as I felt.

I'd become resentful as I pondered all of the ways she must have betrayed me over the years, and it only seemed to grow, until it was difficult to hide even though I knew that I absolutely had to.

Because if this spy for Adelaide had any clue that I was onto her there would be questions that led to consequences that I was not yet prepared to deal with.

"Waitressing. Every role I can find. The usual. They assigned the crew a new lead when you left. She was beastly. I just couldn't take it, so I quit. I bet Leona and Demi won't be far behind."

We were on the hunt for a new sexy little dress for Farrah's hot date that night. It was really just an excuse to shop. Farrah always had a hot date and enough sexy little dresses to cover it, I was sure.

I was helping her because she'd asked, it was my day off, and I was trying to act how I normally would. Normal me rarely said no to shopping.

We'd been at it for a few hours, and Farrah had circled back to the same question five times. I knew she wasn't going to let it go, and I knew why.

Now that I was looking at her with nothing but suspicion, it occurred to me that she was always asking me too many questions, always curious, prying, nosy, with friendly nudges about everything in my life that I'd always just thought was part of her outgoing personality.

I tried to behave as if I didn't know how she'd hurt me and found every good memory I'd ever had with her had turned sour.

Some part of me, the part that gave too much of myself to friendships, was still trying to make excuses for her. Maybe she needed the money. I had no doubts Adelaide could afford to pay well. Maybe she'd agreed to spy before she'd known me, and maybe she didn't share everything with Adelaide. Maybe she'd come to care for me. Maybe she felt bad about what she was doing.

When I wasn't making excuses I was still trying to deny what was becoming more apparent, more undeniable, with every exchange, but even I could only rely on denial for so long.

"Come on!" Farrah nudged me playfully as we sifted through dresses. "Who is he? Dish it!"

I sent her a weak smile and tried to lie convincingly, though I had no energy for it. "Me and Anton, but listen, it's nothing serious. We're just killing some time. It's not worth going on about."

I could tell that wasn't the answer she'd expected, and she gave me a strange, probing stare for it, but at least it got her to drop the subject.

We were done and driving home before she brought it up again. "Does Demi know you're hooking up with Anton?" she asked me, tone careful.

I thought it was a strange question, but I was preoccupied so I just said, "No. Like I said, it's not a big deal."

The irony was I'd been avoiding Anton lately. He'd always been an overprotective friend, and I knew he'd never understand that I was currently shacking up part-time with the enemy. I barely understood it myself.

When we arrived home, I went straight to my room and locked myself in. Since I'd found out there was a spy amongst my roommates, I'd come to hate the apartment.

I felt trapped there whenever I had to stay, because it was simply not a choice anymore. On top of that, I felt like I was being watched all the time, that everything I did would be noticed and reported to someone I'd despised my whole life.

All of that was bad enough, but add to it my pathetic heart, my incessant, weak longing for all the time I was missing with Dante (hadn't we missed enough?), and it was damn near torturous to put in time at the home I'd once found comfort in.

I'd pilfered several soft white shirts of Dante's to

sleep in, and like a deranged addict I made sure that they smelled like him. I wanted reminders of him even when I slept. Needed them. Needed, when I woke up in a panic alone, to have some sort of proof that I wasn't still existing in that old hell where he was completely lost to me.

It used to be that when he was away I could talk myself out of him. We'd gotten way past that point. It was scary how attached I'd become in such a short time.

If I was honest with myself though, and sometimes I was, we'd never really been unattached, not even at the worst of it. I'd hacked at that attachment with a machete more times than I could count, but that didn't mean I'd severed it.

Far from it. Obviously.

I had just changed into one of my stalker Tees when the doorbell rang.

I went to get it myself. If it was someone for me, I preferred to beat Farrah to it. I'd become almost obsessive about keeping as much as I could private from her.

No such luck. She hit the entryway just a beat behind me, which was not good.

I opened the door to find a tired-looking Bastian.

He glanced behind me at Farrah, then back to me. "Have time for a cup of coffee?" He cleared his throat. "Down the street."

"I do," I said without hesitating. I didn't want Farrah to overhear one word of whatever he had to say.

I stomped into some Toms and left the house as is, baggy T-shirt, cutoff shorts and all.

"Mind if I join you?" Farrah asked behind me, sounding frankly curious. Nosy.

How had I not seen her for what she was before? It

was so obvious to me the longer I knew the truth. She wasn't really even trying to fool me.

"Sorry, but we need a bit of privacy," Bastian replied because he didn't know who or what she was.

This is going to blow up in my face, I thought as we shut the door on her.

"She's a spy for Adelaide," I said quietly when we'd been walking for a few minutes. I glanced behind my shoulder, paranoid enough to check if she'd blatantly followed us.

"Your *roommate*?"

"Yes. It goes way back, apparently. Trust me, I was as shocked as you are, but Farrah doesn't know I'm onto her. I'm trying my hardest to keep it that way."

"Dante told you," he observed, tone neutral.

He didn't know, or at least I doubted that he did, that Dante and I had started playing house again. "He did. I guess Adelaide has been getting information about my day-to-day life that only someone living with me could have known. Farrah unwittingly outed herself as the one that must be doing it a few days ago. It hasn't been fun, let me tell you."

"I can imagine," he said, tone so warm and sympathetic that it made me shiver. If the Durant men could bottle their voices and sell it, they'd be rich. Oh wait. "You know Adelaide hates me, obviously," he continued. "She despises all of Leo's bastards, but the loathing she has for you is on another level. Don't you find it strange?"

We were still walking, side by side, but I managed to send him an eloquent look out of the corner of my eye. "She *always* has. But then again, I've always been in love with her only son, so maybe it's just that simple. It had to be her worst nightmare, him falling for the town trash."

No one got the joke more than I did. The town's golden boy and its trashcan girl had never made sense to anyone but us.

"My God. When I think of what she's done to you two. You were always so attached to each other. It was apparent. He's been in love with you since the first time I met him. I think he was ten. That she found a way to poison something like that . . . that shit is evil."

That was certainly an apt description of Adelaide.

"You know," he continued, tone lightening. "Dante and I have been talking a lot lately. We have some common ground now. We're even working together to try to get to the bottom of some of Adelaide's schemes. But there's one thing he won't budge on."

He seemed to be waiting for me to say something, but I just kept walking in silence. I didn't want to bring up anything I didn't have to.

"No matter how I pry," he eventually forged ahead, "how much it would help if I knew, he will not tell me what she's blackmailing him for."

Ah. That. I wasn't surprised. Of course Dante wouldn't share that with anyone. It wasn't his secret to tell. It was mine.

My knight-errant had been brought low with his only weakness. Me. It was so glaringly obvious that I couldn't believe I'd allowed myself to miss it for so long.

Even Bastian seemed to catch on without effort. "I figure it's something about you. Something you did. He's been protecting you, hasn't he?"

I stopped walking, eyes shutting tight. God, it hurt. A new pain, worse even than the old one.

When he started talking again, I made myself open my eyes and meet his. "Let's look at it simply. You and I can figure this out, with or without Dante's help. Obviously, we can't *know* what she has on you or him. All we can do is assume she has everything. We have to think in worst-case scenarios. So tell me, Scarlett, what's your deepest, darkest secret?

I shook my head, blank eyes staring straight ahead. "You don't even want to know."

I could see him out of the corner of my eye. He was wearing a small smile, trying to lighten the mood. "How bad could it be?"

I turned my head and met his eyes steadily. "You don't even want to know," I repeated, because it was the truth.

"What? Did you kill somebody?"

He was clearly joking, but my reaction was not a joke. I tensed up, every part of me arrested, automatically going into auto-save mode, still as a statue.

He studied me, eyes widening. He began to curse and did not stop.

Yeah, that.

"No one worth possessing can be quite possessed."
~Sara Teasdale

chapter thirty-one

PAST

Scarlett

We lasted two years in the apartment together.

The plan was always this: We would live in Cambridge until Dante finished school (and he was working very hard to finish as soon as possible), and then, together, we would move to Hollywood so I could pursue acting.

It was a sacrifice for us both. I didn't want to wait for my ambitions, and thanks to some memorably horrible trips with his father when he was younger, Dante hated L.A.

But that's what you did when you loved someone. You sacrificed. And that's why I made it two whole years in Cambridge.

It wasn't all bad. In itself, living with him was everything I could have hoped for. Sometimes we fought, but sometimes the fighting was necessary. Sometimes it was all that made me feel alive.

Dante was wonderful. It was never about him.

It was about me and the way I felt about myself. At the two year mark I began to see that if I spent much more time being useless I was certain I'd never shake it, that I'd just become some bitter, pointless thing. Like my grandma.

I couldn't do that, not even for him.

I needed to find my self-worth, and for that, I needed to leave him.

"I feel like I'm stuck here," I told him over a dessert I'd made special just to soften the blow. "Like I'm giving up my life for yours. Like the longer I stay here, the more I'm just going to shrivel up into someone I don't recognize."

He stared at me. "You said you'd wait for me," he said simply. He didn't even sound upset yet. He was still in denial.

"I did, and I'm sorry. I just can't stand it anymore. I can't stand myself. I need to be doing something besides serving drinks to a bunch of entitled pricks day after day."

That riled him. "That was your idea. I never wanted that. Quit! Just fucking quit! It's that simple. There's no reason for you to be working, especially at a job you can't stand."

I'd gotten off topic, I could see. "That's all beside the point. It's this place. It's being put on hold. I just cannot stand it, Dante. I'm starting hate myself, and I need to find a way to change that. Can't you understand?"

His soulful eyes were tormented on mine. *"You're leaving me?"*

I could barely stand it. I looked away. "I'm not breaking up with yo—"

"Was that a really an option for you?" he asked, incredulous. "You say it like you thought it over, like it could have gone either way?"

"No." I saw the discussion getting away from me. It was going as badly as I'd anticipated. "No. I never thought of that. We'll be together, of course, but long distance. Until you finish here. Then you can come live with me, and in the meantime, I'm not putting my dreams on hold for yours."

It was bad. He didn't take it well. In fact, he refused to talk about it for days, simply telling me it wasn't an option.

Gently but firmly, I replied that it wasn't a question either.

It's an awful thing to realize that even the love of your life can't make you complete, not when you're as fucked up as me, but I was resolute. It would be torture to be away from him for such a long time, but there was no doubt in my mind that we would find our way back to each other. I had absolute faith in that.

A month later I was packing my things, a sullen but resigned Dante hovering over me.

Just setting up the move made me feel a little more hopeful. I'd saved all of my waitressing money—every cent because Dante never let me pay for anything, and put it toward first month's rent on a small studio apartment in an area I couldn't have paid for by myself. Dante put down the last month's rent. Yes, he was helping me. That was the only way he'd let me go without a harder fight.

That and weekend visitations whenever he could manage to fly out or fly me back. Money had its perks, that was a fact.

He came to visit exactly one week to the day I flew away. He came with Gram's ring in his hand and a proposal on his lips.

Well, it wasn't so much a proposal as him telling me that of course we were getting married.

I put on the ring and didn't so much as consider turning him down. This had been a long time coming. Some promises are made before you ever say the words.

"Your mom is going to lose her mind," I told him later, after our third round of celebrating.

He stiffened, the chest under my cheek going stiff, and I knew I'd struck a nerve. "I won't be telling her. No reason to."

I couldn't blame him but a part of me wanted to tell her myself just to see the look on her face. That part was quickly overruled by any common sense I might have had. Even I knew better than to tangle with his mother.

For a time living apart didn't seem to so much as put the tiniest crack in our foundation. I missed him, of course I did, but I had a purpose now. I started to land small roles my first week, and just kept at it, feeling certain that it was my destiny.

And when he did visit, or I visited him, the reunions were a powerful, heady thing. We were combustible together on a normal day. Add a little deprivation to that and it reached atomic proportions. Addictive stuff, that.

We lasted over a year like that. I can't sugarcoat it. We had our ups and downs. It was as tumultuous as we were volatile. Two insanely jealous people living apart while engaged did not make for a smooth romance.

More often than not when he left me or I him, he had scratches on his back from shoulder to ass.

It wasn't that I thought he'd be unfaithful. It was about ownership, marking my territory.

I trusted him almost blindly, but it took a lot less than the thought of actual infidelity to get me hot with temper. Him talking to other girls, being friends with them, popping up in pictures with them on Facebook, studying with them, you name it, I lost my mind.

Needless to say, he was just as out of hand.

If Dante had had his way, we'd have been married the day we were engaged, but I wanted to wait until we were living together for good. Some strange last throwback to hold onto, I guess, something to save special for after the wedding.

On his birthday weekend, roughly a year after the move I'd saved up enough money to buy my own airline ticket and surprise him with a solid three-week visit starting the Friday before his birthday. I had to be crafty to surprise him, so I showed up at his apartment unannounced and let myself in.

I wasn't certain of his everyday schedule. I could guess based on experience, so at six p.m. I figured he'd be home soon, and I simply waited.

And waited. It was midnight when I decided to go out to find him. I was still trying hard not to ruin the surprise. One text inquiring where he was would surely do that.

I started with the closest bar, the rowdy little place I used to work, and there he was.

But whom he was with could not have shocked me more. He was sitting a table, drinking a beer, and sitting across from Tiffany.

I don't know how long I stood there and stared. I was so shocked that I wasn't even angry at first. What could this be? What could it mean?

And as it started to seep in, still, I wasn't angry. I was hurt. And confused.

It didn't take me long to decide to just walk in and confront them.

I wanted to see what he had to say for himself. Needed to.

He was facing the door when I walked in and the movement caught his eye. He glanced up and saw me first.

His reaction was gratifying. He stood up, moving to me, his happiest smile lighting up his face. He caught on right away. "You're surprising me for my birthday," he said, delight in his voice.

I didn't answer with words, instead I waited until he'd moved close and rubbed up against him, pulling his face down to mine.

I brushed my lips to his, once, then again, until he groaned and started kissing me.

I took it further than I meant to. I'd meant to take it somewhere, sure, but what I did was more than I should have, using my mouth on his ruthlessly, my tongue, my body, making him forget where he was, forget that we weren't alone, forget that he couldn't take me right there, making him lose all sense, intoxicating him relentlessly.

It wasn't un-calculated. Of course not. Territory. Marked. Simple but irresistible.

And all the while, something inside of me had begun to rage, incessantly, powerfully.

Oh yes. I was jealous.

When I finally wrenched my mouth away, he bent

and started kissing my neck, his hands rubbing my ass, over and over, our groins flush, his stiff erection digging into me.

Okay, yeah, I'd let it go a touch too far. We hadn't seen each other in a month. Clearly with that much time apart we shouldn't have had our first meeting in public.

"Dante," I said quietly. I was going for composed, but even I could hear the desire in my voice.

He groaned and kissed his way up to my jaw.

Gently but firmly, I pushed him away.

His glassy eyes just stared at me, dazed, for a solid thirty seconds before they began to clear.

He blinked a few times and started to curse, dragging a hand through his hair.

I gave him and myself some time to compose ourselves before I finally spoke. "I've been at your apartment since six. Waiting for you. How's Tiffany?" I let my tone say what my words didn't.

He seemed to realize for the first time that he was in some deep shit.

"Scarlett!" Tiffany called out cheerfully, still sitting at their table. "So happy you could join us!"

Us. The sting of *that* would linger.

Don't let her see how she affects you, I told myself.

Don't let her see how he weakens you. Don't give her anything.

Nothing had changed between Tiffany and me. I still saw her as the enemy. Time and distance hadn't altered that, though this was the first time I'd caught her infringing on my territory while I was away.

Twice she'd come to visit while I was still living with Dante. I wondered with no small amount of furious dread just how often she came to visit now that I was gone.

"Tiffany," I said without an ounce of friendliness. "What are you up to?"

"Oh, you know how it is. Still attending Barnard. Family tradition and all that, but at least I'm almost finished. Soon I'll be able to visit as often as I please."

Comforting that.

"But enough about me. What have you been up to? Still waitressing?"

I looked at Dante. I didn't have to say a word. My face said it all.

"I was here studying," he told me, tone careful. "She found me here a few hours ago. I didn't know she was coming to town."

"Does she visit you like this often?" I asked, voice sharp, my wide smile sharper. It was a grin meant to dazzle. And cut. It captures the eye and blinds it.

"Never," he said succinctly, fervently, with the intent of a man set on avoiding disaster. "Not since you left."

I looked at Tiffany.

"Oh yeah," she waved her hand in the air. "Whatever he says."

I knew she was trying to goad me, trying to make me think Dante was lying to me. I knew that and it didn't surprise me. It was very typical Tiffany. What I found interesting was Dante's reaction to her words.

He started, staring at her like he was finally starting to fucking get it.

Yeah, you ass, I wanted to say. *That's who she is. An instigating piece of work just like your mother.*

But even with the inner tirade, his reaction was gratifying enough to act as a last ditch effort at averting the fallout that I felt building up in my chest like a scream that just had to escape.

I hated that she was here. *Hated it.* But maybe it would serve some purpose, if it helped Dante see just what she was.

With that thought in mind, I pulled up a chair. "So what are you doing here, Tiffany?" I asked her bluntly, my tone as unfriendly as I felt.

She feigned surprise at my hostile manner. "Oh my. Is something the matter, Scarlett? You seem upset." She smiled.

And just like that. There it was again. Hello, temper.

"What could possibly be wrong?" I asked her, heavy on the sarcasm. My eyes swung to Dante, who'd just taken the seat across from me. "Whatever could be the matter?" I asked him mockingly.

He folded his arms across his chest, jaw clenching, eyes hard on me. I could tell that his own hellish temper was ready to come out and play.

"Again," I said bitingly, "why are you here, Tiffany?"

She pursed her lips and answered, "Just visiting my friend. Is that a crime? *He* doesn't mind when I visit. And who made you his boss? He's not your *property*, Scarlett."

I smiled at her, bringing up my ring hand to tap a finger at my jaw, making sure the huge as hell rock on my finger was given proper notice. She saw it, oh yes. Her eyes widened, and for a second she couldn't hide an honest look of dismay.

My smile grew even as I heard Dante let loose with a soft round of cursing.

"Funny you should mention *property*," I said. Yeah, I was being a bitch.

She needed to be put in her place.

Bitch was about the right speed for that.

She'd gone pale. She looked like she might become ill. "When did that happen?" she asked, nearly spitting out the words.

I didn't even try to touch that one.

"Aren't you going to congratulate us?" I countered with instead.

She didn't bother. The engagement bombshell had been enough to knock her off kilter. It was refreshing to see her usually serene facade slip so completely.

I hoped, quite wholeheartedly, that Dante was taking note.

"It doesn't *matter*," Tiffany said derisively. "You still don't own him."

"It doesn't make you happy," I said with relish. "But it *matters*. And yes, I fucking do."

Her reaction was interesting and if I was being spiteful (newsflash: I was), amusing as hell.

She got up and practically ran from the place, fleeing without giving me so much as a backward glance.

I was still wearing a triumphant grin when I caught the look on Dante's face.

"Do you have any idea what you've done?" he asked, looking beyond pissed and into desperately furious. "My mother will know about that ring within the hour. Do you even understand the kind of hell she's going to raise for this?"

"My God," I said slowly, tone as disbelieving as I felt. "You're turning this on *me*? Somehow you're going to get out of having to explain the fact that I found you at a bar with fucking Tiffany!"

"You're the one that *left*. I wouldn't have been alone for her to join if you'd been with me."

Oh hell no.

If he wanted to fight, he'd come to the right place.

"Is that right?" I asked, tone dangerous.

He was feeling lucky, apparently. "Just stating facts, tiger. If you'd kept your promise and stayed here, you wouldn't be so worried about whether Tiffany was paying me surprise visits or not."

A fight it was. "If I can't trust you—" I began.

"That's not what I said. Don't twist this. It was strange timing. I was here reading—"

I rolled my eyes. "Really? Reading at a bar?"

"Yes. I do it a lot, actually. I don't mind the noise. It's nicer than being alone."

Ouch. Yes. Point taken.

"And she just walked up, sat down. I was as surprised to see her as you were."

I studied him with narrow eyes. "And this is the first time she's visited you? Since I left, I mean."

"Yes," he said without hesitating, eyes meeting mine squarely.

"Where is she staying?"

"I have not a clue. I never asked."

"How long was she here before I showed up?"

"A few hours. We mostly talked about everyone from high school. It was a boring conversation, to be honest. I was just being polite."

His straight answers were getting to me. I could barely hold onto my anger when he just told me the truth without prevaricating.

"What would you have done if I hadn't showed up? Would you have let her crash at your place?"

The look he turned on me was real annoyance mixed with a healthy dose of affront. "Of course not. What are you even thinking?"

And just like that, I felt my anger deflating. I bit my lip. "Were you surprised to see me?"

And just like that, he let go of his own anger and smiled. "Yes. How long do I get you for this time?"

"Three weeks."

His smile grew. "Best news I've had in a year. Holy hell, let's go home and celebrate."

And we did. Oh yes, we did.

I woke up the next day with a nasty cold. Fucking airplanes.

If I'd been back in L.A. I'd have just ignored it until it went away. No such luck with Dante. He nagged me until I went to the doctor, who did nothing but give me a ten day round of antibiotics. I bitched and moaned about it, but three days in, I was feeling human again.

It was a minor thing, quickly forgotten, though I'd have reason to dwell on it later.

The three weeks went by in a flash, and it was harder than ever to leave him again, even knowing he'd be joining me in mere months.

Before I left, we went to a local jeweler and found a ring for him. We had it sized to fit his finger, but he wore it around his neck, right next to the key to the cabin we'd shared on our very first time.

I fingered the key as we said our goodbyes in the airport. "I wonder how that old cabin is doing," I mused.

"Gram tells me it's the same as we left it. The locks have never been changed and only we have keys. But it's not about the cabin. It's the memory this holds for me."

I smiled up into his eyes. I loved his sentimentality.

It never failed to touch a nerve. A good one. "Oh yes, I know. And you're never going to take it off, are you?"

"*Never.*" It was heartfelt, that one word, and I felt it deep in my chest.

"Fighting for peace is like screwing for virginity."
~George Carlin

chapter thirty-two

PRESENT

Scarlett

Dante and I were weeks into our addictive, tentative truce when the shit hit the fan.

He'd found out about my visit from Bastian. I wasn't sure if he knew the reason for the visit or if he was suspecting something worse, but his reaction was bad.

I didn't even have to ask him how he'd found out. I knew. His mother had told him. She'd learned a thing from her spy that would hurt him so of course she'd had to share.

"So Bastian, huh?" he said unexpectedly one night over dinner.

I froze, fork halfway to my mouth. Well, shit. Bringing up Bastian was bad, the look on his face was worse, and

I had no idea what to say, because I didn't know what he knew, and I wasn't going to accidentally tell him more.

"I know he came to your house," he added, tone gone black, his hellish temper out to play.

"Fuck," I said softly, with feeling.

"He came to your house, and you left with him." His rage washed over me, hot enough to scald.

But it's a fact that sometimes I like to burn.

I squirmed in my seat. "We only left to talk. Calm down."

"It was Bastian who told you about the blackmail," he guessed. The words were low, almost soft. He was trying very hard not to raise his voice. "Of course it was."

I didn't answer, kept my face perfectly blank, but he didn't need my confirmation.

"It was him," he said, sounding certain. Dammit. "If it were anyone else, the shit would've hit the fan by now. Sneaky son of a bitch."

I just stared at him, trying to gauge just how angry he was. He'd betrayed his rage with the first few things out of his mouth, but he was doing a very good job now of hiding it.

"It was when he came to see you in Seattle, wasn't it?" he asked. The question was filled with the fire of his temper, warm and awful.

I froze.

"I don't know what you're—" I tried, because when you're just not sure if you're about to set a crazy, jealous ex off into a jealous rage it's always best to lie.

"Save it. I know he came to see you, and that must have been when you found out about the blackmail."

I processed that. "Who told you all of this?" I asked, but I knew. Oh, I knew.

"My mother called me earlier. She's been saving this little bombshell for a while. As you know, Farrah keeps her well informed. Adelaide thinks you and Bastian are sleeping together, and she couldn't be more pleased about it. And of course she wanted to make sure I knew every little detail."

"We are not sleeping together. We never have."

"Not even in Seattle? When you went up to his hotel room. For hours."

His eyes were scary, his hands clenched and shaking on the table between us. If I were anyone but myself, I'd have been worried for my safety.

Dammit. This was all going to end up in Bastian's lap, when all the guy wanted to do was help us.

"Nothing happened," I said, tone as unflappable as I could manage, eyes steady on his. "We did go off together, but all we did was talk. About you. About what your mother's been up to."

"You kissed him at the bar." There was the finest tremor in his voice, but it was a crucial one, like the very first crack in an unsteady foundation. "You were all over him. You rubbed your tits against his chest. She told me everything."

Fucking Farrah hadn't gone easy on the details. *FUCK.*

I thought of that night, the state I'd been in, and my own temper rose to the occasion. I knew I had to be mercilessly honest to take the blame away from his brother. That, more even than Dante's feelings, was what I needed to salvage here. "I was in bad shape, Dante. Because of *you*. Yes, I kissed him. Yes, I rubbed up against him. I have no doubt I'd have done more, just to fucking *spite* you, but your brother had your back. While you're going over the details, go over this: He turned me down. Not because he didn't want me, but because he wouldn't do that to you. He came to see me because he wanted to help us, and that was as far as he let it get."

He wasn't looking at me, his eyes on his fists. They were full of cruel, dark things, not the least of which was anguish.

"We have enough things to hate each other for," I added harshly. Honestly. "We don't need to embellish or invent any. I did *not* sleep with your brother. And you can thank *him* for it. Not me. Him."

"*Jesus*, you never did know how to pull any punches," he said in a voice that *ached*.

I felt my upper lip tremble, eyes blinking rapidly, stinging with the urge to tear up as I fought to look anywhere but at him.

Because wasn't that the brutal fucking truth.

"It's worse with you," I said when I'd regained my composure, trying hard to make my voice light. "You're the only guy who ever dumped me."

"Don't do that," he said, and there was agony in it, enough to fell us both. "Don't put us all into a group like we're the same. There's me and there's them."

He made a very good point. Moreover, this was a subject to avoid at all costs. Why the hell had I brought it up? I was a mess just then is why. Not thinking clearly, not speaking clearly, though I needed to start doing so in order to get my point across.

I tried to get back on topic. "There's nothing your mother would love more than to keep you estranged from the one family member you have who's worth knowing," I said as reasonably as I could. "The one person alive that shares your blood and wants to *help you*. Let me guess:

She knows you two have been getting along lately. She knows there's been a truce. Stop me if I'm wrong here."

He didn't stop me.

"Don't let her win," I implored. "Have the sense not to let this tactic work for her. Don't turn this on Bastian."

"I don't trust him," he told me bluntly.

My mouth curved sardonically. "I don't trust *anyone*. What's that got to do with anything?"

He winced and I didn't blame him. I felt the sting of it myself.

"What are you going to do?" I asked him eventually, when I couldn't stand a second more of the silence.

"It was not his place to tell you anything. He had no right to do that. To put you *in danger.*"

"He didn't know that's what he was doing. He's your brother—"

"Half-brother," he corrected stubbornly.

I glared. "He's your blood, and he's trying to help us. Let him, Dante. Please." It was as close as I'd come to begging, because it was a thing worth begging for. We needed any allies we could get, and there was no doubt in my mind that Bastian was a strong one. He was motivated, resourceful. Spiteful. All things I admired. All things I related to. All things we'd need in spades if there was any chance we'd come out on top of this mess.

Also, any enemy of Adelaide's was a freaking best friend of mine.

I couldn't tell if he was still angry, or rather, *how* angry he was. He was being very quiet, very still, not looking at me.

"I suppose I see your point. As always, Adelaide is trying to manipulate me." His voice was calm enough, but I didn't trust it.

"As always," I agreed.

"And it is a sore subject." His eyes flashed at me and I saw the full force of what was still there, simmering under the surface. He wasn't going to lose it, but he was still furious, and it wasn't just going to go away on its own.

Lucky for us, I had just the thing.

I shifted restlessly, biting my lip as I stared right back. His rage was nothing new, nor my reaction to it.

He glared at me, and it didn't help.

Was I turned on?

Absolutely and abundantly so.

It was twisted. And captivating. Irresistible.

He saw it too, and it seemed to piss him off even more. A flame that fed itself perpetually. No wonder we could never get enough of each other.

"Are you done eating?" I asked him. Neither of us had touched our food since the volatile conversation had begun.

He pushed his plate away. "I lost my appetite."

My breath came faster as I pointedly pushed my own plate away, my eyes on his mean mouth. "I didn't," I said, voice teasing, provocative.

He started cursing and I almost smiled. It told me plainly that, though he wasn't happy about it, he was going to listen to what I'd said, absorb it, comply with it.

Round for me.

He pushed his chair back from the table but didn't stand. "Come here." His voice had changed, gone soft and warm and vaguely obscene.

I went to him slowly, leaving my clothing behind as I moved. This would not be the kind of sex that required foreplay, because that part was already over. The fight had been the foreplay. This next bit would be hell-bent, desperate, rough, quick, intoxicating, and straight to the point.

My favorite.

I reached him, and he was ready for me. I turned around, sinking down onto him, guiding him inside of me with one greedy hand.

He bounced me like that on his lap, both of us facing the same way. His mouth at my neck, weaving pure sorcery, licking, sucking, biting, one hand in my hair fisting, stroking, pulling, aiming my face up at the ceiling, the other at my hip, gripping, pawing, operating in tandem with his thrusting hips to work me on his length in heavy, oscillating strokes.

A liquid throb was beating through me. Faster and faster, heavier and heavier.

I turned my head, felt his breath on my face, then his lips.

I was close, so close, when three words panted out of his mouth and straight to my heart.

With a needy cry, I came hard.

He followed with a rough groan.

It was some time later. I was gathering up the clothes I'd discarded all over the dining room. I'm not sure why it was on my mind, why I was thinking so much when I was sated and content, but it was circling there, always circling, waiting to come out.

"Even after everything I did," I said it idly, almost casually, but that was deceptive if you knew how to read me. Dante knew. "You still never told me. Didn't some part of you want to stop protecting me, even from myself, after a while?

He didn't even bother trying for casual. His voice was low, intense, emotional enough that it ached and I with it. "No. No part of me has ever wanted to stop protecting you. Even from yourself. I only wish I'd done a better job. I wish I could have protected you from *everything*."

That hurt as much as it healed, and I found myself bracing against the table, trying to keep my balance as I reeled. I was too conflicted about this. So much so, I felt at war with myself. There was anger there, oh yes, the things he'd kept from me were unacceptable and detrimental, but also there was regret, so much of it. It nearly took me to my knees.

But overriding all of that, the strongest urge was a pervasive softening, a tenderness for my lover who had fought, at all costs, for my freedom.

Tenderness won for the moment, but only with brute force. It was simple: It was the strongest, so it won.

But I had no doubts that the others would be back to fight another day.

Dante noticed my slip, and he lifted me onto the table, perching me there, cupping my face, and tilting it back to study me carefully.

Silently and solemnly, I studied him back. He was a complicated man.

Manipulative. Ruthless. Savage.

In his eyes was an enigmatic power over me that was exclusive to him.

The king of all of my regrets. The architect of every last drop of joy I'd ever tasted.

My tormentor. My savior.

I looked into his eyes and saw the infinite universe, because everything I needed was in them. It all ended and began right here, with us. It always had.

Now if there was only some way we got to keep it.

I wondered with no small amount of trepidation

whether Adelaide would ruin us this time, or if we'd do it to ourselves.

Dante, clearly, had other things on his mind.

He moved between my thighs, his tireless cock hard and ready again.

He fucked me on the edge of the table, my body jarring sensually, jolting and bouncing tantalizingly with each thrust, his hands anchored on my hips to keep me on the edge, poised at the perfect angle, eyes on mine to the very last.

He only looked away for one brief moment when he came, when his spine bowed backwards, neck arching as he lunged to the end of me and held himself there.

Watching him lose it brought me over, both hands clinging to his nape, eyes devouring him like he might disappear.

Afterwards he carried me to bed, which was fitting. I let him. I was limp, too weak to stand, let alone walk, and it was all his fault.

"If you're losing your soul and you know it, then you've still got a soul left to lose."
~Charles Bukowski

chapter thirty-three

PAST

Dante

The moment I entered my apartment I knew something was wrong. I didn't see anything at first glance, nothing was messed up or askew. It was more of a feeling in the air. A presence where there should have been only emptiness.

But I didn't see anyone. The entryway was empty, as well as the living room. The small dining room, as well.

But it was there that I saw something different.

On the table, splayed out in a fan, was a thick stack of eight by ten pictures.

Something sharp and unpleasant twisted in my gut.

Before I ever saw what they contained, I felt sick enough to wretch.

I knew. Somehow, I just knew that I was looking at my ruin.

I approached the table with no small amount of trepidation.

I didn't touch the pictures. Much like finding the scene of a crime, I didn't dare disturb it or leave behind any sort of mark.

But I could see clearly enough just what they were. Photos of the trailer Scarlett had grown up in. The outside of it. The inside of it. Pictures that very clearly told the story of the darkest day of my life.

Pictures that painted my guilt, and worse, hers, in stark, vivid red strokes.

My mind raced as I tried to figure out how someone had taken them; how I was only just now seeing that we had clearly been found out.

Someone had been watching. Someone had seen it all. The ramifications added a new horror to it all.

Someone had known what was happening to her and hadn't stopped it. Instead they had built a case that I could tell at a glance could not and would not be disputed.

They hadn't gotten shots of anything going on inside of the trailer until after I had carried her out, but that was about all they'd missed.

There was a barrage of photos of me carrying her limp body out that eventually led to pictures of the body still in Scarlett's old bed.

I didn't realized I'd taken a seat, head clutched in my hands, still staring at the horrors in front of me, until Adelaide entered the room.

I looked up, still too shocked to react.

It was offensive how put together she looked, how

polished she'd made sure to be for the destruction of her only child. The crazy bitch was even wearing her favorite pearls.

Her eyes raked over me with spectacular disdain. "Checkmate," she said with relish.

She was my mother and the architect of my destruction.

"We all have a weakness, my son, and I always knew that someday I'd find yours."

"It looks like you managed to find it quite some time ago," I choked out.

I never bothered to ask her why. I knew. Control was everything to her. My whole life we'd been locked in a struggle for power, and while I'd just been fighting for freedom, she'd been playing to *win*.

"What do you want?" I asked her. All was not lost just yet. Perhaps we could negotiate.

"Dump that piece of trash, for starters. Leave her and marry Tiffany."

I wanted to kill her. I looked at my mother and pictured wrapping my hands around her neck and choking the life out of her.

She smiled like she was reading my mind. "I'm not the only one that knows. You think I don't have a backup plan? I have several."

"I could just say no. I'll turn myself in. I'll take the punishment. I'll do the time."

"I know everything. You weren't even there when the shots were fired. She killed him. She killed a cop, and she'd never let you take the fall for her. That girl is a fool. She'd go down with you." She smiled when she caught my unguarded reaction to that. "You know it as well as I do. If you go down, you'll go down together. Pick your poison, son. My way, or yours."

"I won't marry Tiffany. Not fucking happening. Dream on."

She shrugged as though she'd been expecting that. She probably had. "An engagement then. One year. Give it a chance. You might find it's to your liking to be with a girl of your own class. And if it's not, feel free to break it off. Whatever. So long as you don't taint the family tree with that Theroux girl, I'll let you do what you like."

"A year? No fucking way."

"Six months then."

"And that's it? You just expect me to stay away from Scarlett indefinitely? No. I'll take my chances the other way."

"Five years. Stay away from her for five years, and I'll leave you alone. That'll be long enough, I think, for you to realize what a silly idea she was. Time enough for you to grow up and grow out of her."

"And in five years, if I go back to her, you'll just let me?"

She shrugged. "You won't. You'll have forgotten her name by then, but if by some miracle you haven't, fine, you can go play with the trash to your heart's content."

It was a frightfully quick interaction. My entire life changed in a few short sentences, a handful of minutes.

My mother insisted on being present when I called Scarlett. She didn't trust me to go through with any of it on my own.

I had no opportunities to warn Scarlett, to try to make it better, to do anything but what I was instructed to, which was brutal and swift.

I went a little numb as I made the call.

I knew just what to say. That part was simple.

It was too easy to convince her. She was always waiting to be abandoned, to be thrown away. I knew that.

"This doesn't work anymore. We don't work," I heard myself saying at one point. Nonsense like that rolled out of my mouth, my eyes on my mother all the while.

Her freedom or her love. Those were my choices.

It was no choice at all, but it broke us all the same.

"A man can be happy with any woman as long as he does not love her."
~Oscar Wilde

chapter thirty-four

PRESENT

Dante

We'd lapsed into some semblance of normal faster than I could have hoped for.

We had our issues. Of course we did. Our history was long and destructive. I knew we'd be working through some of it for years. I'd never been naive enough to imagine otherwise. Not for one second had I ever been that delusional.

I tried my best to be patient. I tried my hardest to stay hopeful when I saw her internalizing everything when what was needed between us, now more than ever, was communication. I let things slide, let issues drop that perhaps I shouldn't have, all with the assumption that she just needed more time.

It wasn't easy, though.

And it wasn't natural, or right.

I thought I was showing some rather impressive restraint with her and her boundaries, but sometimes I just could not take it.

It was when I caught her face in the moments when she didn't realize I was near. It was what I saw when she wasn't trying to hide that made me realize how much she was keeping bottled up inside.

The haunted look in her eyes, the pain embedded into her every unguarded expression. All of it spoke of the burdens she was carrying. Alone.

That I could not take. That I could not let slide.

It was dark out. I'd just come home, but she'd beaten me to it, for once. They must have wrapped up early for the day.

She was out on the balcony attached to our bedroom, wearing a bathrobe, her hair still wet. She was hugging herself like she had nothing else in the world to hold onto, her posture one of defeat, her face set into stark lines. The eyes she aimed out at the night were full of vile things, old memories, old nightmares.

My God, where did she go when she did this to herself?

I could hardly stand to even guess it.

And I could not take it. Could not take another day with her doing this to herself.

I joined her out on the balcony, loosening my tie as I moved.

She started when I opened the door, turning to me.

She schooled her face when she realized she wasn't alone, but I'd seen it, every last ounce of the despair still written on her.

I held out my arms to her, but she wouldn't even take that.

She shook her head, turning back to stare out at the night.

"Don't be like that, tiger," I teased her, pressing myself against her back, mouth at her ear.

She was in no mood to be teased. "Listen," she said, voice tense and brittle. "I'm not saying this to pick a fight, but sometimes I just need to be alone. I don't want to be comforted. I just want to be alone."

That was foreign and wrong. "Not anymore. That's not what we're doing. We never used to hide things from each other, and we're not going to do that now. If you have a burden, you share it with me. We take the weight together. That's how this works. Whatever's troubling you, we'll get through it."

"No," she said, and I could feel the way her shoulders set stubbornly against me. "I'm in no mood, Dante. Not right now."

Just as she could stir my desire with a glance, she knew how to invoke my temper just as quickly. There was an edge to my words as I responded, "Yes, I know. You prefer being alone. Let's try anyway."

"You don't know," she said, her voice soft. "You really have no idea."

Soft or hard, it was the last fucking straw. I was tired of hearing it, the same words spoken for different reason, all with a meaning known only to her. I was sick of her saying it, but even more sick of her using it as a shield against me. "What don't I know? Let's have it. About the men? I know about *every single one*. And frankly, if there's something that could hurt me more than them I can't *imagine* it."

That set her off. Of course it did. It was unfair of me to mention it, even if it was only the absolute truth.

She shrugged me off, moving a few angry strides away to glare. "What about you? Do you really have the nerve to go *there*? You were no saint when we were apart."

To tell or not to tell. Which thing was more hurtful? More lies or the savage, unbelievable truth?

"A saint? No. Of course not. Not for a day in my life." I took a very deep breath, let it out. This was going to be bad, but I was done dealing with her in lies. "But there were no other women." I rolled my tongue around my mouth and added, "Not *one*."

Simple. Complex. Hurtful.

She sent me a look that was as crushed as it was disbelieving. "What? What are you saying? I saw you. I fucking saw you! What the fuck are you talking about?" She was close to screaming by the end.

Even as she questioned me, I saw that she was starting to understand it, to believe.

"Everything with Tiffany was fake. Part of the arrangement I made with my mother. I agreed to a six-month engagement with her to keep you out of prison, but it was a ridiculous failure. I never so much as kissed her. I agreed to those pictures for the same reason, but it was all fake. I never touched her beyond what you saw."

She was backing away from me, hands in her hair, pulling.

She looked deranged and completely heartbroken.

I couldn't stand it. For every step she retreated, I advanced. We would get this out so we could work past it. It was as simple as it was hurtful, and I was determined to get it done. To put it behind us, if that were possible.

"Liar," she said, voice weak, tears running down her face.

I just stared at her for a beat, two, letting her see in my face my absolute sincerity. "I've told plenty of lies. I can't deny that. But I promise you I'm not lying about this."

She pointed a shaking finger at me. "Tiffany was one. One. I saw the others, too. Woman after woman you paraded in front of me. You think I forgot? You think I'd forget even one of them?"

I winced. It was a stretch to say I didn't have a lot of things to be ashamed of, but that petty revenge had been the most selfish. "Fake. All of them. I took them out, made sure you saw. Took them home. I was a perfect gentleman with every *single* one. You thought I'd betrayed you in the worst, most unthinkable way. You had an excuse for the things you did. And, while I was angry enough to want to *hurt* you, I could never make myself betray you fully. Not like that."

She studied my face, eyes moving desperately over every inch, seeking a lie, almost hoping for it.

She didn't find one.

I was closer by then, but that didn't work in my favor.

She lost her mind. Hitting, scratching, attacking me with blind determination and absolute abandon.

It was awful. I had to subdue her bodily, carry her inside. I pinned her struggling to the bed because I thought that she might hurt herself.

I was holding her down, trying to calm her, my voice soothing, as composed as I could manage.

But make no mistake. I was affected. By her pain. By my own. Shaken by it. Trembling with it.

Nothing seemed to help. I was at my wits end when I

asked her in dismay, "Did you *want* me to be with other women?"

"Of course not," she almost screeched at me. "No. You don't get it at all. Don't you see, though, that it's so much easier to forgive *your* sins than it is to forgive mine? Do you think I needed another score against myself? Do you think I don't hate myself *enough*?"

I did understand something about that. Self-hatred was an old, familiar friend, and this night was rife with it.

I shut my eyes, touching my forehead softly to hers. She allowed me to for a moment.

"We'll get past this," I told her tenderly. "We'll work through it all. The worst is past."

That had her struggling anew. I was so caught off guard by it that she was up and across the room before I could react.

I'd barely risen from the bed when she slammed the bathroom door closed and I heard it lock.

Well, fuck.

I knocked and asked her nicely to come out. She ignored me.

I offered through a clenched jaw if she'd prefer that I break the door down.

"Fuck you!" she called back, the last word a sob. "I'm directly on the other side. If you break it down, you'll hurt me."

Well, fuck. Even when she was near hysterical, she understood well how to stop me in my tracks.

Because I was good at it, I quickly resorted to dirty tricks.

It only took me a minute to walk down the hall, snatch our sleeping kitten from its favorite spot, and carry it back to the bedroom.

I sat with my back to the bathroom door, the still sleeping kitten cradled against me.

I could feel her on the other side of the door, her body propped up against it.

"Diablo is trying to get to you," I told her. "She's crying. She misses you."

Her voice came muffled and forlorn. "No, she's not. I'd hear it if she was."

"She's so sad, tiger. Baby wants her mama."

For some reason, that set her off sobbing the hardest of all.

I turned, leaning my forehead against the door. Sometimes it felt like my whole life was this. Waiting on the other side of the door from her, hoping to be let in.

Diablo was awake by then, rubbing up against my stroking fingers and purring loud enough that I wondered if Scarlett could hear her through the wall.

"She's really upset, tiger," I tried again. "Don't you want to at least check on her?"

"You're mean!" she called back, sounding like a forlorn child.

It made my heart turn to a tender pile of mush in my chest.

"My white flag is up, tiger. I won't say one more upsetting thing tonight if you'll just unlock the door."

"It's not you I'm worried about," she said, dread in her voice.

Wasn't that the damn truth. "I can take it. What I can't take is a locked door between you and me. C'mon, angel. Let me in."

Diablo was a good wing kitten. Suddenly and loudly, as though she'd just realized Scarlett was close, she let out a loud and plaintive *meow*. And then another.

Slowly the door opened behind me. She leaned down, plucked Diablo from my arms, and moved away, not toward the bed but to the chaise in the corner.

She sat down, not looking at me, and restlessly stroked her hand over the kitten's fluffy coat, over and over.

I thought that was the end of it, but our demons were not finished with us yet.

I rose, was about to move to her, when she said, voice low and accusing, "I should have had a choice. You should have *given* me a choice."

I didn't have to clarify what she was talking about. I knew. I fucking knew. And just like that, I was furious again. "A *choice*?" I asked her bitingly.

"Yes. You had choices. You could have told your mother to go to hell, consequences be damned. I didn't have that privilege."

"Privilege? You're going to call that a privilege? To go to fucking prison? That's what you wanted? That was *never* an option. I would *never* have allowed that, and you fucking know it."

"Look at what you did allow! Was that any better? I'd have taken prison over what you let her do to us. That's a fact."

"No. No. No." I felt my head shaking, over and over. She was about two sentences away from me losing my temper. I felt my rage taking over and told myself to walk away. But I just couldn't do it. We had to fucking have this out. "Not an option. Not a fucking option."

"I should have had the choice," she repeated.

I pointed an unsteady finger at her, upper lip quivering with fury. "This is why. This is why I couldn't tell you. I'd have taken the fall for this; it was a solution I could have stomached, but you, you stubborn . . . "

She curled my lip at me. "What? Say it."

"Would you have let me take the fall for you?" I knew the answer. I'd always known. Her stubborn pride had ruined us both.

I could tell she wanted to lie, just for the sake of winning this argument, but she couldn't do it, she was too righteously furious for that. "Of course not. Never. I would *never* have stood by and let you take the fall for something *I* had done."

My eyes were wild, screaming at her. "See?" I was shouting now. "This was why you didn't get the choice! I know you, and I knew what you would do. If you can't forgive me for that, I don't know what to do, but I still don't see that I had another way. I won't apologize for protecting you the only way I knew how."

She knew I didn't. I could see it in the resigned eyes she turned on me.

Even she, the mother of all grudge-holders, could only hold a grudge for so long.

"I'm tired of hating you," she said quietly, a world of regret in it. "When all my heart has ever needed is to love you." Those words were so very hard for her, I could tell, and the next ones were harder. "For helping me survive for so long, for going through hell with me and getting me, somehow, to the other side of it intact, I *will* learn to forgive you. Even with all of the ways you've destroyed me, I could never forget all of the ways you've saved me, Dante."

"You saved me, too. Never forget that, either."

"And destroyed you," she said the words lightly, but they held all the weight in the world. For both of us.

I smiled and it was so bittersweet that she had to look away. "Yes. Broken. Destroyed. But now saved again.

It's enough for me. You are. You always were. I have many demons. But only one angel."

Now the problem, of course, was that she had to learn to forgive herself.

We both did.

It was later. We were in bed and she was tucked securely against my chest.

When I spoke, it was a quiet whisper into the night. "You learn more about someone when you're fighting them than you do loving them. Things you can only learn from war. We know each other in ways we wouldn't have. Maybe it wasn't all in vain. I love you in more complex ways than I did before. I understand you more intimately."

"You're a fool," she said forlornly into my chest.

"I know, tiger. Believe me, I know."

"I love you for it."

"I know, angel. That, too."

"Terror made me cruel."
~Emily Brontë

chapter thirty-five

PAST

Scarlett

It was almost nonsense to me—what he was saying. I only caught snippets, broken off sentences, half-phrases, but my numb brain slowly put it together. He was ending things.

The conversation only lasted minutes, mere minutes to take everything I held sacred and tear it open, rip out the insides, and smash them under his heel.

When he was finished, I felt diminished. Like I was nothing. Like I always had been.

I should have not been so surprised. I should not have been surprised at all, really.

The only real mystery here was that he'd ever tried to love me in the first place.

Even so, my pain was breathtaking.

I was inconsolable, and he did not even *try* to console me. He said his piece and hung up the phone.

It was devastating. Life changing. When you have felt like nothing with that much certainty, you never come back from it. Even if you manage to piece yourself up, a part of you stays in the gutter where you were left. Always.

It was a live or die moment. A get yourself off the ground or stay down and let this end you event. Walk away and leave him behind, or stay and let this kill you, kill yourself just to see if he'll bleed out with you.

I always thought I was too strong to be broken by anything. I always told myself that, at least.

But love changes you. No matter how strong you are, it makes you stronger. No matter how weak you are, it makes you weaker. No matter how hard you are to conquer, it will bring you to your knees.

A part of me held onto a small bit of denial. For days I held onto it. I couldn't get out of bed, but I held on. It couldn't be real.

It had been Dante's voice, but it hadn't been him. An imposter had broken me. Somehow Dante would make it right.

I was holding onto that delusion for dear life when I started receiving the texts. One after another. The first was only words, short and to the point.

This is Tiffany. Dante and I are getting married. Just thought you should know before it's announced publicly. He would like Gram's ring back.

I was still staring at that bit of evil when the next message came in.

Oh and I thought you should see these. Enjoy.

What followed was a furious flow of picture texts, one after the other, all showing roughly the same thing.

Him with her.

My God. *Her? Tiffany?*

Turns out it was right there in our foundation all along—the thing that would break us. *Her?*

The intimacy of it is what killed me.

He was supposed to be mine. Inarguably. Irrevocably. Every part of him, inside and out, belonged to me.

I'd never seen him so much as touch another girl's hand, and there he was, in picture after picture.

Sprawled on his back, being straddled, hands on her slender, naked hips.

That's what felt like the biggest betrayal, that he'd hidden it so thoroughly from me, this other side of him.

That his devotion to me could be nothing but a lie.

And just like that, the delusions, the denial, were gone.

I won't deny it. Those pictures broke me, took something precious inside of me, and left a hollow shell behind.

I did some terrible things after. Unforgivable things. Because I was lost, broken, and afraid.

Nate was just too easy of a mark. Too convenient. Too perfect for my purpose; which was, of course, revenge.

He came to me, flew all the way out to L.A. just to comfort me.

I let him, or at least let him try, let him go through the motions, hugging me, holding me, whispering reassurances.

I let him think he seduced me. I let him think that I wanted him back, as much as he wanted me, that I cared, that I was even capable of feeling, that anything he said or did or felt got through to me.

Nothing did, but I must have faked it convincingly enough.

I let him think that I loved him. I let him think that I would marry him.

I did it all for one reason. An obvious, vengeful one.

Nate was in the shower when I intercepted a call for him from Dante.

I was feeling particularly hateful when I answered it with a purring, "Hello, Dante."

Silence on the other end.

That was fine. I had enough to say for both of us. "Nate's in the shower. He's not like you. He doesn't like to wear his sex, always has to get cleaned up right after. Can I take a message for you?"

He managed to make out some word-like noises, something like, "Don't. No. Please, no."

"Too late. We did. Many times. Did he tell you? He proposed. I said yes. You're not invited to the wedding."

"Oh my God. What did you do, Scarlett? *What did you do?*"

I shuddered at the awful, anguished sound of his voice. I could feel his pain, reaching out across the distance, over the miles that separated us. Moving north to south. East to west.

Racing over mountains, across roads and through cities, flowing down from him to me.

It pounded out to me until it felt like my own pulsing hurt.

Every gory bit of us was strewn and twitching in the space between us.

"I think that's pretty obvious," I managed to get out. "Do you want me to spell it out for you? Would you like me to send *pictures*?"

"You're heartless," he told me, sounding like he couldn't quite believe it.

Like he thought I would deny it.

I did not. "Of course I am. Did you think I wouldn't be? You were my heart. And you left."

The sounds he made then were almost comforting in their familiarity, anguished, desolate noises that matched perfectly just how I'd felt since he'd left and taken not just my heart, but my soul with him.

So he wasn't over me. He still felt something.

It was humiliating how relieved I was.

I needed him to feel. Needed him to hurt, needed his wounds to throb in time with my own.

Needed to bring him to my hell.

At least then I would not be alone here.

A small distinction but a real one.

So I couldn't have him. At least I would still have the satisfaction of knowing that we suffered together.

"And what about you, Dante?" I finally managed to choke back at him. "Where did *your* heart go?"

"You still have it." He lobbed it at me like an accusation.

The bastard.

"And you can *keep it*," he continued, voice ragged, breath uneven. "But I'm *finished* with you. *Finished*. We are done."

And that was that. As he'd said, we were finished. Of course we were. We were beyond all repair.

I broke it off with Nate—he'd served his purpose. I wasn't kind about it. I didn't tell any pretty lies to soften the blow. I'd never loved him. I didn't want him. No, it had not been good for me. I'd only slept with him to hurt somebody else.

A week after I sent him from my sight I got a call from Nate's mother. He was in the hospital. He'd tried to kill himself with a bottle of pills. He'd live, but he was a mess.

She blamed me as much as I blamed myself and told me to stay the hell away from her son.

I was only too happy to comply. Relieved was an apt word for it.

And so it went. I became completely rootless for a very long time.

And I hated Dante with what little there was left of my heart.

"Your task is not to seek love, but merely to seek and find all the barriers within yourself that you have built against it."
~Rumi

chapter thirty-six

PRESENT

Scarlett

I should have never brought it up. Okay, I didn't. It wasn't like it was a choice.

Nate called me while I was in the bathroom. I'd left my phone out on the bed.

Dante saw. It was bad.

Worse than rage, though that was there. It hurt him, wounded him deeply that I was in contact with his old friend.

"You know what happened after I broke it off with him," I told him, attempting to explain myself. "I was on a warpath after we ended, and I wasn't just callous with him. I was cruel. I felt—feel bad for him. At Gram's funeral he said he wanted to start talking again—as friends—and so I agreed."

"What happened between me and him," I said falteringly. "You shouldn't take out on him. It was me. I'd have done anything back then just to get your attention, just to hurt you how I was hurting."

He was shaking his head, lip curled up in disgust. "No. Bullshit. Did you know *I* sent Nate to you to comfort you? He was supposed to help you, because I couldn't. Instead he took advantage. I'll never forgive him for that."

My God. I hadn't known that. Just when you think a thing can't be worse, some new evil is added into the mix just for panache.

Story of my life.

"I won't stand for it. You need to stop talking to him." His voice was clipped, curt to the point of rude, demanding to the point of ordering. "Cut off all contact. Immediately."

I opened my mouth to argue with him, just on principle I suppose, instinctual contrariness, but then I stopped myself. He was right. If we were going to work, there were some things you couldn't take back, people you couldn't have around, reminders that you couldn't keep close—not for any reason.

It took one insanely jealous person to be sensitive enough to understand another. "Fine," I said carefully.

I made the mistake of thinking that was the end of it, but it seemed fated to be one of those days. The phone call had started it, set the tone, and after that, we were just at each other's throats. Thin-skinned and feeling destructive.

It was some random dig he made over some silly thing that had me taking it a step too far, delving into things I wasn't ready for.

"God, can't you *ever* just say you're sorry? For *anything*?" I asked him heatedly, but more than temper, there was pain in it.

"You want apologies? I see. What exactly should I apologize for? Tell me, tiger, please. Where would I *even* begin?"

Hello, temper. Again. Because every sentence out of his mouth held something in it, some bit of appeal that was the apology in itself, that told me he was sorry for everything, that somehow he'd taken it all on himself, added it to his cursed martyrdom, and I was supposed to have known it.

"I'll apologize for anything you ask," he said quietly, "but that's not the issue. What you're missing is not my contrition, and I think you know it."

I waved him off. "You're blowing things out of proportion."

"You need to find your faith in us again," he said with quiet intensity.

And just like that, he had me. I'd gone from annoyed and argumentative to sad and desolate. "I don't know how," I said, voice raw with the helplessness of it.

His eyes softened, and just like that I was in his arms. We were out on the back porch, and he sat down in one of the loungers, cradling me on his lap.

He stroked a hand over my hair, then again. "Do you remember when my touch used to comfort you? Do you remember when it brought you peace?"

I couldn't even speak, my eyes closed. I remembered too much.

It filled my whole being, the remembering.

Eventually I nodded, but not before rogue tears were seeping past my eyelids.

"I can be ruthless." His voice was quiet but vehement. "I can be mean. I can be jealous, and wrathful. I have a hellish temper." Whisper soft, his fingers traced over my tears. "We both know this too well. There have been times where I was *so angry* with you that I didn't think I ever wanted to set eyes on you again."

He paused, just stroking and stroking my hair, his touch tender and steady, and it seemed he wanted some response from me.

Finally I nodded.

He continued. "I can be manipulative, and I know I've done some things you don't agree with, things you don't understand. Things that sorry does not, and will not, cover. I know that at times your faith in me has been lost."

For some reason one tiny, hapless sob escaped me at his last sentence, and he paused for a moment, comforting me, before he continued. "But search your heart, angel, and tell me, and yourself, if you believe that any of my actions, no matter how messed up, or misguided, no matter how *unforgivable* they may have been . . . Ask yourself, do you truly believe that any of the things I did weren't for you? We can disagree on my methods, but do you have any doubts that what I did, I did to protect you?"

I didn't answer, just let him rock me, and stroke me, wipe my tears, and comfort me. All the while, I was doing as he said, searching through my ravaged heart.

"Find the answer to that question, and you'll find your faith again."

I'd had my eyes closed for a long time, but when I opened them, I found him doing something that helped me to see the truth.

He was rubbing the chain around his neck, rolling the key and rings between his fingers—Gram's ring had been added—over and over, like it was a very old habit. For the first time in years, I let my hand cover his, let the pad of my index finger trace over the objects, let it linger on them, remembering them.

His shoulder jerked as he shook off a shudder. "You get it. I know you do."

"You never took them off. Even at the worst of it, you kept them on as reminders."

"Touchstones, yes. They help to calm me. And they help me remember what we are. What we're supposed to be. That no matter what, we'll find our way back to each other."

I was crying, but so was he. "No matter what," I agreed quietly.

I'd been so blinded by my own hurt and fear for so long where he was concerned, but when I let go of my doubt, my pain, my insecurity, I really did know him.

His soul was mine and always had been. I couldn't deny that if I tried now that the truth was out.

"If all else perished, and he remained, I should still continue to be; and if all else remained, and he were annihilated, the universe would turn to a mighty stranger."
~Emily Brontë

chapter thirty-seven

PAST

Scarlett

Hollywood parties were the worst. I hated them, had relegated them to one of the more miserable parts of networking in tinsel town. A necessary evil that had to be borne with a big fake smile and plenty of liquor.

This one was being thrown in one of the trendy new clubs in Hollywood. It was a big space, surprisingly well-lit for a den of iniquity, and it was full to the brim with people I needed to meet.

I was still taking it all in, scoping out the best place to mingle/network. My bored eyes swept across the room for maybe the third time as I tried decide where I wanted to spend my energy and charm, when they landed on a pair of cold eyes that I had not expected to see again.

Eyes that were more familiar even than my own.

I froze, drink halfway to my parted lips.

No. Oh no, please. Not now. I haven't had a moment to pull myself together. It's not fair. He's not allowed to see me first, to catch my initial reaction.

Because it would surely be the most telling.

I blinked, recovered, then took a long drink.

It had been well over a year since I'd seen him, and the things that had occurred since our last parting and now . . . I couldn't even stand to glance at him across a crowded room.

But some part of me, the lovesick, pathetic part that I'd have cut out of myself if it were possible, rejoiced at the sight of him.

And the way he looked then, it was something to behold.

There was a woman clinging to him, a beautiful black-haired woman, and as I studied her, I realized it was an actress. No one terribly famous, more of an up and comer who was talked about often in the industry of late. Her name was dropped in a lot of gossip rags for potential roles, but nothing she'd done had panned out in a big way yet.

Still, she was certainly more famous than I was. No contest. And he'd come here with her. It was clearly the most hurtful scenario he could dream up.

Well, close to. Tiffany would have been the *most* hurtful, obviously.

Always.

The actress was, of course, young and lovely, wearing a clingy, red Versace dress I could remember ogling in this month's Italian Vogue. She was fashionable and beautiful and would likely be the next 'it' girl, and Dante barely seemed to notice that one of her perky little tits was trying to permanently meld itself into his bicep.

Of course the too good-looking for his own good Durant heir could have any woman he set his sights on. I'd never had any doubts about that.

His eyes were on me, his body stiff, his fists clenched as he watched me like we were the only two people in the room, and just the sight of me had stopped him in his tracks.

I smiled. Maybe there was some fun yet to be had in this misery trip down our fucked up memory lane.

I could do this. I could suffer through this pain if it was for the sake of making him suffer with me.

Ah, love. Isn't it grand?

I finished my drink and tore my eyes from his, seeking my date for the night.

Justin was a screenwriter who had developed a pretty devoted crush on me when I'd first moved to town. He got me into all of the parties I hated to attend but could never say no to. In exchange I'd been stringing him along rather relentlessly.

I spotted him doing a line off the bar a scant ten feet away. He was still wiping his nose when I finally caught his eye. I called him over with a crook of my finger.

He blinked a few times, swallowed hard, and came to me looking hopeful enough to stir some pity in me.

Not enough. But some.

He was very cute, tallish and trim, but muscular, with nerdy glasses that only seemed to add to his boyish handsomeness.

"Darling, something's come up," I purred at him, grabbing the lapels of his jacket and moving our faces close. "I've got to run."

He looked confused, but didn't ask questions and didn't try to stop me. He was my favorite kind of man, the kind that let me do whatever the hell I wanted without protesting. He was just happy to be along for the ride.

Until, of course, I left him on the side of the road, as I inevitably would.

I pressed my chest to his and gave him a brief, warm kiss. It stirred nothing in me.

Hardly anything did these days.

It was a show, no more, but I could tell as I pulled away that he'd taken something from it that he shouldn't have.

I'd given him hope.

"When will I see you again?" he asked me.

I wanted to pat him on the head, the poor guy, but I just pursed my lips and shrugged. "Who knows? I'll text you sometime. Or you can call me when there's another good party."

I walked away from him and headed straight for my real target.

It was pure misery to walk toward Dante, to make my body move closer to him instead of *away*, but at least there was some gratifying thrill to be had in the way he looked at me. That little kiss had done the trick, taken him from incensed ex-lover to enraged mess.

Perhaps I'd win this round after all.

His date had stepped away, to network no doubt, and so it was easy to move right up to him. I strutted close, not stopping until I was a mere foot away, going straight for the kill.

He was here to mess with me, so I'd mess right back.

And I happened to be better at making messes than he was, if I did say so myself.

I looked up into his face, letting every bit of the spite, the pure, concentrated hatred in my eyes pour out to him.

"If I were you, I'd stay far away from me," Dante warned.

The way his voice quavered, the weakness in him, the unchecked violence in every line of his body, was nothing but blood in the water.

I stepped closer with a smile. "You're not me." It was that simple and that devastating. We were not one anymore.

We were two. Two very separate people now with little to connect us.

And it was all his fault.

I was not done making him pay for that.

Not even close.

He was almost panting as I brushed my body against his. "Your date is not going to be happy about this." His voice was a low rumble, his eyes aimed over my head, at Justin, I presumed.

"No, he won't be. He wants me, can you tell? He's been obsessed with me for a while now and seeing me with you will only add to it. But I'm too curious to pass this up. What are you doing here? Are you really going to try to tell me that this is a coincidence?"

"Yes," he lied, not even trying to convince me, his voice too full of raw emotion. "I'm dating an actress, and she wanted me to come to one of her Hollywood parties. That's the only reason I'm here." He said it robotically, as though he'd rehearsed the phrase, but his delivery ruined it all.

I saw right through him.

I believed that he was dating that actress, and I believed he'd been invited here. What I did not believe was that he hadn't known or suspected that I'd be here.

What I did not believe was that he hadn't come here for *me*.

"Did you bring your own car?" I asked him, my smile now mischievous bordering on malevolent. "I rode with my date, so either he takes me home or someone else does." I was daring him to tell me no.

I wanted, *needed* to see if he even had it in him.

I wanted to *wound* myself on that knowledge, to use the sharp finality of it to cut myself free.

But alas, he did not, which was why I would *never* be free.

He didn't even answer, just grabbed my wrist and started moving, leaving his date and mine to watch on in baffled affront.

We were in his car driving furiously away before I spoke again. "Where are you taking me?" I asked him.

His eyes were wild, his hands clenching the steering wheel so hard that his knuckles were white. "Does it matter?" he finally asked.

I touched a hand to his leg and his thigh muscle jerked in agitation. "Take me somewhere outside. Somewhere with a view. I want to watch the sunset while you're inside of me."

I studied his face intently while I said it, saw him flinch then harden. "I didn't come here for this," he uttered softly.

"Well, then you're a fool. What did you come here for?"

His mouth twisted so bitterly that I had to look away. "To see you. Just to look at you and see if there was still any part of you left that I recognized."

My head snapped back and I leaned toward him,

grabbing him crudely. "I found something of *you* that I recognize. The only part of you that I miss seems to be about the same."

He tore my hand off him, flinging it away. "How could you?" His voice was wretched with agony as he finally got to the point, to the ugly, rotten root of it all. *"How could you?"*

I felt nothing but fury at his pain. I was too wrapped up in my own. "How could I? *How could I?* How could you? *How could you?*"

He was shaking his head, over and over. "You don't understand. You don't know anything."

"I know you were engaged to fucking Tiffany, and that's all I ever need to know for the rest of my fucking life. You wanted to break me? Well, you did it, and today is your lucky day, because now you get to fuck what's left. Are you happy?"

His face was flushed, his eyes blinking so rapidly that I thought for a moment that he was going to cry. *"Jesus.* How did it come to this? *Jesus.* How did *we* end up like *this?"*

"If you don't know then nobody does, because you fucking brought us here."

"I know, angel," he whispered. "But believe me, I am *not* happy. If it makes you feel better, you can be sure that I will *never* be happy again."

It was something. A few drops of cool water to dampen the inferno that lived inside of me.

He had thrown me away, but at least he could *never* move on from me, not completely. He was no more capable of that than I was.

It wasn't long before he pulled the car deep onto the shoulder and put it in park. He'd taken me to a spot that fit what I'd described. He'd found me a nice view and a bit of privacy. Despite his animosity, he'd accommodated me.

I thought it was a tell of how I still affected him.

It was enough, for the moment.

He didn't move, though, didn't even take his hands off the steering wheel.

It didn't matter. I opened my door, stepped out of the car, slammed it shut, and walked around the front of it slowly, my movements sinuous, seductive. I made my way to his side, leaning over the hood, bracing my hands as I leveled my gaze on him through the windshield.

I watched his gorgeous, sinister mouth as he shaped a curse and then my name, the sight making me smile. Not a happy smile. There was no joy to be found in this. It was the opposite.

This was about killing anything inside of me that was capable of that emotion. Stomping it to death under my vicious, spiteful heel, then grinding it unrecognizable with my sharpest stilettos.

It was nothing new. I'd been at this for a while and doing a stand up job of it, if I did say so myself.

His door opened and the sound of his cursing matched the words his lips shaped.

It was music to my ears.

"I hope you brought condoms," I interrupted his rather creative diatribe, tone as abrasive as I could manage. "You aren't getting inside of me without."

The cursing stopped, and his silence was somehow much more hostile than even that had been.

The last time we'd had each other, no protection had been necessary, and the significance was not lost on either of us.

The difference between then and now was more brutally apparent than ever, and if he thought his bitterness could match my own when it came to this, *this particularly*, he had a lot to learn.

Finally he answered with a choked, "I brought some."

I flashed my teeth at him in my most sadistic/masochistic grin, "Well, then. Wrap it up, lover. I don't have all night."

He didn't even try to kiss me at first. I was so relieved that I didn't question it.

Instead he moved behind me, and I braced my hands against the car as I listened to the bittersweet sounds of him getting us both ready.

The rustle of my dress as he pushed it up to my waist. The whisper of my panties coming down. A zipper being undone, the crinkle of a foil wrapper, the snap of a rubber rolling into place.

I squirmed as I listened, but didn't move to help. I didn't want to look at him. Feeling him would be more than enough. Too much, on its own.

He seemed to agree, butting up against my entrance with no foreplay at all.

Good.

I was wet enough for him to ease inside of me. Just the idea of this hate sex did that to me.

Still, the size and suddenness of him was almost painful at first.

I welcomed the discomfort, leaning down to press my cheek hard against the hot metal of his car as he invaded me. I hadn't wanted this to feel *good*. That was not the point of *this*.

He pressed a hand to the small of my back as he started to move heavily, his breath ragged as he pounded his rage straight into me with succinct, brutal thrusts.

The brutality I welcomed. Every savage plunge in and out, every jarring contact of my hipbones against heated metal, every rough slide of my nipples against my thin dress as they rubbed into the hood of the car, my cheekbone digging in until I was sure it would bruise, my nails scoring into his perfect paint job with enough zeal to break them.

All of it only added to my perverse pleasure in the damaging exchange.

Hate sex at its finest.

Unfortunately, it was stimulating enough to get me off and fast. I told myself it was the booze that'd primed me so quickly for it, but of course I knew better.

I tried to hold back, bit my lip and tensed up, but each forceful plunge in, every perfect drag out, all of the sounds he was making, the helpless moans escaping him with every desperate movement, were too much for me.

I came, fast and sudden, letting out an anguished cry.

He cursed, thrusting harder, faster, again, again, again, and started to come, calling out my name as though he had the right.

After, I just lay there for the longest time, eyes wide open, staring out at the night with Dante draped heavily against my back, still inside of me, his mouth close to my ear.

I listened to the familiar pants of his breath as they went from jagged and wild to soft and even while we slowly recovered from the destructive encounter.

Eventually he spoke, "You didn't even look at the sunset. You kept your head down the entire time."

I shuddered. The bastard's casual, almost amused tone got to me.

His release had helped him get his temper in hand, which had *not* been the point.

"Get off of me," I snarled at him.

He didn't listen. Instead he brushed my hair to the side and started kissing my neck, his lips tender, devastating, as they began to move down to my nape, then along my shoulder.

"Time's up, lover," I made my tremulous voice as hard as I could manage. "I need to get back to my *date*."

He didn't like that. In fact, he stiffened and straightened, sliding out of me with a decisive swiftness that made me gasp.

Good. His rage was back, which had been my intent.

I wanted, expected, *needed* him to get off me then, to go away, to never touch me again.

But of course that was not what he did. Not even close.

His big, strong, familiar, despised hands turned me over onto my back.

As my torso was exposed, my body instinctively started to curl in on itself.

He wasn't having it. He pinned my shoulders, moving his hips between my thighs before I could muster up the energy to maneuver away.

His chest pressed to my breasts right as his lips took mine.

My hands, of their own volition, began to tug at his tie, seeking skin even while I gasped out a ragged, "Don't kiss me."

Please, I almost said, almost *begged* for that one small mercy.

But it would have been pointless, precious pride spent for nothing, because there was no mercy in him, not today.

He kissed me with the same fevered longing that he always had. The same despairing hope.

The same passionate reverence.

Like nothing had changed. Like we hadn't destroyed each other and *ourselves* with determined, spiteful abandon since our last parting.

I let him have me again, and this time it was, much, much worse.

More than fucking or release. More than hate sex.

More than masochism or revenge.

It was the give and take that only occurs when the heart is involved.

When the heart isn't yours to give, because it already belongs to someone else.

Because it always fucking did.

I barely got his tie off, his shirt open, as he tugged the scant top of my dress down, dragging the thin straps off my shoulders.

He took me face to face, mouth to mouth, bare chest to bare chest.

It was smoother this time. With more finesse. This was not merely him consuming me. It was not just his body partaking of mine. This time he seduced as much as he owned.

It lasted longer. And felt better.

There was more pleasure to be had within his expert, knowing touch.

There was more delight to endure under his relentless, familiar body.

There was more torment to suffer from his unstoppable, merciless lips.

The first time had been more than enough to mess with my head for the foreseeable future, but the second time ruined me.

Utterly. Completely.

If I'd built up any believable delusions that I could move forward from this, from him, he'd just blown them all to little, twitching, unrecoverable bits.

Was there some piece of my heart left intact inside of my miserable chest before that encounter?

Some tiny fragment of my soul?

I couldn't remember.

But I felt like *nothing* when he finished with me. Whatever had been left, he'd just carelessly taken.

There was some trivial bit of comfort to be taken in the fact that he seemed to be as affected. He couldn't muster up the energy for a casual one-liner after that round. Instead, when he caught his breath, he wrenched out of me, staggering away, his devastated eyes making a connection with mine for a few horrible beats before he strode off, heading opposite of the road, straightening his clothes as he took some crucial moments to compose himself, giving me his back.

It was a mistake on his part, because I recovered faster, or at least, I got my act together quickly enough to make the first move.

My only regret was that I didn't get to see his face as I drove away, leaving him stranded on the side of the road.

In the middle of fucking nowhere.

I'd driven about a mile before I took some pity on him, slowing the car, rolling down the driver's side window, and tossing his phone out. Maybe he'd find it and get himself a ride.

If I were smart I'd have kept the car, used it for a spell. It was very nice, a brand new Audi. I could have driven around in style for a change. Even with how he felt about me now, I couldn't imagine him reporting it stolen.

Still, I *wanted* him to report it, because I didn't keep it. I left it in an empty parking lot a few blocks from my apartment, hoping he'd somehow get it back and find the present I'd carved for him on the hood.

I FUCKING HATE YOU. QUIT STALKING ME.

Subtlety had never been my strength. Why try to change now?

"There's nothing half so real in life as the things you've done… inexorably, unalterably done."
~Sara Teasdale

chapter thirty-eight

PRESENT

Scarlett

We'd been living together in our love nest for a few months when it all came crashing down around us.

I was resigned to being together in secret for the foreseeable future, or forever if need be.

Hell, I was thankful for it. Even with the fighting, some of it horrible, messy, disastrous—some of it damn near too painful to take, I was still grateful for every second granted to us, only hoping each day that we could have another, and another.

We'd never had much luck with hope.

The movie was going well, scheduled to wrap up in days, and I'd just gotten into to my trailer and was changing to go home when I got the call.

It was an unknown number, and I automatically ignored the first few times it rang. Finally annoyance had me answering with a curt, "Hello?"

"Hello, Scarlett."

I hadn't heard the voice in a while, not since Gram's funeral, and then only briefly, but I recognized it instantly. "Hello, Adelaide," I said, voice gone cold with no effort at all. I had nothing but ice in my veins for this woman.

"How long did you think this could last?" she asked, poison dripping from the words. "How long did you think you could hide it from me?"

"I don't know what you're talking about," I said evenly and unflappably. I was an actress, after all, and there was only one person, one man to be precise, that I couldn't fake it in front of, in a pinch.

"Cute. Very cute. I have a man waiting for you, right outside of the gate at your studio. Get in the car. It's time we had a talk."

"Not likely. Why the hell would I want to talk to you?"

"Don't be coy. I'm in no mood. You'll do what I say because you know what I know and I'm just *looking* for a reason to turn you in."

"I don't know what you're talking about." Yes, I was still faking it for the simple reason that I didn't know what else to do.

"There's no statute of limitations on killing a cop," she said, tone flat. Dead. "Go get in the car."

Checkmate.

I changed and left the property.

I saw her car and driver right away. A man in a suit leaning against a Rolls Royce. Yeah, no brainer.

He opened the door for me as I approached, holding

out his hand. "Your phone," he said without expression.

I eyed him. He was middle-aged and nondescript, head to toe—brown hair, dark shades, medium build, face deadpan.

I had a very bad feeling. "Fuck you," I said succinctly, eyeing the open door narrowly.

My cell started ringing. It was Adelaide again. "Do you have her?" she asked by way of greeting.

"He doesn't," I said, my temper boiling. I really wanted to hit something. Adelaide's face particularly.

She made a tsking noise over the phone. "Always difficult, even when you don't have a leg to stand on. Give him the phone and get into the car."

"What do you want?" I was already so fed up with her that I was ready to say to hell with the consequences.

It was a problem, except that my rage was almost a comfort just then, for the simple reason that the alternative was worse. If I was focused on my anger, I wasn't worrying about the fact that my life, and my options had just narrowed drastically.

"As I told you, I'd like to talk," Adelaide said into my ear, sounding almost reasonable, which let me know that she was full of it. "In person. I think we can work something out. I want you out of my son's life, and you want to stay out of prison. We're both motivated. This can be productive."

I wasn't sure what I could have done, I felt pretty cornered, but I was saved from having to decide by the sudden and very welcome appearance of Dante.

His car pulled up, he jumped out, and whisked me away. I barely had time to hang up on his mother before he'd bundled me into his car and started driving away. It was over in seconds.

His hands on the steering wheel were shaking. "What was that? Was that one of my mother's henchmen?"

"Yes. She was trying to get me to go with him. She said she wanted to talk. She knows about us, Dante."

He started cursing and did not stop until we were nearly at the house. "Were you actually going to go with him?" he finally asked incredulously.

"I don't know. Maybe. She wasn't exactly giving me a choice."

"*Never* deal with her by yourself," he told me. "Never go anywhere with her. Never engage her. If she bothers you, and I'm not around, you fucking wait for me."

We were home by then, and he didn't even allow me to respond. He was out of the car, on his phone, pacing.

"Adelaide knows," he was saying. "Yes. She tried to grab Scarlett. Sent one of her henchmen to pick her up right outside the studio." He paused, gripping a hand into his hair. "Yes. Fine. Fine. We need to figure this out and fast. We're running out of options here." He hung up and looked at me. "We need to meet up with Bastian. We've been working on some things, but we thought we had more time. Now we need to focus on plan B. Do you want to grab anything from the house before we go?"

"Where exactly are we going?" I worried about filming, but felt silly about it. What would the movie even matter if I went to jail tomorrow?

"Not far. Bastian's already here, so we'll meet him at his hotel."

This was news to me, and so was the plan B. And the plan A, for that matter.

We were driving again before I brought it up. "You're getting into that habit again. Keeping things from me. I know you think it's to protect me, but I want to know the truth more than I want to be protected, and I think you owe it to me to start respecting that."

He just nodded, mouth tight. "I do. I know it. And I'll bring you up to speed on everything tonight. If it makes you feel better, I don't even know some of it. Bastian's been doing some dirty work of his own, but he seems to think he has a solution for us."

It was becoming clear that Dante had nothing on Bastian in the scheming department. It was almost impressive. One thing was for sure, they were both, without question Durants.

The hotel was only twenty minutes away. Bastian was on the top floor, and he didn't have a room, he had a penthouse suite. And he wasn't alone.

He opened the door for us and led us straight into a large room with a bar.

A bar and a drunk Leo.

"Oh God, why is he here?" just sort of slipped out. Because Leo.

He shot me a very unfriendly look.

I returned it in spades.

"You can all hate each other later," Bastian said reasonably. "Right now, you need to work together. Leo has some pieces of this puzzle and a vested interest in seeing justice done. Isn't that right, Leo?"

He glared at his favorite son. His normally styled, dirty blond hair was sticking out all over the place, eyes squinting, his clothing askew. He looked ridiculous. "Em your dad. You're s'posedta call me Dad."

I arched a brow at Bastian. "Oh yeah, he seems to be in a very helpful state."

Bastian grinned and shrugged. "He'll sober up

eventually. In the meantime, we have a whole lot of ground to cover without him. So Adelaide tried to grab you off the set?"

"More or less," I said tensely.

Dante and I still hovered at the entrance of the room, not advancing, not sitting, just standing side by side with near identical poses, arms crossed over our chests.

When I realized how we'd copied each other, I almost smiled.

Bastian was even more amused. He waved a hand back and forth at the two of us. "Feeling a little defensive? There's no need to be. Come on in. Make yourselves comfortable. Have a seat. Have a drink."

Well, he was certainly in good spirits. I sincerely hoped that meant he had some good news for us all.

Dante and I looked at each other.

"We're fine."

"We're fine." We said it almost in tandem.

My mouth twisted wryly. Dante grinned. We'd been spending a lot of time together lately, and it was starting to show. Like old times.

"Have it your way." Bastian waved us off. "But don't say I didn't warn you; you might want to be sitting down for some of this."

He took a deep breath and began, "I strongly suspect, and have since it happened, that Adelaide killed Gram. Or at least, had her killed."

I was floored. The thought had never even occurred to me. I don't know why. No one had ever accused me of *not* being paranoid and suspicious.

But it had still never crossed my mind.

I looked at Dante and found some comfort in the fact that he looked just as floored.

"It is a very hard thing to prove, but I have found a lead that's given me some hope that we'll see *justice* done for this. There's just one small hiccup in my plan. Or there was. I think I've got a handle on her now, but you're going to have to trust me here."

His wording was off, wrong somehow, but that wasn't what either of us focused on.

"I thought it was proven that Gram had a stroke," said Dante.

Bastian's mouth twisted. "It's complicated. There was extreme trauma to the back of her skull, and the coroner told us this was done post-mortem, meaning she had a stroke, fell, and hit her head, which is on its own suspect, because according to experts, generally you'd fall forward, not backward, so I certainly had some questions. But said coroner has since disappeared. Whether he was buried in the woods for knowing too much or given enough money to retire in Fiji, we have not been able to figure out."

"Adelaide," I breathed, feeling murderous.

"That fuckin' cunt," Leo said from the sofa where he was still drunkenly sprawled. "She was ne'er even worth the trouble. Terrble inbed."

"Nice contribution, princess," I told him, because Leo.

"You're a fucki—" he began.

"No," Dante was shaking his head. "Not fucking happening. Say another word to her, Leo, and see how much I don't have a problem beating your drunken ass."

Leo glared at me for that. "She started it."

He had a point.

Bastian sighed. "Back to the point, I've been chasing that trail since the funeral. Exhaustively. I'd just about given up hope. But then something even better came along." He smiled and there was triumph in it. "I've secured some additional insurance. For both of our issues, ironically enough. It wasn't cheap, but some things are worth paying heavily for." For some reason his eyes were sad and on me as he said it. He cleared his throat, and called out, "Tiffany!"

"Enemies are so stimulating."
~Katharine Hepburn

chapter thirty-nine

The bane of my existence came striding into the room. We shifted to the side automatically. To let her by or just make sure she didn't accidentally touch us, take your pick. Probably both.

"What is she doing here?" I asked slowly and with absolute venom.

Dante's arm wrapped around me, and he gripped my shoulder firmly.

Preemptively holding me back, of course.

Because he knew me.

"Hear me out," Bastian said, ever reasonable.

I glanced at him. He'd earned at least some of my trust, so even with her in the room, I was willing to let him explain. I nodded my assent.

Tiffany seemed particularly pleased with herself. Preening. Yes, that was the word. She was preening as she walked across the room to stand beside Bastian.

Her smile grew when she laid her eyes on Dante. "Nice to see you, Dante," she began.

I hated the way she looked at him, still with such warm interest. Still with frank infatuation. Even knowing everything had been fake between them, I still wanted to spit at her, to shout in her face, break her nose again.

I felt Dante stiffen at my back. *"Fuck you, Tiffany,"* he growled back.

Well, hell. This was all going to go downhill pretty damn fast if I was supposed to be the calm one here.

Leo started giggling.

"Shut up, Leo!"

"Shut up, Leo." Dante and Bastian both said, which almost made me smile.

Leo shut up. For good measure, Bastian took away his drink and made him a cup of black coffee, ordering him to finish it.

"But I like it with milk," Leo complained, sounding like a whiny child.

"Shut up and drink." Even Bastian was losing patience with him.

"Tiffany has kindly agreed to switch sides," Bastian explained when he was finished tending to his father, making it sound like it was the most reasonable topic in the world. "And as she has been very firmly entrenched in Adelaide's camp for many years, and holds many, many of her secrets, this is very good news for us."

I glared at her. I just didn't believe it. Not for one second.

"Why?" Dante asked, sounding as suspicious as I felt. "Why would she turn on Adelaide?" He looked at Tiffany. "Why now? After all this time? After all of the *vile* things you've done for her?" Disgust was dripping from every word he addressed at her directly.

The look she gave him was filled with vulnerable

reproach and even that made me want to do her violence. I was not okay with her looking at him with any personal thing written on her face. She wasn't entitled to *any* of that.

I owned him and she didn't. She fucking didn't.

"Since I was young I thought I would marry you," she told him, sounding sad and sweet, and like she'd fucking rehearsed it.

Dante's arm tightened around me.

Because he knew me.

"I was told I would, and I let myself want that, let myself fall for you, always thinking you were my future. You were promised to me."

Dante had both arms around me at this point, in a firm hold disguised as an affectionate bear hug. Or maybe it was both.

"You're delusional," he told her disdainfully.

"Promised to me," she repeated, tears in her eyes. "I was planning our wedding when I was fifteen. I even had the dress picked out. The jewelry. The shoes. Since I can remember, Adelaide promised me I'd be a Durant. You were never supposed to fall in love with her." She pointed an accusing finger at me. "And you certainly weren't supposed to *stay* in love with her. *You were promised to me.*"

I was about done with that. I looked at Bastian, whose steady eyes were on me. "Is there a point to this?"

"Unfortunately, yes." He sounded resigned. Tired beyond his years. "It is our solution. Continue, Tiffany."

She sent him a teary smile. "You can call me Fanny."

Barf.

He didn't even roll his eyes. "Continue, Fanny."

"She promised me this, and I wanted it more than

anything. She held it over my head, year after year, scheme after scheme. You wouldn't believe the things I did for her, all for this promise."

I was pretty sure we would, but I kept my mouth shut. I just wanted her to finish.

"And then it happened. I was engaged to him. But it only lasted six months, and it wasn't even real." Tears were pouring down her face, and silly or not, they were real. "But she told me to be patient, that she'd fix that too. But he wouldn't even kiss me."

"I told you then," Dante said with chilling animosity, "and I'll tell you now. I was never attracted to you. Far from it. Kissing you would be like kissing my mother."

She flinched but kept talking. "It's only recently that I realized that Adelaide is just keeping me on a string. She can't deliver the things she's promised me. If I want to be a Durant, I need to do it *myself*."

I was staring at her, my face stiff, expression filled with hate. I opened my mouth, to say what, I hadn't a clue, something bad, when Bastian spoke.

"Tiffany," he began.

"Fanny," she interrupted.

He merely nodded. "Fanny here knows things about Adelaide that would make your skin crawl. She's been a close confidante for quite some time.

"And an accomplice," Dante added.

"Perhaps," Bastian agreed. "But that's beside the point. We have bigger fish to fry. Fanny is a witness, and more, she recorded Adelaide talking about Gram's death and what she says on it is as good as a confession. At the very least, it will forever ruin her reputation. In addition, Fanny has agreed not to testify against either of you in the death of Detective Harris, which is a valuable thing, being that she personally witnessed parts of the crime. It was one of the most damning pieces of evidence Adelaide had on you, that in addition to the pictures taken, the photographer of said pictures," he waved his hand at Tiffany, "was a witness in her pocket."

"It won't matter whether she takes Adelaide's side or not," Dante pointed out. "Those pictures say enough. Enough to need an explanation."

"Ah. But there it is. There's no proof at all at this point that Scarlett was involved. They can prove what happened. And where. Everything else is debatable, even with the pictures. All of the DNA has deteriorated by now. Anyone could have done it.

"I doubt that will fly," I said. "She brings those pictures in, they're going to want a culprit, and they won't have to look far beyond me."

"Yes. True. But you didn't even live in that trailer at the time, correct?"

"Correct," I agreed, staring at him. His attention to detail was kind of scary.

"Someone else lived there," he continued. "Correct?"

"Yes, but it was just my grandma."

He nodded, eyes steady on me. "And we will get to that. Step one is Tiffany's cooperation. And we have it. All she wants is the Durant name."

My eyes were on him when I caught it, when I saw what he was getting at. His mouth twisted when he saw he'd gotten his point across. "Yes. Me. I'm a bastard, which she does not prefer, but I've still been allowed to carry the name, and so will she."

"No, Bastian," I said, and I couldn't hide my horror or my weakness in the words. It was too much of a sacrifice. It was too unfair.

"Yes," he countered. "It's the solution to our problems, and it's better me than Dante. If I had what you had, I would not do this. I'm doing this to save what you have. I'm doing this because I believe in it, even if it's something I can never have for myself."

There was such a deep-seated sentimentality to his words. They felt so personal, and a hundred things I'd overlooked clicked into place at once.

Bastian had feelings for me. Old and deep ones. He must have for some time, though we hadn't spent any real time together in years, and never without Dante.

Dante. So that's where the resentment for his half-brother came from. Not from some family rivalry or Durant snobbery. It was always about me.

"I'm so sorry," I said to Bastian, and it had too many meanings for me to ever articulate.

"I want you to be happy," he said simply. "I want you to finally get back what was stolen from you."

That was impossible, but even so, his sacrifice was significant. Life changing.

Unacceptable.

"Don't you feel a little pathetic blackmailing someone into marrying you?" I asked Tiffany.

"*Winning* doesn't make me pathetic."

Jesus, some people you couldn't even insult.

"No." I was shaking my head. "We can't let you do this."

"You also can't stop me," he said it with resigned bitterness. "This is a part of the solution that cannot be screwed up. Without Tiffany, all of the rest could easily get away from us."

He had a very good point. But it was so wrong. He deserved *so much* better.

I swallowed the bitter pill and tasted it all the way down.

"We have two confessions. And a witness," he said, as though that settled it all.

"You should have been a lawyer," I told him.

"Yeah probably," he agreed with a sad smile.

It took me a minute to catch it, but then, "Two confessions?"

He was back to studying my face intently as he said, "Yes. Two. Adelaide incriminating herself in the death of Gram. And, I'm sorry I'm the one to tell you this, there's no easy way to say it, but also, your grandma."

I was so confused I thought I'd misheard him. "My grandma?" The words made no more sense to me when I said them.

"Yes. Glenda's going to confess to killing Detective Harris. In self-defense."

If Dante hadn't still been holding me, I thought I'd have needed to sit down. I doubted I was holding any of my own weight. "I don't understand," I said finally. Nothing made sense.

"This can no longer be used to hurt you, to be held over your head, if someone else confesses to it. Glenda has agreed to confess. We worked on the story. It doesn't incriminate you in any way. You're free and clear."

I realized suddenly that Dante had had no reaction to anything for quite some time. He'd known most of it. I shouldn't have been so shocked by that.

Actually I wasn't. I was still just reeling from the idea of my grandma doing something completely selfless that would help me.

"Why would my grandma do that?" I asked no one in particular.

Bastian cocked his head to the side. "To help you. To keep you from being on trial yourself." He looked away, appearing suddenly uncomfortable. "Again, I'm sorry to have to be the one to tell you. She wanted me to, though, actually. She said she hates doing things like this herself. But ... she's been diagnosed with pancreatic cancer. Late stages. Her doctor's given her six months to live, perhaps a little longer. She's willing to spend that time on trial, in prison, however it goes, if it means you'll be free of the burden. Again, I'm sorry to have to tell you like this."

I didn't know what to say. What to think. "Why would she do that?" I asked again. It didn't match up with anything I knew about her.

"She wants to help you," Dante said into my ear. "She's sorry for the way she treated you. She's stopped drinking, and while no one will ever accuse her of being a pleasant woman, she's not as awful as she used to be. She does love you, Scarlett. In her own way, she does."

"You did this," I said to Dante. "You talked her into this."

"Yes. Of course. But, you may not believe this, it wasn't that hard of a sell. She knows more than anyone that she has some making up to do. She's feeling very mortal, and she'd like to leave this world knowing that she did some good."

I was still taking all of that in, still reeling from it, when they dropped another bombshell on me.

"And now we come to Leo," Dante said to his father with resigned scorn. "Are you sober enough to say your piece, Leo?" he asked him.

"I'm perfectly sober," Leo said, sounding less than perfectly sober.

Still, he was markedly less drunk.

"So what does Leo have to add to this?" I asked no one in particular when the silence had gone on too long.

Leo glared at me. I glared back. The usual.

"I know what happened to your mother," he said, sniffing, and I was shocked to realize he was fighting back tears.

"What happened to my mother?" I asked automatically, almost robotically.

We'd shifted gears so quickly, information overload, and I hadn't given my absent mother a thought in years, so I wasn't really even committed to the question.

Leo changed that pretty quickly. "Your father killed her. Jethro. He beat her to within an inch of her life and left her on my doorstep."

"Tell the whole fucking thing, you asshole," Dante gritted out at him. "Start at the beginning. She deserves to know it all."

Leo glared at his heir but complied. "Renee was a few years younger than me in high school. She was a freshman when I was a senior, but we went steady for a year." The childish phrase sounded silly from him. All of it did. But I didn't care. I wanted to hear. He'd effectively caught my interest. I wanted to know anything, everything I could about my mother.

He waved a negligent hand in my direction. "She looked like you. Prettiest girl in school. By far. Prettiest thing in the whole town. She's still the only woman I ever loved. But I was young, and once I graduated high school, the last thing I was going to do was wait around in that Podunk town.

"I left, went to college. I didn't forget about her, but I just sort of got distracted. That's when I met Adelaide. At Harvard. She was as conniving then as she is now.

She got knocked up quick. I don't even remember how, but she talked me into marrying her. I got sick of that quick, and after the first year of college I went back home to visit. Not gonna lie, I was hoping to see Renee, to start things again. I was already planning to leave Adelaide. To divorce her as soon as humanly possible."

He took a deep breath, looking around suddenly, and I think everyone in the room knew that he was searching for his usual glass of Scotch.

"No liquor until you finish, Dad," Bastian said, voice quiet but firm.

Leo glared at him. "Long story short, I show up and Renee is seven months pregnant. I was pissed. Really pissed. Especially when I found out that the daddy was that piece of trash Jethro. I didn't talk to her for a few days, but I caved pretty quickly. I still wanted her, and she was already avoiding Jethro, said he scared her.

"We lived together over that summer break. I was planning to take her back with me. We had a lot of plans, actually, but one day Adelaide showed up, newborn Dante in tow, and threw a fit to end all fits, and scared Renee off.

"I was planning to fix it, to get Adelaide to leave, get the divorce and everything, but then Renee went missing. Couldn't find hide nor hair of her anywhere for three days. I was really worried, since she was due any day."

He took a very deep breath, looking distraught, and for the first time in my life, I felt sorry for the prick. "It was the worst timing, but that's Adelaide's specialty. Some part of me thinks she orchestrated the whole thing. Hell, it'd be hard to convince me otherwise. She came to my house one night and started a fight. I was so over her by then. I didn't even care. I just let her go crazy. She was pulling out her hair, bashing her head and face against the wall. She was deranged, and I did try to stop her at some point." He waved a dismissive hand at Dante. "She *was* the mother of my child. But I couldn't stop her. She beat the crap out of herself, and right at the worst of it, my doorbell rang.

"It took me a while to get it. Adelaide threw herself in my way. But when I finally did, I found Renee on my doorstep, beaten bloody. I brought her inside. I wanted to call the police, an ambulance. I wanted to help her, I swear, but she was in active labor, and I just reacted, helped her deliver the baby." He pointed at me and sneered. "And Renee died before I could ever make that phone call."

He sighed and started looking around for his drink again.

"Finish the story," Dante ordered him.

"You can guess the rest. I wanted to call the police. I wanted to have Jethro fucking drawn and quartered, but there was Adelaide. She told me that if I called the police she'd say I beat her, and that she'd watched me beat Renee to death, too. You know how she fucking is. She had her proof all lined up. It was a setup, all of it. All so I wouldn't divorce her. I was a wreck. A sad, terrified wreck. I agreed to everything she asked, even got rid of the body, took it where she told me. Did everything, *everything* she said. A fucking life sentence with that cunt. Then she took the baby and left. I didn't even know what she was going to do with it . . . with you. But I can't say I was even slightly surprised when I found out you ended up in a dumpster."

I thought, no, I knew, that I couldn't have held my

own weight at that point. I was literally floored.

Dante was all that kept me upright.

It was sad, but a part of me, a big part, was relieved to hear the tragic story. At least she hadn't abandoned me on purpose. Maybe someone had wanted me. Maybe my mother would have kept me if she'd had a choice.

Leo was still Leo, but I asked him anyway. I needed to know. "Did she want me? Was she going to keep me?"

He was looking around for his drink again, but he answered quickly and absently enough for me to think it was the truth. "Oh yeah. She was real excited about you. She was a bit impulsive, but I think she'd have been a good mother. Wasn't meant to be, though. Obviously."

We left soon after that. I was feeling numb but somehow okay as Bastian walked us out.

I faced him when Dante went to turn in his valet ticket.

"We can never thank you enough for doing this, Bastian," I said sincerely.

He touched my face. "Be happy with him. That's my thank you." He smiled and it was sad. "It could've been us. If you hadn't met him first, it may well have been."

I couldn't have agreed or disagreed with him, because I simply didn't know. My heart hadn't belonged to me since I was ten and a beautiful blond-haired boy had shown me that I wasn't alone in the world. I couldn't imagine another life than that, but I nodded solemnly at Bastian, because it seemed to be what he wanted, and he deserved that.

"Did you always know?" I asked Dante on the drive home. "That Bastian had feelings for me."

"Yes," he uttered succinctly. "Imagine if you had a friend, or a sister, that had feelings for me, and you knew it every time you saw them. It has not made things peaceful between us."

"Yeah, I get it. Believe me. I get it. It's just so sad. Especially now. God. Tiffany?"

"We'll fix it. One thing at a time, though. He and I will figure out something. Tiffany is conniving and ruthless. She feels no guilt, and she'd do anything to get what she wants. Like my mother. But she's not that smart. Or complicated. She's simple. She thinks she's good at this game, but she never sees the whole board. Sooner or later, Bastian and I will find her weakness and exploit it."

"God, you two are scary enough on your own. Put you together ... "

He grinned and it was bloodthirsty. "Yes. We work well together. As Adelaide is about to find out."

He sent me a sidelong glance, his hand going to my knee. "Don't you feel like a weight's been lifted off you? We can live our lives again. Scarlett, *we're free.*"

I couldn't quite meet his eyes.

It's time, I thought. *I have to come clean now.*

Because I didn't have one excuse to keep it from him any longer.

"In three words I can sum up everything I've learned about life. It goes on."
~Robert Frost

chapter forty

PAST

Scarlett

I'd never felt so utterly hopeless in my life.

I'm not even sure how I ended up on a park bench, watching a playground full of strange children, bawling my eyes out like the world was ending.

The truth was, my world had been ending for months now, crumbling to pieces around me, and I'd just now received the last blow, the final bit of information that I absolutely, emphatically, could not handle.

It was one month to the day I'd last spoken to Dante. Since I'd destroyed us both over the phone, since I'd used Nate to make Dante bleed, to make him suffer and then callously broken up with him as soon as I was done.

Four months since I took antibiotics while on birth

control and then completely forgotten that the one canceled out the other.

I could barely support myself. How the hell was I going to be responsible for someone else?

Not just someone else. A *child*.

A child without a father. A child whose father had stated, plain as day that he did not want its mother so much as calling him anymore.

I was wearing shades, but even with that buffer between my eyes and the world, I knew I kept not even one ounce of composure.

I was lost. I had no clue what to do with myself.

How could I be so stupid?

What was I going to do?

I'm not sure how long I carried on like that, arms hugging myself as I rocked back and forth, feeling profoundly alone in the world. It felt like hours, when in reality it may have been only minutes.

When I noticed the outside world again, I realized that there was a woman sitting next to me on the bench, just a few feet away, which was not unusual on its own.

What was unusual was that she was crying, like me, sobbing like her heart was breaking, clutching her hands together as though in prayer.

She seemed to notice me at about the time I noticed her. She wasn't even wearing shades, her grief laid even barer than mine.

She wiped her eyes, studying me. My suffering seemed to have calmed hers, as though seeing someone else in need gave her purpose.

And so it did.

It was the type of meeting that imprinted itself on

your memory, and looking back on it I realized that it was indicative of her nature—Gina was a woman who always put others needs before her own.

"Every act of creation is first an act of destruction."
~Pablo Picasso

chapter forty-one

PRESENT

Scarlett

The first time I brought Dante to Gina and Eugene's was the hardest.

They greeted us at the door, and Mercy was with them, flinging herself at me with abandon.

I stroked her hair and let her hug me to her heart's content, my gaze wary on Dante.

The look in his eyes as he saw her for the first time broke my heart all over again.

I knew what he was feeling, and I felt it with him, knew precisely what he was seeing as he took her in.

Mercy was a gorgeous doll of a girl, a lovely mix of her biological parents.

She had her father's blond coloring and the same gorgeous ocean eyes.

And there was no doubt where her wavy hair texture came from, her high cheekbones, her stubborn jaw. Her mother.

But that was all they had in common.

No one called Mercy trash. No one would. No one thought of her that way, she was the opposite, in fact.

And only once had anyone ever thrown her away.

You never make peace with being abandoned. This I know. But we would do what we could to take responsibility for it. To never let her feel the way I had. She was loved deeply, and not just by the parents that raised her. That was a fact.

Dante had known what to expect, or at least he'd had fair warning.

But knowing and seeing are two different creatures.

Not to mention feeling.

It was hard, perhaps even as hard as telling him had been.

He hadn't taken either thing well.

Who would? Who could?

We'd had a bad few days after I told him, a few miserable moments where I wasn't sure we'd make it out the other side.

Of course he resented my decision. Resented that I'd made it without him, but even he knew that that was as unfair as it was natural.

The night I'd told him is one I'd never forget. Neither of us would. It had been as horrible as I'd dreaded. As painful as I'd known it *had* to be.

"How could you do that? How could you do a thing like that just for spite?" he had asked when I told him, his immediate gut reaction.

I'd been expecting something like that, but I was still offended, still taken from reasonable to messy with those two sentences.

"It wasn't for spite," I told him, voice quavering in something akin to dread. This conversation could ruin us. That fact was not lost on me. "It was for survival. You were engaged to Tiffany when I found out. What was I supposed to do?"

Something awful wrote itself on his familiar features in all caps. His mouth twisted.

Shame.

"You should have told me," he gasped out. He couldn't even look at me. His eyes were aimed up at the ceiling, blinking over and over. *"You should have at least told me.* Jesus, how could you go through that alone?" I shook harder with every word out of his mouth. "How could you give our child away *without even telling me?"* He was weeping by the end.

"I didn't know how. And I thought you'd reject me. Us. I was sure you never wanted to speak to me again."

"You know, *you know,* that if you'd come to me, that *no matter what,* I'd have helped. You know that if you'd come to me, pregnant with our child, *I'd have helped."*

God that hurt. And I couldn't deny it. Even I, the queen of denial, couldn't choke out the words.

We were in our bedroom for the conversation, and by then we were both huddled in opposite corners, crying our eyes out, and I, for one, was wondering how the hell we'd ever get through this.

Of the two of us, Dante was by far the forgiving one. If he couldn't forgive, how could I even begin to try?

But somehow we found a way. Dante made the first move, coming to me, picking me up, and carrying me to bed. We held each other as we wept until our tears ran dry, then set about trying to heal. It would be a long journey, but if we were committed enough, I knew we could do it.

We were committed enough.

"You need to meet them," I said eventually. "When you meet her parents, you'll understand. Or at least, it will help. They were there for *everything*. For me and for her. Her mother was the first to hold her, her father the second. It's not *possible* for them to love her more."

That had comforted him, but even so, nothing could have fully braced him for the shock of meeting our daughter for the first time.

The second Mercy had her fill of hugging me, she approached Dante. She didn't seem the least intimidated by the tall, solemn man that was staring at her with eyes that matched hers.

She held up her hand in a wave like he wasn't right in front of her. "Hi. I'm Mercy."

He lowered down to his haunches and tried very hard to smile for her. "I'm Dante."

"Are you Scarlett's friend?"

"Yes. Her very best friend. I'm going to be her husband. Would you like to come to our wedding?"

She beamed at him. "Can I dress like a princess?"

He nodded, still trying to smile. It was strained, but he got an A for effort.

I had to look away and cover my mouth to keep from sobbing aloud.

"You can," he said, the words unsteady. "If it's okay with your parents, we'd love for you to be the flower girl."

"Of course," Gina said, sounding less than steady herself.

Mercy was thrilled, and completely oblivious to our anguish. Also, she was an instant fan of Dante's. She'd always wanted to be a flower girl, she told him.

"What color do I get to wear?" she asked him, sidling closer.

"Whatever color you want," he said.

She clapped her hands. "Can I pick more than one color?"

"Of course. You can pick them all."

And just like that, they were buddies. She wanted to sit by him at dinner. She wanted him to cut up her meatballs into little tiny pieces and then her spaghetti.

They were fast friends. It was hard to watch but necessary.

We stayed much longer than I normally did, and I knew without having to ask that this would be the new pattern.

It was hours later, and Dante and I were sitting on the back porch swing, our hands clasped hard together, every finger entwined, hips glued like we were attached, watching Gina and Eugene dig through a large outdoor sandbox with Mercy.

"It's so strange that we can just visit her like this," Dante said, his eyes on the mother of our child.

"It is an open adoption."

"That's what you wanted," he stated.

"It's not," I contradicted. "It's what *she* wanted. She thought, and thinks, since it was an option, that when the question arises, I should not be a mystery. *We* should not be a mystery. They are fans of total honesty. They want to keep no secrets from their daughter."

"It seems harder this way. The idea of her and the reality . . . are two very different things."

"Yes. Harder indeed. As I've said, it's not what I wanted, but I didn't trust at the time, or even now, that what I wanted was what was *best*. I was wounded . . . *am* wounded, and I longed for the easy choice, but the fact is that there wasn't one. So I tried for the best choice, for her, her mother, and her mother I trusted to know what it was."

Gina taught me what angels were, and that maybe, just maybe, Gram was right about prayers, that no matter your sins, sometimes life sends you the answer you need.

Not the answer you want, perhaps, but need is the thing. The thing that matters most, no matter how it hurts.

epilogue

Scarlett

I dreaded going to visit my grandma, but I didn't put it off. Her time was limited, and I had enough regrets and guilt in my past that I'd learned not to add to it.

Everything had happened very fast. The Durant men had made their move, maneuvered the first chess piece, gone after Adelaide, and the rest of the moves had come fast and vicious.

Adelaide was arrested and charged for the murder of Vivian Durant. No bail was granted. It was a cold, cruel world when all of the Durant influence was suddenly being used against instead of for you. Her trial would be long and complicated, and no matter how it went, her reputation was forever in tatters.

It was going kind of beautifully. More stakes had been nailed into Adelaide's coffin within hours of her arrest. Three of her henchmen had been implicated and instantly turned on her. I ate up each piece of this news with absolute relish. Yum.

At nearly the same time, Glenda turned herself in preemptively, confessing her rehearsed speech. Her spiffy, Durant paid for attorney brought her in and coached her through every word. She was charged and booked.

Even her more expensive than God lawyer was surprised when she was granted bail.

It was for a million dollars, but that was small change in the world of Durant schemes.

All of this made it possible for me to visit her in her new and sumptuously appointed apartment.

She greeted me at the door solemnly and I don't think either of us knew what to do. We'd never hugged, so that didn't seem right, but it felt like we should do something.

We settled for nodding at each other and then she showed me around her new house.

"Nicest place I ever lived," she said. She sounded awful. Old and sick. She looked it too. "They even got a nurse checking in on me, helping me out every day. Never been treated like this before. Don't know what to do with myself, but mostly I just watch TV."

I'd figured as much. The TV was on even while she led me around, as though she never even thought to turn it off. "You should try out a show called Kink and Ink. Pure TV crack," I suggested.

She told me, looking dubious about it, that she would.

She made us tea, something I'd never even seen her drink, and we sat at her cute little dining room table and stared at each other.

"I don't know what to say," I told her. "I'm still not sure why you're doing this for me."

She stared at me, and while she did look awful, her gaze was more lucid than I'd ever seen it. Perhaps it was being terminal, but she seemed more human, more normal than I could ever remember.

"I owe you some words. I ain't good with words, but I'll try to explain myself. Bear with me."

I nodded because she seemed to expect it.

"I've been homely my whole life," she said. "You see me. Homely and awkward. All the pretty girls at school always loved to make fun of me. I was an easy mark. Mean enough but no good at articulating it.

"And then one day, when I was fifteen, the most beautiful boy in town, his name's Verne Hawn, set about seducing me. I fell for him in about a second flat, but two weeks after he got me on my back, I heard the real story. He did it on a dare. He made fifty bucks to sleep with the ugliest girl in school, and I got a broken heart and a baby out of it.

All my life pretty people been tormenting me, and all a' sudden, there I was raising one. She was a sassy little piece, too, always knew she was better than me. Then she runs off soon she can, leaving me with her own pretty baby. And I took it all out on you. It wasn't fair, and the only defense I got is that the horrible things I said to you, the ways I brought you down, in my own twisted way, a lot of it was just my way of trying to guide you, to keep you from being like me."

It didn't make it better. It didn't even make it okay. But it helped. At least now I had an explanation. At least now I knew that the way I'd been treated wasn't all me and my own defectiveness.

"And about that cop." She wasn't done talking. "I didn't know. I just didn't know. But at the very least I should have been the one to protect you. This is my way of making that right. That I didn't do my job."

And still she wasn't done. It was the most I'd ever heard her talk in my entire life.

"I been off the drink for a while now," she continued. "It helps. Well, on some days it helps. I ain't as bad as I was.

"I know what I am. I know what I did to you. I'm an unpleasant, bitter woman. No one understands this more than I do. I was a terrible mother, and my daughter hated me for it. That hate made me cruel, and I took much of it out on you. I didn't mean to, but that's no excuse. You don't want anything to do with me, and I don't blame you for that. I'm doing this because it's the right thing, and for once in my miserable life, I want to do the right thing. Please don't try to take that away from me. And please consider letting it make up for some of the harm I've caused you."

I had no clue what to say to that, but unbidden tears welled up in my eyes, and I'd never been so shocked as I was when I saw twin tears building up in hers.

"I have no right to ask anything of you, no right at all, but I just want you to know that if you ever wanted to visit me in these few months I have left . . . it would mean a lot to me. It doesn't have to be a long visit. I won't talk your ear off every time like I did just now. I just want to look at your beautiful face, to hear your voice and even . . . get a chance to tell you I love you a few more times."

"I can do that," I told her slowly. "I'd like that," I amended. It was strange, us being nice to each other, but I was certainly on board if she was. "And thank you for doing this."

"To be honest, I'm looking forward to the break. I'm sick of cleaning that rich bitch's house."

We laughed hard. I tried to recall if she'd ever made a joke before and couldn't come up with any. Still, it was a good start.

*"One word frees us of all the weight and pain of life:
That word is love."*
~Sophocles

Dante

Scarlett straightened my tie. "You're so decorative. Arm candy. I'd take you over any bag."

"Well, that's reassuring," I said wryly and she looked up and smiled.

I wanted to kiss her, head to toe, starting with her lush pink mouth, but I knew better than to screw up the makeup she'd just had painstakingly applied.

She properly interpreted the look I was giving her and made a little noise in her throat.

It didn't help.

She took a step back, biting her lip.

It was an effort, but I kept myself from going after her.

My phone dinged a text at me, and I checked it surreptitiously. And smiled.

Good. The night was going to be perfect.

The surprise hadn't been hard to finagle. The owner of the casino that housed the Kink and Ink tattoo parlor was an old family connection, generations deep. I'd even met the famous James Cavendish several times, and we got along quite well. We had lunch whenever we were in the same city, as a rule.

I'd passed the invitation to Frankie Abelli through James, and her response had come swiftly: a resounding yes.

She was a huge fan of Stuart Whently and only too happy to attend one of his movie premieres.

And Scarlett, being Frankie's biggest fangirl (she'd recently made me marathon watch the entire show with her) was going to lose her ever-loving mind. I couldn't wait.

She'd dressed with utmost care for tonight. She looked edible. Opulently beautiful. Completely flawless and abundantly ravishing. Sin draped in sheer lavender Givenchy.

This was her introduction to the world and she was about to knock 'em dead, and it was about goddamned time.

She was made for this.

She'd left her hair down, and I couldn't keep my hands off it for long. Nor my lips from her skin. I saved her makeup by focusing on her shoulders, her collar, her cleavage. There was way too much of her perfect flesh exposed, and I wasn't sure how I was going to make it through the evening without falling prey to her lavish charms.

"Stop it," she said, her tone telling me that she wanted the opposite. "You're such a tease. We have to leave in like five minutes."

"I can work with that," I told her sincerely.

She threw her head back and laughed.

It was flooring. Spectacular. I'd been through hell and back more than once just on the faith that I'd see it again someday. It was worth every second of suffering to be on this side of it, to see her smile every day, to hear that laugh.

I'd do it again if I had to. Every bit of it. For this.

"Come here," I told her gruffly.

She came, her eyes suspicious on me, but I just held her for a few drugging moments, lips at her hair.

Heart in her hands.

Soul joined with hers. In perpetuity.

We were in the back of a limo that the studio had sent, headed to the premiere when I said, "I have a surprise for you."

She shot me a saucy grin. "Is it oral?"

That surprised a belly laugh out of me. "Is oral on the table?"

"Only if you're doing it. *You* don't have any makeup to worry about."

I started shifting lower in my seat, all too ready to accommodate her, but she stopped me with a hand and giggle.

"I was kidding! You know I'm too nervous right now."

"I'm pretty sure an orgasm will help with that."

"You're incorrigible."

"Yes," I said, tone succinct. "Also, I'm *very* good with my tongue."

When I handed her out of the limo, she was only slightly mussed and *much* more relaxed.

She took to the red carpet like a natural. A queen taking her throne. A goddess.

Gram would have been so proud and not the least bit surprised. Just like me.

I was just as Scarlett had said—arm candy. An accessory for the evening. I was fine with that. It was refreshing and stress-free in comparison to my usual social functions. I didn't have to conduct any business, didn't have to do much aside from stand close to the love of my life and smile for the camera.

She really, sincerely disliked her co-star, and she made sure I stood next to him in several photos to illustrate how much taller I was.

I was game. Any enemy of Scarlett's was on my shit list, as ever.

"We heard you're engaged? When are you tying the knot?" was asked often, or some version of it.

"As soon as I can drag her to a courthouse," I'd say, or, "How late is Vegas open?"

These answers were always met with chuckles, but the truth was, I wasn't really joking.

"Your surprise is here," I murmured into her ear when I spotted Frankie Abelli approaching.

Scarlett's eyes twinkled mischievously up at mine. "I thought the killer limo oral was my surprise."

"As tempting and accurate as that is—my oral is killer," Frankie said directly behind her. "I'm taken by this spicy little Brazilian babe on my arm."

Scarlett turned, recognition lit her face, and she squealed in delight.

Totally worth it.

The women, all three of them, hit it off. How could they not, after that introduction?

I'm biased, of course, but the movie was brilliant. Scarlett stole every scene.

There were a few parts that I had a hard time watching. A bit more skin than I'd have liked to share with the world, a lot more touching than I wanted to see, but I bore it in silence and with good grace. It was my issue, not hers. This was her art, her craft, and I'd be *damned* before I'd be the ass that told her how to express it.

She'd always been one that took self-criticism to new extremes, but even she admitted that she was happy with her performance and with the movie as a whole.

When the lights came on, she was watching my face, a grin on hers.

There was a twist to her smile always, but just then, she was happy.

As was I.

"Scarlett Theroux," I told her with quiet reverence. "I will love you to the end of my days. There aren't a lot of guarantees in life, but that is one of them."

"I know, lover. I don't doubt it for a second. You've earned that."

"They say marriages are made in heaven. But so is thunder and lightning."
~Clint Eastwood

Scarlett

For months I'd waffled between wanting a huge wedding and saying to hell with it and just eloping.

But Dante had promised Mercy that she could be a flower girl, and I really, really liked dressing up, so we settled for small but lavish.

And most importantly of all. Quick.

We took a small entourage to an extravagant Durant property in southern Italy and threw one hell of a party.

I wore a champagne lace Givenchy number that made every other dress in the room have a small, intense orgasm as I passed by.

And red Louboutins, of course. Because shoe porn.

Leona was my maid of honor, Demi a bridesmaid.

They'd both been even more shocked than I had when they found out about Farrah. Shocked and disgusted.

The girls hadn't even had to kick her out. She'd disappeared one night amid the Adelaide fallout. None of us heard from her again. Good riddance.

Gina was my third and final bridesmaid. When I asked her to do it, she cried like I'd just granted her a wish. I still wonder all the time what I ever did to deserve such sweet, amazing people in my life.

Bastian was the best man, but his fiancée was not invited. Just no. Never. I was still waiting for her to die in a fire.

I live on hope.

The groomsmen were rounded out with Eugene and Anton. I was more surprised than anyone was when I introduced Dante to Anton and the two men actually became friends.

There weren't many attendees beyond the wedding party, and that was perfect with me. It was a beautiful, happy day, filled with laughter, friends, and love.

We both had tears in our eyes as we watched our gorgeous little flower girl decorate the small path to the altar for us. But they were happy tears. Progress.

"Marriage is the most valuable, treasured friendship of your life," the officiate began.

I won't lie, we barely heard the rest, but at least it was a strong start.

Dante and I were having a moment, staring at each other, thanking the powers that be that in spite of everything, in spite of ourselves, somehow we'd ended up here. Together. Joined.

Whole again.

"Dante Durant, love of my life," I said at the end, still drowning in his ocean deep eyes, my mascara a mess down my face. "There aren't a lot of guarantees in life, but I promise you this: I will never lose my faith in you again."

I saw in the way his face fell and lifted, the way his eyes melted at me, that I'd said the right thing, what he'd needed to hear. What I'd needed to say.

It took me time to make peace with the decisions Dante had made, even after I'd come to understand them. He hadn't had a lot of choices and his priority, as ever, had been to protect me.

It took me longer to come to terms with the fallout I had caused as a result.

Some wounds time couldn't heal, this I had always known.

But what I learned, even as I learned what it meant to forgive, was that some wounds it could.

It was a revelation to me.

I had forgiven him and he me.

But perhaps most important of all, I had learned to forgive myself.

BOOKS BY R.K. LILLEY

THE LOVE IS WAR DUET
BREAKING HIM
BREAKING HER

THE WILD SIDE SERIES
THE WILD SIDE
IRIS
DAIR

THE OTHER MAN
TYRANT - COMING SOON

THE UP IN THE AIR SERIES
IN FLIGHT
MILE HIGH
GROUNDED
MR. BEAUTIFUL

LANA (AN UP IN THE AIR COMPANION NOVELLA)
AUTHORITY - COMING SOON

THE TRISTAN & DANIKA SERIES
BAD THINGS
ROCK BOTTOM
LOVELY TRIGGER

THE HERETIC DAUGHTERS SERIES
BREATHING FIRE
CROSSING FIRE - COMING SOON

THE BISHOP BROTHERS SERIES
BOSS - COMING SOON

Made in the USA
Coppell, TX
12 March 2024

30012121R00236